ONE OF
OUR OWN

THE GREGOR DEMARKIAN BOOKS
BY JANE HADDAM

ONE OF OUR OWN

OUR OWN

A Gregor Demarkian Novel

JANE HADDAM

MINOTAUR BOOKS
NEW YORK

First published in the United States by Minotaur Books,
an imprint of St. Martin's Publishing Group

ONE OF OUR OWN.
Copyright © 2020 by the Estate of Orania Papazoglou.
All rights reserved.
Printed in the United States of America.
For information, address St. Martin's Publishing Group,
120 Broadway, New York, NY 10271.

www.minotaurbooks.com

The Library of Congress Cataloging-in-Publication Data
is available upon request.

ISBN 978-1-250-77049-3 (hardcover)
ISBN 978-1-250-77050-9 (ebook)

Our books may be purchased in bulk for promotional, educational,
or business use. Please contact your local bookseller or the Macmillan Corporate
and Premium Sales Department at 1-800-221-7945, extension 5442, or by email
at MacmillanSpecialMarkets@macmillan.com.

First Edition: 2020

10 9 8 7 6 5 4 3 2 1

for
William L. DeAndrea
July 2, 1951–October 9, 1996

PROLOGUE

1

Tommy Moradanyan was late.

Tommy Moradanyan had been late all day, starting with breakfast, which wasn't much of a nervous breakdown. These days, his mother expected him to be late. She said it had something to do with puberty.

She meant it had something to do with Russ.

The other parts of being late were more serious. He'd hitchhiked his way north this morning. He'd hit the highway well after rush hour. There were virtually no cars, and even fewer of them were willing to pick him up. That meant it had been five minutes into rush hour by the time he'd presented himself to the guard station. Then Russ had been Russ. It had been another ten minutes before he'd accepted the fact that Tommy wasn't going to leave until they talked.

Russ had been Russ.

What a laugh.

Pickles was standing on the counter, already tricked out in her green plastic raincoat. The veterinary nurse was named Kelsey. She was cooing like she had a real baby in front of her instead of a dachshund.

"She's so precious," Kelsey said brightly. Kelsey said everything brightly. "I put her picture up on Facebook. Father Kasparian said I could. I put her picture up wearing her raincoat here. She's so proud of her raincoat. People don't realize how much of a difference it makes, when a dog gets rescued."

The phone went off in the pocket of his jacket. It was a Samsung Galaxy S10+. He'd been worried about it the whole time he was hitchhiking.

Kelsey was putting on Pickles's little plastic rain booties. Tommy turned his back to her and propped himself against the counter. Right across from him was the clinic's plate-glass window. He could see the lights and the rain and the cars. It was after five o'clock.

Tommy looked at the screen, but he didn't have to. The ringtone was Beethoven's Fifth. That was the one he had assigned to his mother.

He took a deep breath.

He was late, and she was going to be furious.

"Yeah," he said, picking up.

"Where are you?" she said.

He turned around and looked at Kelsey and Pickles. "I'm at the vet. Pickles is getting her booties on."

"You were supposed to be at St. Catherine's half an hour ago."

"I know. I've been running late all day. I'm getting there."

"You've been running late all day."

"They didn't have Pickles packaged up when I got here. There was a bunch of discussion about the wardrobe. They finally decided she needed a sweater under the raincoat. Then they had to dress her up. Then she's got luggage."

"Luggage."

"It's not going to help to repeat everything I say."

"I got a phone call."

2

"He said he was going to."

"Tommy—"

"I'm standing in a waiting room. It's crowded. Fifty million people are admiring the dog. If you want to yell at me, wait till I get to St. Catherine's. Or wait till we all get home."

"Tommy—"

"Stop," Tommy said.

Then he cut the line and turned his attention to Kelsey. Pickles was all dressed up, the plastic rain hood up over her head, the little umbrella attachment fastened to the hood. She looked as proud of herself as Vivien Leigh playing Scarlett O'Hara.

"Here she is," Kelsey said. "All ready to go."

"Thanks."

Tommy had already put Pickles's little bag in his backpack. Now he fastened the leash to her collar and put her on the floor. She stretched and preened. Two middle-aged ladies with a cat came over to tell her how wonderful she was.

Tommy headed for the door. He wasn't a child. He was fourteen. He didn't need a keeper. He didn't need anything except to get some things figured out, which weren't going to get figured out, because none of it made any sense.

He stepped out onto the street. There was rain, almost sleet. There was cold. There were too many cars. He turned right, in the direction of St. Catherine's.

He should have taken Pickles with him up to the state prison this morning.

That would have been a trip.

2

Marta Warkowski did not like going out alone in the dark. She had never liked going out alone in the dark, even when she was young, even when the neighborhood was still . . . normal.

Marta had grown up in this neighborhood. She had been baptized at St. Catherine's Church. She had made her First Holy Communion and her confirmation there. She had attended St. Catherine's parochial school. She was seventy-two years old. She could remember Masses in Latin and nuns in habits. She could remember when the outrage in the world was over the fact that the Irish archdiocese insisted on calling the church St. Catherine's instead of St. Katerina's.

These days, there was no help for it. She had to go out in the dark. And she had to go out alone. In her day, the old women went to Mass at seven in the morning. There were big clutches of them, most of them in black.

Marta didn't wear black. That would be coming right out and saying she was a widow. She had never married. She just wore her ordinary "weekday" clothes and carried her big pocketbook. In the pocketbook she carried exactly one dollar. She couldn't be too careful.

She carried her keys, too, of course—one key for the street door, one key for her apartment door. She had grown up in this apartment as well as in this neighborhood. She had laid out her mother in this very living room. The priest had come and blessed the wake.

In English.

The light was out in the vestibule. It always was. The lights were out on the stairs, too. Her knees hurt. It was getting harder and harder to climb.

She saw Mr. Hernandez waiting for her on the landing. She supposed she should call him *Señor* Hernandez, but she didn't want to.

She brushed past him without saying hello. She did not put her key in the lock. She did not want this man coming into her apartment.

Mr. Hernandez let out with a stream of Spanish. He knew she didn't speak Spanish.

"It's not that I have to have an English Mass," she said. "I grew up when the Masses were all in Latin. I didn't understand that, either."

"Miss Warkowski, please."

"I want to go lie down now. I'm very tired."

"Miss Warkowski, please. We have to talk about the apartment."

"We don't have to talk about the apartment."

"Miss Warkowski, please. It doesn't make any sense. It's a three-bedroom apartment. You're all by yourself."

"I'll be dead soon enough. That ought to make you happy."

"I could give you another apartment in the building. I've got a one bedroom on the first floor. You wouldn't have to climb the stairs."

"I'm going to be laid out in my living room when I go. Just like my parents were."

She stared at the key in her hand. Who would lay her out when she was dead? All her people were gone. Even the priest was gone. The priest at St. Catherine's these days was Spanish, like the rest of them.

"Miss Warkowski," Mr. Hernandez said. "I have a family that needs an apartment. There are two parents and two aunts and four children. I can't put them in a one-bedroom apartment. You have to see that. You have to see that you should—"

"I should nothing," Marta said. "You can't tell me what I should do. You don't own this building. You're just the super."

"But there are children!"

Then there was a stream of Spanish again, the sound of frustration. Marta waited for it to be over.

"You can't tell me what to do," Marta said, when there was silence again. "I pay my rent on time. I have a lease. I don't even deal with you. I bring my rent to the company downtown. I know you want me out of here."

"I only want to make sense."

"They think I don't know," Marta said. "They think because I don't speak Spanish, I can't tell what they're saying about me. And those boys. Trying to lift up my dress. Trying to lift up my dress at my age."

"Miss Warkowski—"

"I don't want you here when I open this door. I want my privacy."

Mr. Hernandez stood, silent for a change. He was a short, muscular man with a tattoo on the side of his neck. The tattoo was of Our Lady of Guadalupe. They told you in church that there were Catholics all over the world, that all Catholics were Catholics together. It wasn't true.

"This is my home," Marta said. She said it firmly. She wanted to believe it.

Mr. Hernandez turned away from her and headed down the stairs.

Marta put her key in the lock, and opened up, and went inside. Then she locked all four of her security locks, including both bolts. It wasn't just lifting up her skirts, or shutting her inside a circle and chanting, or cheating her on the price of potatoes. Sometimes she thought her neighborhood had been invaded by space aliens. They hated her.

She dropped her pocketbook on the couch. She went to her little shrine to the Virgin and lit the candle in front of it. Her mother had lit the candle in front of this same shrine and left it lit, day and night, whether anyone was home or not. Marta didn't dare do that. Leaving a flame lit with nobody in the apartment might be some kind of "violation," might be an excuse for forcing her out. Mrs. Gonzales kept hers lit day and night, but that was different. There were different rules for Mrs. Gonzales. She was one of their own.

Marta closed her eyes. She was still both cold and damp. She wanted to die right where she was.

No, that wasn't true.

She only wanted to spend one single hour feeling at home again.

3

Sister Margaret Mary had learned a lot of things since she was first posted to St. Catherine's, but the most important thing was that there was no sense to be made out of it, ever.

There were no solutions, either, but that was inevitable. If there was one thing the Church had taught consistently through the centuries, it was that the world was a mess whose only solution was Christ returned in glory. Christ did not seem to be returning any time soon.

Now she stood in the doorway to St. Catherine's School and looked across the asphalt playground to the street. It was dark, and cold, and miserable, but the boys were still out there. They clutched up in little groups and smoked cigarettes. Nobody bothered to tell them not to. Everybody knew they wouldn't listen.

The boys smoking cigarettes were nine and ten years old. When they got older than that, they would disappear. They would go into basements and abandoned buildings. Some of the girls would go with them. By then they would be finished with St. Catherine's School and over at the high school across town.

Next thing we should do is start a high school, she thought. She thought that often, even though she knew it couldn't happen. Carmen Gonzales and Lara Esposito came running up the street, dressed in Junior Girl Scout uniforms, their vests festooned with badges and awards. It wasn't a good idea to let young girls come out in the dark by themselves in this neighborhood, but they came anyway. The sisters had tried to talk to the mothers about going with them. The mothers had to work, or had three more children at home, or both.

The boys in the clutches along the street called out things in Spanish Sister Margaret Mary was glad she didn't understand. Carmen and Lara slowed down long enough to say hello and then raced inside, toward the back.

Sister Margaret Mary stepped back into the foyer and closed the door. That should be the lot of them. Everyone had at least gotten here safely tonight. Maybe they could spare a couple of sisters to see some of them home.

She heard the sound of steps on the stairs behind her and turned to see Sister Peter coming down.

"Are the Girl Scouts all in?" Sister Peter asked. "They're right underneath the Sodality Chapel. You wouldn't believe the racket."

"They're all in," Sister Margaret Mary said. "I'm more worried about Javier. I found him in the church again, did you know that? Just sitting in the side chapel, watching the Virgin."

"There's nothing wrong with dedication to the Virgin," Sister Peter said. "Maybe he has a vocation."

"He doesn't pray," Sister Margaret Mary said. "He just stares. You've got to worry with these children. We've got no idea how much trauma he's been through. We've got no idea what's happened to him. This could be PTSD. Or something worse."

"Have you changed your mind about the Demarkians?"

"No," Sister Margaret Mary said. "I don't know who we could have found who would be better than Bennis Hannaford. And that doesn't even take into account that she's got almost as much money as God, which means anything he needs he's going to get. No. It's just—things."

"Things?"

Sister Margaret Mary looked back toward the door. "I must have stood out there for fifteen minutes. I'm a block of ice."

"And?"

Sister Margaret Mary shrugged. "I don't know. It's the street. It's the neighborhood. There weren't any signs tonight. Of either one of them. I don't think. There was a van."

"There are lots of vans. You're getting paranoid."

"It kept circling around. Four times. A big black van. Brand

8

new, too. That's why I was out there for so long. I wanted to see if it would come back again. But it didn't. Or at least it hadn't yet."

"ICE isn't usually that subtle, you know that, don't you? They come screaming in with their initials on their vests in neon yellow and guns drawn. What they think they're doing with the guns is beyond me. Somebody's going to get hurt if they keep that up."

"People do get hurt," Sister Margaret Mary said, "and the vultures can be subtle, and I wouldn't put anything past them."

"I agree," Sister Peter said, "but can Child Protective Services afford a brand-new van?"

Sister Margaret Mary sighed. "I'd better go over there and collect Javier before the Demarkians get here. I hate to say it, but I'm not entirely sure it's safe even in the church at night. And we've got to look out for Father Kasparian, too, and there's supposed to be a dog. Tell me again we're right to be doing this."

"We're right to be doing this," Sister Peter said. "Somebody has to. And you don't have to worry about Javier being alone in the church. There's a Forty Hours' Devotion in progress. The place is full of old ladies who could give the evil eye to Satan himself."

"Right," Sister Margaret Mary said.

Sounds came drifting down the hall from the Girl Scout meeting.

Sister Margaret Mary opened the front door again. "I'll see you in a couple of minutes," she said.

Then she stepped all the way out into the rain and shut the door behind her.

The street was still the street. The boys were still the boys. The rain and sleet pounded against her veil like tiny bullets.

There was no sign of the big black van anywhere, but somehow, that didn't make Sister Margaret Mary feel any less apprehensive.

4

Meera Agerwal was so sick, she almost didn't understand what she was seeing. She had a fever of 102. The girls in her office had taken it right before they had packed up to leave, right on time at five o'clock, like good little Americans. Americans made Meera furious. They didn't expect to really work for anything. They started on time. They finished on time. Then they wanted everything, and if the company wouldn't give it to them, they voted for stupid politicians who promised to make the company do it.

Her body was freezing cold, but there was sweat running down the back of her neck. She'd ended up leaving work "on time" herself, because she couldn't think straight with this fever. She came down out of the building and headed in the direction of her apartment. It was only five blocks away. The sleet was slick and sharp. It stung against her face. Then all of a sudden there was this hulking shape in front of her, this woman in a thick coat that fit as tightly as a sausage casing, just there, and she crashed right into her and fell.

"Watch where you're going," the woman said, and stomped off.

The sidewalk was hard and wet. People walked around her without stopping. She got on her hands and knees and tried to push herself up. Then a man did stop and held out his hand.

"Are you all right? Can you get up? I could call 911."

Meera took one of his hands, and then the other. She pulled against him until she had one foot flat on the pavement. Then she pulled some more until the other foot came up. She was upright. She was also unsteady.

"Are you sure you don't want me to call for some help? You don't look too good."

"I will be fine. Thank you."

The man was black. Meera was never sure how to feel about

American blacks. This man was extremely polite. He was also almost elderly. She took a deep breath. It hurt her to breathe.

"Thank you," she said again. "I have a cold. I need to go lie down."

"I could walk with you if you wanted, just to make sure you don't fall again. Most people aren't like that—that person. I can't believe the way some people behave. My grandson would say it's because you're black. We're black, so white people don't see us."

"I am from Mumbai," Meera said. She felt as if somebody had reached up and snatched the caste mark right off her forehead.

"Mumbai," the man said. "I bet it's warm there. Warm and sunny. Not like this."

"I can get home on my own," Meera said. "I need to go home now."

"Then I'll let you get on your way. As long as you're sure."

"I'm sure. Thank you for helping me up."

"No problem. You get some rest now."

Meera made herself start walking. He wasn't going to leave if she didn't start walking. It hurt her to walk at the beginning. There was dirt on her hands. She would have to check to see if he was following her. You never knew with American blacks. Maybe he was just being helpful so that he could get her home and get into her apartment and then rob her, or worse. American blacks were supposed to be very prone to the worse. All her friends from Mumbai who had come to America before her had told her about it.

She made it to her red brick row house. She made it up the stoop. She made it up the four flights of stairs to her apartment. The apartment took up half the floor. She let herself in. She forced herself to make it a little farther, across the tiny foyer and into the living room, and collapsed in the very first chair.

It was then she realized that the woman who had knocked her down had not been a stranger. She knew that body. She knew that coat. The woman had not seemed to recognize her. What could that mean?

She wanted to fall asleep where she was. Instead, she made herself get up again. There was a contraption in the kitchen for making coffee. In Mumbai there would have been somebody at home to help her. She wouldn't have had to make her own coffee or cook her own meals. Even students didn't have to fend for themselves, and students were poor.

She got the coffee started, sat down in a kitchen chair, and took out her phone. Then she hit two on her speed dial and waited.

Cary was a typical American in many ways, but he had irons in the fire, as he put it. He stayed late at work.

He picked up. He said "Cary Alder" and nothing else.

The rudeness of Americans was mind-boggling. In Mumbai, even untouchables didn't talk to each other this way.

"This is Meera Agerwal," she said. He wanted her to call him Cary. She wouldn't do it.

"Meera? You're calling me? Why didn't you just come down the hall?"

"Because I'm not in the office."

"At home? I don't believe it. You never leave before I do."

The little timer thing on the coffee maker went off. She left it. She shouldn't have coffee in the state she was in. She should have tea with honey in it. Later.

"I have the flu," she said. "I need to tell you what happened to me."

"Something happened to you? Are you all right? Do you think you should call a doctor? Do you need to go to the hospital?"

Then she closed her eyes and counted to ten. In Hindi. Finally, she said, "Please, listen," and launched into the story of the woman who had knocked her down.

After that, there was a long stretch of silence.

"Damn," Cary said finally. "Are you sure?"

"Yes."

"Marta Warkowski."

"Yes."

"Did she come to the office?"

"Not while I was there. And when I left, I closed up. The girls had all gone home. If she went to the office after she ran into me, she would have found it closed. And you're in the back. You wouldn't have heard her knocking."

"Hernandez says she never goes out in the dark. She comes home after Mass and locks herself in and won't answer the door."

"Well, she was here tonight. And I don't see what business she'd have in that neighborhood except for us."

"True."

Meera couldn't do this anymore. "I need to lie down now," she said. "I just wanted you to know. And to tell you you should be careful. Maybe she came up and she's waiting right there outside the door, waiting for you to try to leave."

"Crap."

"I am going to hang up now. But I am going to tell you what I always tell you. Dealing with her was a mistake."

Meera turned the phone off and put it down on the kitchen table. She would have to take it with her when she went into the bedroom. She would make tea and go there and lie down. If somebody tried to wake her up, she would pretend to be dead.

It was Cary Alder himself who had told her, when he'd first hired her, that it was always best to deal with illegals when you could. Illegals have no options. They can't go to the authorities, for fear of being spotted and arrested and deported. They have to do what you tell them to. They have to work cheap. They have to keep their mouths shut.

Marta Warkowski couldn't keep her mouth shut if she sealed it with superglue.

5

Bennis Hannaford Demarkian had never really thought about having children. Unlike many of the girls she'd gone to school and college with, dreams of a family had never been front and center in her plans. She hadn't spent the early part of her career obsessively reading articles about her biological clock. Even so, she'd always really liked children. She'd always been happy to babysit for Donna Moradanyan. She'd always been happy to coo over Lida's photographs of her grandchildren. In a way, children had been to her like the setting of a science fiction novel—a vast and alien landscape, both endlessly fascinating and endlessly foreign.

Now that there was to be a child in her life, however, she was beginning to wonder if she had fallen down on the job over the last few years. Gregor had been married and widowed before they met. No children had resulted from that, and Bennis had, without realizing it, just assumed that that was because Gregor had not been interested. She thought she probably should not have taken that for granted. They should have sat down and had a talk. They should have gone about it all deliberately. Instead, they were standing on the doorstep of St. Catherine's School in the cold and dark, coming to pick up a seven-year-old they'd never met and whose language they couldn't even begin to speak. The language was going to be a problem. Technically, Father Tibor Kasparian spoke Spanish—but apparently, it was the wrong kind of Spanish.

St. Catherine's School was unlocked during the daytime, but locked tight once it got dark. The church next door felt an obligation to keep its doors open. Father Alvarez felt strongly that a church should always be open for people to pray, and to be a refuge on the worst of nights for those who had nowhere else to go. The school had no such obligation. After a half dozen incidents of theft and vandalism—computers ripped out of their terminals and hauled away; expletives written on the walls of the first floor in feces; the Sodality Chapel torn apart and all the paintings of the Virgin slashed to ribbons—Sister Superior had put her foot down. The doors were locked after dark.

Bennis and Gregor had to ring the bell and wait. Bennis looked at the side of Gregor's face.

"Here we go," she said. "Are you sure you're all right with this?"

"I'm very all right with it. I was all right with it when Tibor first asked us."

The door in front of them pulled back and there was Sister Superior herself, Sister Margaret Mary, in her "modified" habit that left her neck and the sides of her face clear but sported a long black veil that fell down her back to her waist. Sister shot them both a vague smile. Then she stepped out onto the little stoop and looked up and down the street.

"Is everything all right?" Bennis asked.

Sister Margaret Mary stepped back inside and opened the door wide. "Come on in," she said. "I'm sorry. We've been having a kind of weird evening."

"You've been having trouble?" Gregor asked.

"No, no. It's been nothing, really. I was out earlier, watching for the Girl Scouts. It's the neighborhood. I wish we had enough people to see them here and see them home on the nights when there are meetings. It's the neighborhood, if you see what I mean. Anyway, I was out there watching them come in, and there was this van. This big, black, shiny, new, expensive-looking van. It came through four times in less than fifteen minutes. Let's just say it wasn't the usual kind of thing."

"Maybe it was something official," Gregor said. "A police vehicle. Something unmarked."

"I'll admit, I worry a lot more about sex trafficking," Sister Margaret Mary said. "A van that size. With things the way they are these days, you don't know what's going to happen. It could be some perfectly innocent person who got lost. If you call the police, if you take the license number and turn it in—well."

"Did you get the license number?" Gregor asked.

"No," Sister Margaret Mary admitted. "It didn't occur to me until it was all over. Never mind. It really was most likely nothing. And Javier is in the auditorium waiting for you. We've got four new foster families picking up tonight. Javier's already getting acquainted with the dog."

"Father Tibor's dog?" Bennis was confused. "I thought Tibor wasn't going to be able to make it in until seven thirty."

"The dog came with the boy," Sister Margaret Mary said. "He said he was with all of you, so we let him in and he's been talking to Javier ever since. And they've been talking to each other, too, although I'm not sure how. The boy speaks English. Javier speaks Spanish. They seem to be making it work."

As they were talking, Sister Margaret Mary had been walking them down the main first floor hall to the back of the building. The hall ended in a set of double fire doors. She pushed these open. The room in the back was a large square space meant to serve as an auditorium on some occasions and a gym at others. The space was full of people. There were nuns. There were children. In one case there was a couple, sitting on folding chairs and talking to a very little girl with ribbons on the ends of her braids.

"Over there," Sister Margaret Mary said, pointing all the way across the room.

Bennis looked across. There was Tommy Moradanyan, sitting on the bottom bench of the foldaway bleachers. Next to him was a very small boy dressed in jeans and a white shirt and a cotton crewneck sweater. Bennis recognized the clothes, because she'd sent them. She thought the boy looked scared to death.

"I keep telling myself that of course he's scared to death," she said. "*I'm* scared to death."

"He may be a little more scared than most of them," Sister Margaret Mary said. "It's a difficult situation. I did try to tell you—"

"No, no. That's all right," Bennis said. "We understand all that. To tell you the truth, I'm a little flattered that you think we can help. I wouldn't have said I was the most obvious person to take care of a traumatized child. I supposed they're all traumatized."

"Of course they are," Gregor said. "What else would they be?"

They all watched. On the other side of the room, Tommy leaned down to pick up Pickles, who was out of her raincoat and booties and was wearing only her turtleneck sweater. Javier put out his hands. Tommy put the dog into them. Pickles settled into Javier's chest as if she'd been born there.

Javier's face lit up.

"Well," Gregor said. "That worked."

Sister Margaret Mary started moving again, but Bennis put out a hand to hold her back.

"Just one more thing," Bennis said. "Did you have a chance to check on any of the things I asked you about? I know it may not be possible, but any information we could have would help. At least it would be a start."

"I know," Sister Margaret Mary said, "and I did try checking again, but it's as I told you. We just don't know. Nobody knows. He just showed up at Our Lady of Peace one morning, sitting in the side chapel. That's run by Maryknoll. They've set up a mission at the border to provide water and food and some facilities to migrants coming in. Anyway, the usual thing is that the people come in and some of them are what are called 'unaccompanied minors.' The Maryknolls separate them out and then see if they can do something for them so they don't end up in a detention facility. But Javier wasn't with any of those groups. He was just there one morning."

"And he didn't say anything about where he was from or what he was doing there?" Gregor asked.

Sister Margaret Mary shook her head. "When he talks, he mostly talks about the Holy Mother. That she's the mother to all of us. That she will keep and protect us. From what he knows, I'd say he'd at least started religious instruction wherever he came from. But that doesn't help, does it? We don't even know if he's actually undocumented."

"You're not worried he could have family somewhere who are looking for him?" Bennis asked.

"I don't think so," Sister Margaret Mary said. "We've asked him about family. He just says the Holy Mother is his mother and the mother of all of us. I've been wondering if he came north with family and saw them die along the way. Saw them killed. Except—"

"Except?" Gregor asked.

"Except when that happens, the coyotes always take the kids. And they don't leave them alone. But among the other things the Maryknoll sisters did was to get him to a doctor for a complete examination, and there's no sign that he's been sexually molested in any way, and no sign of physical abuse. No scars. No broken bones. One day he was just there. And we don't know anything about him."

They all looked across the room again. Pickles and Javier were squirming around each other. Javier looked immensely less tense than he had when they first walked in.

"Well," Sister Margaret Mary said. "We might as well get this started."

6

It took Cary Alder a full hour to get in touch with Hernandez, and even then, it was like talking to a wall.

"You must have done something," he said, listening to the sounds of children and women in the background. "You're the only reason she ever comes down here."

"I don't ever do anything," Hernandez said.

Cary was standing just inside his private office door. The door was mostly shut, but he had it open just a sliver, so that he could see out across the carpeted reception room to the frosted windows next to the front door. The reception room and his office were outfitted in tune with the public face of Alder Properties: upscale everything, probably too expensive for you to afford. His father had taught him that. Rich people didn't want to believe they had anything to do with poor people. If the city made you put "affordable" units in your buildings, you very carefully made sure there was a separate entrance to them, so that Those People never appeared in the marble-floored lobbies.

And Cary Alder didn't blame them. You worked all your life to make something of yourself—and then what? You were supposed to live practically in bed with the muck and the filth and the failure? Who had thought up this whole thing about cramming "affordable" units into premier properties? And why did anyone expect they'd get away with it?

She was out there, pacing back and forth in front of those frosted-glass windows. Cary could see her from where he stood at his office door.

If it had been up to him, he would have had nothing on his books but those premier properties. He'd have had high-rises full of duplexes and acres of McMansions in Bucks County and on the Main Line. Unfortunately, his father had taught him something else that turned out to be true.

Those apartment buildings downtown, the ones with nothing in them but "affordable" units, made money.

He'd have smoked a cigarette, but he'd quit them over a year ago. You couldn't smoke around rich people anymore. You couldn't eat a Big Mac, either. It was incredible how many people these days were turning out to be vegan.

"Listen," he said. "You were the one who told me she never went out after dark."

"To Mass," Hernandez said. "She goes to Mass. There's an English Mass at four o'clock."

"This isn't Mass. This isn't even the same side of the city."

"I didn't do anything."

Forget the cigarette. Cary wanted a scotch. Laphroaig would be good. He didn't have any.

"Let's try this," he said. "Did you talk to her today?"

"Only once. When she was coming back from Mass. She came back from Mass. She went into her apartment. I didn't see her go out again."

"Did you talk to her?"

"Only for a couple of minutes."

"What did you talk about?"

There was no real silence on the other end of the line, because there was all that noise in the background. How many people was Hernandez shoving into that super's apartment? It was only supposed to hold four.

"Hernandez."

"It doesn't make any sense," Hernandez said suddenly. "It's the biggest apartment in the building. She's there all by herself. She could take the one bedroom on the first floor."

"Jesus Christ," Cary said.

"I have a family that wants to move in. You could make a lot more money."

"And I keep telling you, no I couldn't. She's been living in that apartment since before I was born. She pays her rent on time every single month. She brings it right down here and gets a receipt. You know why she does that, right? She thinks you won't give it in so that we can get her in trouble."

"I hand all the rent checks in. Every time."

"She comes down here because of you. I have to have that—gargoyle—in these offices at least once a month because of you.

When I've got serious clients here. Who are not used to that sort of thing."

"It's a three-bedroom apartment," Hernandez said. "She's a crazy woman."

"She's a crazy woman with paperwork. If you keep this up, she's going to go straight to housing court. She's already taken us to housing court. More than once. We don't want to have it happen again."

There was no response at all, this time.

"Listen to me," Cary said. "The only reason you have a job at all is that you look legal enough on paper to give me plausible deniability. But you're not really legal, and you and I know it. Nobody else knows it. Even Meera thinks you've got a legitimate green card. But you don't, and I could do something about that if I wanted to."

"I am a very good worker," Hernandez said. "I give satisfaction for money."

"You give me a pain in the neck. Now pay attention. I don't want you talking to her again, not unless there's some ordinary business. Fix the plumbing—and none of that crap you were pulling last year about taking forever to get around to it. Change lightbulbs. Keep the stairs clean. But don't ever say a word to her about moving out of that apartment. Ever. Got that?"

Nothing.

"I'm going to hang up now," Cary said. And he did.

He pulled his office door open wide. She was impossible to miss, out there, on the other side of the frosted glass. Given her age and the shape she was in, Cary was surprised she could keep up the pacing for so long. He wondered what she'd told the security guard so that he let her pace and didn't bother her. Cary was stuck there, too. You couldn't have the security guard throw out a legitimate tenant. Even a legitimate tenant in a building you wished you didn't have to own.

He went out across the reception room and opened the door to the hallway. She'd tried the door when she first came up, but she hadn't knocked. He wondered why not.

He put on the best face he had. It wasn't a very good one. "Miss Warkowski," he said, "I thought I heard somebody out here."

She brushed past him and went right through into the reception room.

"I'm going to talk to you."

"Well, yes, I assumed you needed to talk to somebody, but I don't know if you noticed, but we're actually closed. Everybody's gone home for the night. I was just about to go home myself. If you could come back in the morning, there will be people here who could help you a lot more than I can—"

The huge wiggling hulk of her whirled around.

"I'm going to talk to you," she said yet again. "And it's going to be for the last time."

7

Father Tibor Kasparian remembered everything about the day he arrived in America. He stepped out of the tunnel from the plane into a space so cavernous he could almost see the echoes. It was 1980. The Department of Homeland Security did not exist. The long lines for TSA screening didn't exist either. He had a Greek passport, because the Greeks had been willing to give him a passport after he'd slipped into their country one night under cover of darkness. The Greeks liked the Armenians, more or less. At least both peoples belonged to the Orthodox Church.

There was a welcoming committee waiting for him when he got through the checkpoint. There was a small priest from the archdiocese, another immigrant from Armenia. All priests had to be imported in those days, because it seemed to be impossible to get American boys to go to seminary. Tibor always wondered about that. Armenian priests could marry. What was the disincentive?

There was also a small group of women from some kind of benevolent association. At the time, Tibor hadn't been used to the American habit of forming these organizations of laywomen who were not directed by priests and did not intend to be. The women were all American born and raised, and they showed it in their every movement. The way they stood. The way they walked. The way they tilted their heads. Tibor had seen all that in the American movies he had watched over the years, but he had always thought that was just Hollywood. That was the day he discovered that American women behaved with authority and didn't care who knew it.

Now, crossing the last street before he turned onto the block for St. Catherine's Church and School, he couldn't tell if anybody walked with authority anymore. Maybe it was just the sleet and the bitter cold, but the people around him all seemed to be hunched. They were all closed off within themselves, as if they were trying not to be seen. Tibor sympathized. He wished he could close himself off and not be seen. It was as if, in the last two years, the entire world had blown up. Nothing was the same. Nobody was the same. Nothing made sense anymore.

Sometimes I think Russ is making sense, he thought. He caught sight of the lit-up fronts of the church and the school. The buildings were halfway down the block and with all the security lights and safety lights going full blast, they drowned out the more timidly glowing streetlamps. There was a metaphor for you. The light of God was shining in the darkness. It was calling out to you.

Forget Russ, Tibor thought, *I am going crazy all by myself.*

He reached the steps of the school just as an enormous black van came down the street beside him. It kicked up a spray of wet from the asphalt and disappeared.

Tibor rang the front doorbell and waited. A few seconds later, Sister Peter opened up. American nuns moved with just as much authority as all other American women. Tibor did not envy their bishops.

23

Sister Peter practically pulled him through the doorway.

"You look absolutely miserable," she said. "You should at least have worn a hat. Well, don't worry. I'll get you a cup of coffee to warm you up. Or tea? I'd offer you hot chocolate, but the children have been drinking it, and I don't know where we're at."

"Is everybody still here?"

"Oh, absolutely. Even your dog. And there's a buffet out. I don't know how you'll feel about it. It's mostly Mexican food, because of the children, you know. They're not usually from Mexico these days, of course, but none of us has ever been to Central America. I think we're just hoping the food will be similar. And maybe it is. Everybody's been eating like crazy."

"I like Mexican food very much," Tibor said. Then he thought: Mexican food made by Irish nuns in a Spanish neighborhood.

"Listen," Sister Peter said. "I know Sister Superior will say it herself if she hasn't already, but I really have to tell you how wonderful I think it is that you're taking part in this project. I know it seems useless sometimes, what with all those pictures on the news with children in cages and I don't know what anymore. Not that we watch a lot of television, really, but you know what I mean. You can't avoid it. It takes everything we have just to get these few children to some kind of safety. And you'd be surprised how hard it is to find sponsors."

"There are no sponsors in the local communities?"

Sister Peter flushed. "A lot of the local families are mixed. Some of them are here legally and some of them aren't. And ICE checks sponsors these days. And you can't be a sponsor without oversight by CPS. Most of these families will do anything to stay away from CPS."

"It was called the Immigration and Naturalization Service when I came," Tibor said.

Sister Peter ushered him into the auditorium and pointed across to the benches. The small boy was there, methodically eating his way through a plate piled so high it looked ready to tip over. Pickles was sitting on his lap.

"I think the food is very satisfactory," Tibor said.

Just then, Gregor Demarkian, who was standing a little off to the side of the group, looked up and saw him. Gregor leaned down to say something to Bennis, who was sitting in a folding chair, then stood up straight and started over.

"Krekor," Tibor said.

"Did you make your weekly phone call?"

Tibor nodded. "And it went on and on, Krekor. There have been developments."

"You mean he's started to make sense?"

"Tommy went up there for visiting hours today."

Gregor threw his head back. "Dear God. Does Donna know?"

"If you mean, did she know before he went, Krekor, no. After he left, Russ called her and left a message on her machine. She won't talk to him directly."

"Of course she won't talk to him directly. How the hell did he get there?"

"Russ believes he may have hitchhiked."

"Hitchhiked. To the state penitentiary."

Tibor was afraid Gregor was about to explode. "It is not safe, Krekor, I know that."

"Not safe? It's outright suicidal. He's fourteen. He looks twelve. He's practically asking to get picked up by the worst sort of—I thought Donna had one of those tracking things on his phone."

"I think she thinks she has. I think she put one there, but Russ tells me there are things you can do about it if you know how."

Gregor rubbed his face. "And Tommy would know how. God help us. Look, come over and meet Javier. He's a very interesting small person."

"The meeting has been going well? There is not any—antagonism?

I am told that in some cases the foster families and the children do not mix, there is tension—"

"There's a lot of tension, but not that kind. And he loves your dog. Oh, and he also sort of loves Tommy. Hero worship 101. Like I said, come on over. We're due to go home in half an hour. You should get something to eat before you go."

"Krekor."

"What?"

"Krekor, maybe you should at least think about it. Going up to the prison to see Russ. He wants to see you. He wants to see everybody. He misses—everything."

"He ought to miss everything," Gregor said. "What the hell else did he expect?"

8

Clare McAfee had wanted to change her name as soon as she came to America. Her Lithuanian name was too hard for Americans to say, and too hard for Americans to spell, and just not American enough. Clare had been twenty-two at the time. The Soviet Union had just fallen apart, and she didn't care. She didn't just want to leave Lithuania. She wanted to *be* American, with everything that implied in her then very confused mind. She thought the name thing would be simple. She'd read a million stories about people who had their names changed at Ellis Island. She thought it was just a thing you could do in the United States, like eating at McDonald's or buying Starbucks coffee.

All this time later, she couldn't come to an assessment of the experience. She was still glad to be here and not there, but here had been both more and less successful than she hoped. On a career level, it had been very successful indeed. She had started at a small bank as a teller, moved up to assistant branch manager at a slightly larger bank a year and a half later, and then moved to the Mercantile

Mutual Trust on a career track that led her right to where she was now, vice president in charge of commercial lending. This was the result of a confluence of circumstances. The United States was crazy on the subject of "equality," and especially the equality of women. Women who had graduated from the very top universities were very expensive to hire. And anyone who had not graduated from the very top universities was so badly educated they were painful to listen to.

To tell the truth, even some of the people who had graduated from the very top universities were badly educated. The president of the Mercantile Mutual Trust had graduated from Yale, and he knew less about American history than Clare had in first form. Clare didn't know what was going on with that. Lord knows the Americans spent enough on education, far more than Lithuania ever had. They just didn't seem to do much of anything with the money.

What had been less successful had been Clare's attempt to find a place for herself in New York. It was New York she had always imagined herself living in. It had turned out to be far too expensive, insanely expensive, so that even the tiniest little box of an apartment would have cost more money than she could make. If she'd found the same kind of job she had now, at the same salary, she might have been able to rent something smallish and derelict in Queens—but she didn't want to live in Queens.

Philadelphia was a livable second best, but Clare could never forget it was second best. And her apartment was beautiful. It was large, and new, and had three bedrooms and a beautiful view across the city. Still, people with jobs like hers in Philadelphia didn't usually live *in* Philadelphia. They bought houses in the suburbs and invited people to cocktail parties they held next to their pools.

It was incredible how much everything cost in America. She had this very good job, and full benefits, and a 401(k), and her little . . . side efforts . . . and it still wasn't enough.

27

Sometimes she thought she was balancing on the very point of a pyramid, and any moment now she was going to fall off.

She didn't keep the records for her side efforts at the office. That would be far too dangerous. She didn't keep them on her computer, either. All she needed was to be hacked. She had a set of old-fashioned ledger books, carefully disguised to look like old-fashioned atlases. *Maps of South-Central Europe. Topographical Guide to the Mediterranean Nations.* She didn't know if they would be effective if everything blew up, but at least they wouldn't be all that easy to find.

She was making notes in the ledger about the new complex going up on the edge of Society Hill when Cary Alder called. She was thinking they were going to have to restructure the mortgage in at least three places if this was going to work. Her boss might be an idiot, but he was not a fool about this kind of thing.

She picked up the phone when it rang. She wasn't surprised to hear Cary Alder. He called all the time. He was always afraid he was going to screw something up and his father was going to come back from the grave to murder him.

"Listen," Cary said. "She's back again. Hernandez pulled one of his pieces of crap, and she's back again."

Clare put down her pen. "We can't afford to do this right now."

"Don't you think I know that? I've told him and told him. He won't listen."

"I have the semiannual audit in just two weeks. There shouldn't be any problem with it. They're not really looking for anything. But if we gave them any reason to be looking for something—"

"She's on the warpath. You wouldn't believe it."

Clare closed her eyes and counted to ten. Then she counted to ten again, in Russian.

"I wish you'd regularize your situation," she said. "If I'd had any idea what kind of a mess you were in when we started this, we wouldn't have started it. What do you do with all the money you get? I've seen your books. I've seen more of your books than you ever wanted to show me. Why you thought I wouldn't check into all that—"

"We've had that argument."

"I still want to know what you do with all that money. Even you can't be spending it all. I'd understand it if you were addicted to gambling, or cocaine, or—"

"Don't be ridiculous."

"What did she want?"

"She wanted me to fire Hernandez."

Clare considered this. "That's not necessarily a terrible idea. He won't go to the authorities. He isn't legal even if he pretends to be. He wouldn't risk it in this climate."

"There are other considerations. I've . . . used him for a few things. Off and on."

"Used him."

"Things have to get done sometimes. You know what I mean."

"Do any of these things you've used him for concern me?"

"Do you remember when the copper pipes were stolen? That big pile of copper pipes? We put in a claim on the insurance, and—"

"He couldn't have done that all by himself," Clare said. "That stack of pipes was as tall as a normal house."

"I think he gets friends to help."

"So, on top of everything else, you got Hernandez to help you commit insurance fraud, and he brought in a bunch of people you don't know, or sound like you don't know. What happened to all those pipes?"

"Oh, they're back at the site. I wasn't going to waste them. We put in the claim and then had them hauled back there and said they were new ones, you know. There's no point spending for them twice."

Clare was counting to ten in Russian again. This should have been simple. There was nothing to complicate it. Except that Cary Alder always complicated everything.

Clare had never seriously considered what would happen if she got caught. She knew these things didn't last forever. Everything unraveled eventually. Now she had to wonder if they would put her in prison, or just revoke her citizenship and send her back to Lithuania.

"Did you ask her if she would rather move into one of the affordable apartments at the Alder Arms, or one of those places? It would be more expensive than she could afford, but it would be a nicer apartment in a nicer neighborhood."

"I tried that once. She wants her own neighborhood. But it wouldn't work anyway. Those apartments are under the control of the city welfare agencies. You can't just put anybody in there. You have to go through the agencies, and they're all running their own hustles."

"Of course."

"I just called to let you know. I don't see what we're going to be able to do about it. Calm her down for the moment, maybe. If she goes to the housing authority again—"

"Yes," Clare said. "Yes, I understand the situation. When are you due to get the next scheduled payout?"

"Monday."

"All right," Clare said.

"I'll let you go now," Cary said. "It's like I told you. FYI."

The phone went dead in her ear.

It was always so hard to know what to do next.

But she was going to have to do something.

9

Tommy Moradanyan knew he was in for it as soon as Mr. and Mrs. Demarkian and Javier and Pickles took off for Cavanaugh Street in one direction, and Father Tibor grabbed his arm and took off for Cavanaugh Street in another.

It was after nine o'clock by then, and the sleet had morphed into a full-blown ice storm. The neighborhood was deserted. The people who normally hung out on stoops and sidewalks had disappeared into shelters of one kind or another. The streets were deserted, too. Either the city had issued one of those no-vehicles-on-the-streets-without-serious-necessity orders, or drivers were being a lot smarter than they usually were. The sidewalks were slick. It was hard to stay upright on the pavement, and it was going to get harder.

"Tcha," Father Tibor said, after a while.

But that was it. Just "tcha."

It took a little over a block before Tommy couldn't stand it anymore.

"I'm not a child," he said finally. "No matter what the pack of you think, I'm not a child."

"You are fourteen," Father Tibor said.

"Which is not a child," Tommy said again. "It's old enough to think. It's old enough to need to know."

"You could always think," Father Tibor said. "Even as an infant, you could think. Sometimes you could think too well for your own good. Or your mother's."

"I know Mom is—I mean, I know this is—"

"Did you hitchhike because you didn't have the money for the bus?"

"I had the money for the bus one way. I used it to take the bus home. I thought that made more sense. It was more important to get back on time. I started off early enough in the morning to give myself a lot of leeway getting there."

Father Tibor nodded. "And you have faked identification?"

"Uh—I did a license."

"And this license says you are how old?"

"Eighteen."

Father Tibor nearly stopped dead on the sidewalk. "They believed that? At the prison? That you are eighteen?"

31

Tommy flushed. "I was a little worried about that, too, but it wasn't any problem. They barely even looked at it. I think it could have said I was a penguin and they wouldn't have noticed."

"The next time you decide to go up there," Father Tibor said, "you will come to me, and I will give you money for the bus fares. You will not hitchhike."

"It really wasn't a problem—"

"It is not safe. I am not your mother. I understand this, a little. I talk to him, too."

"I don't have your advantages. I can't claim to be his priest and get a designated hour every week."

"That was Krekor. But yes, I know."

"And I wanted to see him. Face-to-face. I wanted to look at him. All that stuff happened and Mom packed us up and took us off and it was like one minute he was there and the next minute he'd just vanished. She wouldn't even let us see the news. I don't know. Maybe there wasn't any news. He pled guilty. There wasn't any trial."

"There was some news."

"Father Tibor, he was the only father I ever really had. And I thought I knew him."

"We all thought we knew him. Your mother says he was very tense there, at the end, in the last eight months or so. I think back and I cannot remember."

"I can't either. I think back and it all seems normal to me. Maybe he was treating me a little more like an adult, if you know what I mean, but there's nothing odd in that. Does it matter that I think that woman he killed deserved to be dead?"

"I think it matters that you think anybody deserves to be dead."

"But what she did. Taking money to give kids longer sentences in juvenile hall so the for-profit-prison people could make money off them. Okay, I've never really figured out how that worked. But I have the gist of it. Right? That was very bad."

"Yes," Tibor said. "That was very bad."

"But then in a way it doesn't matter," Tommy said, "because he didn't kill her because she was doing it. He didn't kill her to stop her from doing it. He was part of it, too. Sometimes I sit around and think about it and I get feeling crazy."

"You must remember that there were other things besides the woman. He tried to kill Krekor, too."

"Does he talk to you about all this crazy stuff he thinks? About how everything is falling apart and there's going to be a civil war and blood in the streets and if you don't have money you're going to die or be worse than dead and Mom is the perfect target and—it went on and on. I was there for twenty minutes and he never stopped."

Father Tibor nodded. "Yes, I know."

"Do you believe any of that stuff?"

"I believe he believes it."

"Do you think he's insane?"

"No," Father Tibor said definitely. "No. You must not do that. It is a very American thing to do, and I care very much for American things, but in this case it is wrong. To say he is insane is to say he did not know what he was doing, that he did not have control of himself. It is saying he is something less than a human being. But that is not true. He is as human as everybody else."

"Even if he did the things he did because he thought the world was about to end and he was trying to get enough money to— I don't know. Build us a bunker? Build us an entire private army? Did he even know where he thought all that was going?"

"Probably not," Father Tibor said.

"I don't know if I want to go up again," Tommy said. "It was depressing. And scary. It was like something out of a science fiction movie. One of the dystopian ones. And he was—different."

"Yes," Father Tibor said.

They were right at the intersection where, to get to Cavanaugh Street, they would have to turn left. They had left the Spanish neighborhood behind them by a couple of blocks. They were in a small area of shop fronts, all of which had those metal security barriers over their plate-glass windows. It was not as depressing as the prison had been, but Tommy thought it was pretty depressing.

Somewhere in the not-too-distant distance there was a squeal of brakes. Tommy looked into the weather and could just see the pinpoint glare of a pair of headlights.

"I hope that's a police car," he said. "They catch anybody out here in this, they'll have fits."

"The sanders should be out by now," Tibor said.

The vehicle wasn't a sander. A sander was a truck. This thing sounded like an ordinary car. Tommy adjusted his backpack on his shoulders. He was exhausted.

"I suppose I ought to go home and face Mom," he said. "I'm going to have to do it eventually."

"I will walk you to your front door. I will watch as you go inside. I will call and tell her you are coming in the door."

"I don't know where you think I'd go in the middle of all this, Father. I haven't even seen a diner open."

There was another squeal, closer now. They both turned in the direction of the noise. The headlights got bigger. Then they got bigger still, and the vehicle was finally close enough—about a block and a half away—to be recognizable in the storm. It was a big black van, one of the ones without any windows in the sides, and it was picking up speed.

"What the hell does that idiot think he's doing?" Tommy said.

"Tommy," Father Tibor said.

The engine revved and the van shot forward. Suddenly it was right next to them. It was fishtailing wildly, its rear end swinging back and forth. Tommy grabbed Father Tibor by the chest and pushed him back against the walls of the stores behind them. Didn't vans like that usually have four-wheel drive? But even four-wheel drive didn't work on ice. Russ had taught him that.

Russ had taught him practically everything he knew.

The squealing was almost as loud as a siren now. Then the driver seemed to get a clue and began to turn into the skid. The turn was a wide circle. There wasn't space for it. The van came around and the driver hit the brakes. It didn't help. The van came around again and then suddenly the side of it hit the streetlamp on the corner. The noise was metallic and enormous. The van's back doors popped. They hung there in the air for a moment, flapping.

Then the van righted itself. The engine revved again. The van aimed straight ahead and shot off past them.

And as it went, an oversized black garbage bag came flying out of its interior and landed on the street.

And then it was over. The street was empty except for the garbage bag. The ice storm was bad. There was nobody to be seen anywhere. Tommy moved back out onto the middle of the sidewalk and stopped.

The garbage bag was not empty. There was something inside it, lumpy and unpleasantly familiar.

"Tommy," Father Tibor said, grabbing his arm.

Tommy hadn't noticed that Tibor had moved back onto the sidewalk, too. Tommy shook off the arm trying to hold him back.

"*Tommy*," Father Tibor said.

Tommy went out into the middle of the street.

He knew that there was a human body in that bag before he got anywhere near it.

What he didn't know until he got right on top of it was that it was alive.

PART ONE

ONE

1

Gregor Demarkian took Pickles out for a walk the long way around, starting at his own house and going all the way up Cavanaugh Street and then back again. The ice storm was over but still a problem. The sidewalk was slick. The utility poles all looked like they were frosted. Pickles was not enamored of this bit of exercise. Gregor was surprised she was willing to get her business done at all.

What Gregor wanted was to take a look at Donna Moradanyan's house, the same house where Tommy Moradanyan and his sister lived, the same house where they had all lived together with Russ Donahue. He had no idea what he expected to see. There was a time when any house Donna Moradanyan lived was a spectacle for the neighborhood and beyond. She liked decorating for holidays, and her idea of decorating was to wrap entire buildings in lights or colored tinfoil or shiny paper or whatever else occurred to her to carry out a theme. Sometimes she wrapped her own house this way. Sometimes she went on to another building or two on the street. One Groundhog Day she had decked out the Ararat Restaurant with plastic grass and flowers and added a mechanical groundhog that sprang up to celebrate spring. On Valentine's Day she had covered Gregor's own house in wriggling cupids with red and white hearts on the tips of their arrows. Stories and pictures appeared on the local news stations. People came from as far away as Bucks County and the Main Line to see what she was going to do next.

This morning the house was dark, with nothing to cover it but its own red brick. There had been no decorating since Russ had gone to prison. In some ways, there had been no Donna since Russ had gone to prison. She went about her day the way she always had. Her children were well dressed and well fed. Tommy got halfway decent grades in school. Charlotte was the star of her ballet class. Donna herself had taken a job as an editor at a small local newsmagazine. Gregor had heard she did well there. Even so, it was like Gertrude Stein said—there was no there there. The Donna Moradanyan of today was a competent, organized woman. She just wasn't really Donna Moradanyan.

Pickles decided to do her business right in front of Donna's house, which Gregor thought was a statement of some kind, he didn't know about what. Gregor used the pooper-scooper and cleaned up after the dog. He half expected Tommy to come barreling out to talk to him. There had to be a lot left to say after the mess of the night before. There was always the chance that Gregor, with his contacts, might have heard something about what it all meant. As a matter of fact, he hadn't, but Tommy didn't come out anyway.

Gregor gave a last look at the brick facade and started back toward his own house. He got as spooky as Donna sometimes these days. He didn't know what to do about it. Things just seemed . . . wrong, somehow. He couldn't put them right.

He let himself into his front foyer and heard sounds from the kitchen. A moment later, Javier came running out, and Pickles snapped against the leash hard enough to break free. Javier was talking a mile a minute in Spanish. Pickles was licking his face and scattering wet drops of melting ice everywhere.

Bennis came out, too. "Hey," she said. "The Melajian boys were just here. We have breakfast."

"The Ararat delivered breakfast?"

"Just this once for the special circumstances," Bennis said. "I talked to Linda about it a couple of days ago. I thought it would be a bit much to take Javier to the Ararat first day out, so she put together a few things for us to have here."

"Did she send eggs?"

"Scrambled only. She said sunny-side up doesn't travel well. There's sort of a lot of it."

Javier and Pickles had disappeared into the kitchen. Gregor followed Bennis back there and saw Javier sitting at the table in front of a plate piled up with pancakes, waffles, hash browns, sausages, and toast. Next to him, Pickles was being presented with a small plate of pancakes with butter and syrup.

"Oh, no," Bennis said. She grabbed the small plate and put it on the floor. Pickles followed it. "No dogs at the table," Bennis told Javier. Then she leaned over and told Pickles the same thing.

"Of course, I don't know what Tibor does," she said, "and I've got a suspicion that pancakes aren't what you really want to feed dogs, but we'll work it out. He's going to bring over some of her things later. Do you mind Pickles staying a few days?"

Gregor sat down at an empty place and started going through the plastic containers of—everything. "Of course not. She seems to be acting like a therapy dog. I hope Tibor doesn't mind."

"I don't think he minds. I don't know if he's making much sense this morning, though. You're making a lot more sense than I expected you to."

"All I did was go down and check things out. I probably didn't even need to. It isn't like they got arrested. They were just witnesses. They talked to the uniforms. They talked to the detectives headquarters sent out, or maybe the precinct. I don't even know. They gave their information and we all came home. It was just a weird incident."

"You were the one who said it was an attempted murder."

"I can't think of what else it would be," Gregor said. "But the woman was alive when she was taken away in the ambulance, I'm just glad Javier wasn't there."

"I'm just sorry Tommy was," Bennis said. She looked toward Javier. Gregor noticed that the boy had started in on the fruit jams. There were five or six different kinds. He was using all of them.

Bennis had tea and a plate with a piece of melon on it. She sat down herself, saw Javier was struggling to reach the big tub of hash browns, and pulled it closer to him. Javier said *gracias* and went at it.

"Lida called. She and Hannah are coming over sometime today. They baked cookies. Father Tibor is sleeping in. I suppose Tommy is sleeping in, too."

"Did you talk to Donna?"

"Sort of. And the weather is awful, so I was thinking we'd just stay in today. Javier and me, I meant. You can do what you want."

"Is there somewhere you wanted to go?"

Bennis shrugged. "There are things that need to be done. Clothes, for instance. I have all his school uniforms, that was easy, but I don't have that much in the way of stuff for him to wear otherwise. I didn't want to go out and pick up a bunch of things I liked and just stick him with them. Even children have their own tastes. I don't know what he wants in colors, or if he likes jeans or khakis, or any of that sort of thing. And he needs a backpack. I can get that off the Internet at L.L.Bean, but then there's that color thing again, and there are different kinds. There are a lot of things to think about."

Gregor looked over at Javier. Pickles was in his lap, and chomping down on something. Bennis got up, took the dog, and put it back down on the floor.

"No dogs at the table," she said to Javier, very emphatically this time. Then she sat down again. "I've got my suspicions about the language thing," she said. "I think it's like the first time I was by myself in Paris."

"He speaks Spanish," Gregor pointed out.

"I know. But I was in Paris on my own for the first time, and I was getting kind of frantic, because I didn't speak the language and I kept seeing myself starving to death in the street because I couldn't figure out how to order any food and the French are really such jackasses about pretending they don't know what you're trying to say. And then I was in this bakery, patisserie, you know, and I was trying to buy some pastry, and it suddenly hit me. I wanted to buy pastry, and the girl behind the counter wanted to sell me pastry, and given those circumstances, we'd find a way."

"You aren't making any sense."

"I think Javier's ability to understand what I'm talking about sort of waxes and wanes with how motivated he is to get the message."

"Ah."

Somewhere out in the foyer, the landline rang. Bennis stood up.

"I'll get it. And I was thinking just last week that we ought to get rid of the landline because we never use it anymore."

"It'll probably be a robocall. You can hang up."

Bennis left the room. Gregor turned his attention to Javier. Pickles was back in his lap, but she wasn't chomping on anything this time, so Gregor let it go.

Javier stroked the dog's head.

"You don't know it yet," Gregor told him, "but you're about to be surrounded by a bunch of Armenian ladies who were born to be grandmothers. They're going to be all over you. You're going to have cookies."

"Oreo," Javier said, almost solemnly.

Gregor laughed. "Those, too. But there are going to be cookies they make themselves. In big batches, bigger than you can get at any grocery store."

"Chips Ahoy!" Javier said. "Fig Newtons!"

Gregor laughed again. "We've got Girl Scouts around here," he said. "We'll get you some of those, too."

43

"Mallomars."

Just then, Bennis came back, looking puzzled.

"It's for you," she said. "It's John Jackman."

2

Over the years Gregor Demarkian had known him, John Henry Newman Jackman had become the most famous politician in Pennsylvania. He had started as a detective of homicide in Bryn Mawr, a position that had made him joke that racial stereotypes didn't work in Bryn Mawr, because the only black man in the suburb was on the side of law and order. He had moved from there to become head of homicide in Philadelphia, and then police commissioner in Philadelphia, and then mayor. Until Barack Obama came along, Gregor had been sure he had been looking to become America's first black president. At the moment, he was having to settle for a seat in the United States Senate and more interviews on CNN than most people could handle without losing their minds.

There was a little chair next to the telephone table in the foyer. It was solid enough to sit in, but ornate in the way furniture was when Bennis didn't expect anybody to use it. Gregor sat down and picked up the receiver.

"John? Are you calling from Washington? Why are you calling on the landline? Nobody calls on the landline. I don't understand why we still have it."

"It was the number I could remember," John said. "Besides, I figured somebody would be home. I don't mind talking to Bennis."

"You still haven't told me what's wrong."

"There's nothing wrong," John said. "At least, not exactly. Believe it or not, I'm calling for a friend. And no, I'm not in Washington. We're on recess. I'm spending the holidays out in Bryn Mawr. At the moment, though, I'm downtown."

"All right. Downtown doing what?"

"Like I said. Calling for a friend. Do you know who William Jefferson is?"

"Of course I do. Took over as police commissioner after that whole thing blew up."

"The whole thing blew up," John Jackman said. "Well, that's one way of putting it. Biggest corruption scandal in the history of the Commonwealth and it happens while I'm on the job. Do you know I've introduced a bill to make private prisons illegal?"

"I have been following your career, John, yes. But—is that back again? Is there another judge out there shanghaiing people to keep the prison populations up?"

"No," John said. "No, I'm sorry. I wasn't sure how much you knew. You got shot. You were in the hospital. I understood you had a long rehab. I didn't know if you were keeping up. Bill Jefferson thought you probably had been keeping up, which is why I'm making this phone call. He thinks you might not be interested in talking to him."

"I'm a little tired," Gregor said. "This is sounding like gibberish."

"I'm supposed to reassure you that the department is no longer a cesspit of corruption, and it's safe for you to deal with them."

"It was safe enough for me to deal with them when they *were* a cesspit of corruption. What's going on here? Has he got a murder he wants a consultant for?"

"Not a murder, no. It's that thing that happened last night."

"The woman in the garbage bag," Gregor said.

"Exactly."

Gregor stretched out his legs. "You do realize, both of you, that I wasn't actually there? It was Tibor Kasparian and Tommy Moradanyan who witnessed whatever that was? Tibor just called me and asked me to come on out and help. Meaning stand around and listen to the cops question them. I did see the woman and the garbage bag on the ground, but by the time I got there the ambulance men were there already. They were packing her up to get her to the hospital. I take it she didn't die."

"Not yet."

"It's that close?"

"I don't know where we're at now," John said. "The report I got said she was a complete mess, but that's to be expected. You always want people to live, of course, but I think the issue here is the same whether she lives or dies. Things are kind of complicated. Jefferson wants some help."

"All right," Gregor said. "Put him on."

"He wants some help down here."

"You want me to come down there."

"We'll send a car. I take it you still don't drive. We'll send an unmarked, don't worry. Just come down here and talk to Bill and the two detectives we've got working this. You don't have to go on with it past that if you don't want to."

"But you wouldn't call me in if you didn't want me to."

"Yeah, well."

"How fast do I have to be ready?"

"We could pick you up in twenty minutes." There was a long pause. Then Jackman said, "You can't have changed that much, Gregor. This is you. You're up. You're probably in a suit and tie already."

Gregor was in a suit and tie already. Gregor pulled his legs in and stood up. "All right. Just ring the bell when you get here. Do you know Bennis and I have a foster child? He came to us last night."

"Jefferson really does need help, Gregor. This really is a complicated situation."

"Just ring the doorbell. Actually come up to the door. I'm not going to keep everybody's cell phone clear just so the cops can call me from the curb."

Gregor hung up. Then he went down the hall again to the back of the house and the kitchen.

Javier and Bennis were still at the kitchen table. Javier had started in on fruit and cheese. He was handing thick slices of cheese to Pickles, who was sitting patiently on the floor next to his chair. Bennis was just putting down her cell phone.

"That was Ed George," she said as he came in. "He's on his way over. He has paperwork."

"Hadn't we decided we were going to make this a nice calm day, get acquainted with Javier?"

Javier looked up. Pickles put her paws up on Javier's leg and looked over the surface of the table. Javier reached for a strip of bacon.

"What did John Jackman want?" Bennis asked.

Gregor sat down and told her. His plate was still where he had left it, and still mostly full of food. He got a strip of bacon for himself and gnawed on it halfheartedly.

"I think it'll be all right," Bennis said. "I don't think he wants us to sign anything right this minute. I think the point is for us to read it over and then go get it signed in front of a notary. At least he said something about a notary, and he didn't say anything about bringing a notary."

"And Lida isn't here to try to introduce him to every gay man she's ever met in Philadelphia so she can get him safely married and—I don't know what she wants. I'm sorry. I really didn't mean it to be like this. I really did mean to take the month off so we could concentrate on this."

"Don't worry about it," Bennis said, leaning over to take yet another strip of bacon out of Javier's hands before he could feed it to the dog.

3

Edmund George showed up before the police did, which meant he had to have been just around the corner. He was wearing a fedora over a black cashmere coat and a plaid cashmere scarf. He looked like a model for *GQ* magazine, the Absolutely Youngest Partner in the Absolutely Most Prestigious Law Firm in the world. The chances were he wasn't that young. There had been a few lost years back there when Gregor first met him.

He came through to the kitchen with his attaché case held out in front of him. He put the attaché case on the kitchen table and surveyed the wide spread of food there. Then he sat down in front of the nearest empty space.

"Good morning," he said to Javier.

"*Buenos días,*" Javier said.

"He looks better than the last time I saw him," he said to Bennis. "Is that Father Tibor's dog?"

"The general consensus is that he's using it sort of like a therapy dog," Gregor said. "Tibor doesn't mind, and the dog makes Javier happy, so—"

Bennis put a cup and saucer down in front of Ed. "Eat all you want," she said, "but do us a favor and don't feed the dog. Javier's been feeding her all morning. She's going to end up throwing up all over the living room."

Ed ignored the food and started to take papers out of his attaché case. "These are mostly from the Department of Homeland Security," he said, "and that's just busywork. I don't know why they think we're all going to be safer if we fill out enough forms, but they do. I've looked into the whole thing about Javier's background, and I don't know what to tell you."

"Do we really know much of anything about the backgrounds of any of these children?" Gregor asked. "This is the part of all this I don't understand. They come up here, 'unaccompanied minors,' they call them. Who knows where they're from or what they've been through?"

Ed George shrugged. "Gregor, most of these kids, they may be unaccompanied, but you can talk to them. They'll tell you where they're from. They'll talk about their lives at home."

"You can't verify any of it," Gregor pointed out.

"No, you can't," Ed said. "But you can punt. You at least have something to say. Angela Gonzalez from Honduras. Jose Gomez from El Salvador. It gives you something to write down and it makes everybody feel better. Unless you've had better luck than the rest of us, we don't even have a last name for this one."

"I wonder if we just couldn't make up a last name for him," Bennis said. "We could call him Santamaria, because he's always sitting in the Mary chapel in church."

"He's going to have to have a last name for school," Ed said. "What are you using there?"

"Demarkian," Gregor said. "It seemed like the most sensible thing to use."

Ed shook his head. "You might as well use that on this stuff. I've been fudging it for weeks now. They haven't been happy with me. That's why you have all this, now. I've been putting off doing it until we could decide what to do about a surname. And it's not safe to let it go too long."

"We really have to worry about that," Gregor said, feeling completely disoriented. "Do you realize how many people this neighborhood has brought over from Armenia just since I came back to live here? Never mind before that. I can remember all kinds of snags and problems and I don't know what else. Armenia was under Soviet control for a lot of the time. But I don't remember anybody ever worrying about raids from immigration."

"It's a new world," Ed said.

"Is it just because he's, you know, Spanish?" Bennis asked.

Ed shook his head. "It's everybody, everywhere. Except Canadians. Nobody seems to care about the Canadians. But we've got a guy in the office doing immigration from the UK, and they're threatening one of his guys with deportation over a DUI from 1982. Granted it was a pretty spectacular DUI and the guy spent a month in jail, but we'd never have had that kind of problem even five years ago."

"Sister Margaret Mary said they keep watch for ICE vans over at the school," Bennis said. "They've never had ICE there, but some of the other schools in the city have. It seems insane to me."

Ed George got another sheaf of papers out of his attaché case. It was smaller, but also more *official* looking in some way. Gregor picked it up and looked at it.

"Department of State?"

Ed took the sheaf of papers back. "We're going to try something. If it doesn't work, it can't hurt us. If it does work, we're going to be able to protect Javier here, at least in part. We're going to make his visit official."

"Whatever Javier's story," Gregor said, "I don't think he was the Honduran minister of agriculture."

"And we don't know who his parents were, so we can't say his father was the Honduran minister of agriculture, either," Ed said. "We're also stuck with not knowing his country of origin. But maybe that's a good thing. We're going to guess that he's Mexican."

Gregor nodded. "That's the most logical thing, if you think about it. I've been thinking that he can't have come far. He wasn't hurt or abused. That's almost never the case with kids who take the long trek up here from Central America. They get preyed on."

"My interest is that the Jesuits have an educational exchange program going on with Mexico," Ed George said. "Javier is actually a little too young to qualify, but it's like everything else in his case. We don't know his age, so we can fudge it a little. I've talked to the Maryknoll nuns down at the border and the sisters here and the head of the program in Philadelphia and we worked something out. You can use Demarkian as his last name. That's all right. That won't matter. But from now on we have to be consistent. This at least has to look good."

"So the State Department will think Javier is here on an educational exchange program?" Bennis said. "And that will protect him from ICE?"

"Sort of," Ed said. "Unfortunately, there's nothing we can do

50

about the raids. If ICE decides it wants to swoop in somewhere and check everybody's documentation, there's nothing we can do about it. And they sometimes pick up people who are here perfectly legally but can't prove it. After all, can either of you prove you're in the United States legally? I couldn't. I don't carry my birth certificate around and I keep my passport in my safe-deposit box. And if ICE does stage a raid and scoop him up with a bunch of other people, he won't necessarily be given a chance to phone you. Assuming he knows how to phone you."

"We're getting him a cell," Bennis said.

"In that case, if he suddenly goes missing, you're going to have to go looking for him. If I were you, I'd make sure somebody walks him to and from school every day. And the office is all set up to go looking for him if he gets snatched. But what this will do"—Ed pointed at the State Department paperwork—"is make him not exactly undocumented. He'll have paperwork he can carry and you'll have paperwork you can keep, saying he's part of this program. But it would be a really good idea if you could hurry."

"Why?" Gregor asked.

"Because," Ed said, "we probably can't get this backdated. He's supposed to have done all this before he ever crossed the border. And we're not going to send him back down there to cross the border again, so we're going to have do a few dipsy doodles so it isn't clear that he came in illegally first. You fill those out today, if you can. When I come back to get them, I'll bring a notary from the office. And I'll come back at six."

"I'll do them," Bennis said quickly.

Out in the hallway, the doorbell sounded, playing the first few notes of "Für Elise."

"I'll get it," Gregor said.

TWO

1

Meera Agerwal got to the office late, still sick, and still in a very bad mood. The sick was even worse than it had been the night before. She had taken ibuprofen before she left home, and also had a cup made from one of her mother's special tea packets that was supposed to cure everything because it was Indian. She had no idea what was in the damn thing, and she didn't care. Her head was pounding. Every muscle in her body ached. She seemed to have both fever and chills at once. Then, to tear it all, she was finding it nearly impossible to balance on her high heels. There were two things that were better in India than in the United States: you didn't wear high heels with a sari, and it didn't get this kind of cold.

The girls in the office were already seated at their computers and talking away, jabbering nonstop about nothing that mattered. They all had pictures in frames on their desks. The frames were cheap and thin. With one exception, the pictures all seemed to be of animals. The one exception was on the desk of the only woman in the office with children. She had a girl and a boy, and they were posed together in front of a backdrop that looked like sky. The rest of the photographs were all of dogs and cats. The girls talked about the dogs and cats as if they were children.

Meera had her own little office. It was nothing much, but it distinguished her from the girls out there, in what was called the bullpen. She sat down and put her purse on her desk. Her ankles ached from negotiating the sidewalks. The city was still full of ice. She put her head in her hands and tried to steady herself. Any American in the company would have stayed home on a day she felt like this. That was why Meera was here. If they'd wanted an American, they would have hired one.

Rita Antonelli came in without knocking. They were supposed to knock. Meera wanted to scream.

"Miss Agerwal?" Rita said. "Are you sure you're all right? You look like you're feeling worse than you were last night."

Meera put her hands down. "I am feeling all right," she said. "Thank you."

"Well, I don't mean to bother you, but your mother called," Rita said. "We've been a little worried, because it was really long distance. She said it wasn't anything important, but—"

"I will call her back," Meera said. Except she wouldn't. She wasn't about to call Mumbai from the office phone. She wasn't about to call Mumbai from her cell phone while she was in the office, either.

"Well," Rita said, hesitating. "She did say she would call back. And she said she had some good news. I took the call. She sounded happy."

For God's sake, Meera thought. "We need to file the rent receipt reports today for the places downtown," Meera said. "I need you to start putting them together and sending them to me, and I'm going to go over them so they can be corrected before they're officially filed. I don't want a repeat of last month. There were so many typos, Mr. Alder could barely read them. And we're going to have to make an eviction list."

"I always think it's sad," Rita said. "Evicting people at Christmas."

"It's not at Christmas, it's after Christmas. And everybody will get the usual thirty days."

"Still."

"Mr. Alder is a lot more lenient than I would be," Meera said. "Some of these people, it's incredible. It's as if they thought apartments sprang up out of the ground like grass. It costs money to build an apartment building. It costs money to run it. Where do these people think the money comes from?"

"Yes," Rita said, looking uncomfortable. "Yes, well—"

The phone on Meera's desk rang. Rita looked infinitely relieved.

"I'd better let you take that," she said, and fled the office.

Meera picked up. "Hello," she said.

If her head hadn't been pounding so badly, she would have realized that her mother couldn't have called with good news. The times were all off. God only knew how late it was in Mumbai, or how early. Meera could never keep it straight. But her mother never called her at the office, either.

"Meera?" Her mother's voice was floaty and high.

"Mai," Meera said.

"I tried to call you at home, but you weren't there. And then I tried to call you at your work, but you weren't there, either. I didn't know what to do?"

"What's wrong?"

"Nothing is wrong!" Meera's mother sounded triumphant. "I thought there must be, but here you are. So nothing is wrong!"

"Okay." The ibuprofen was doing her no good at all. There was a sledgehammer going off inside her head. "Maimai, listen. I have a flu. I am feeling very ill."

"You should drink—"

"I did, already, before I left the apartment. And before I went to bed last night. But I'm still very ill, and I don't understand—"

"It was on the CBS. I listened on the Internet."

Meera tried to sort this out. "You were listening to CBS on the Internet," she said. This made a sort of sense. Her mother had bookmarked a local CBS news site. She checked it on and off to find out what was going on in Philadelphia and what the weather was and that kind of thing.

"It was that woman in the garbage bag," her mother said. "They didn't say who she was. They didn't show a picture. Somebody put a woman in a garbage bag and threw her away on the street. It could have been you."

Compared to Mumbai, there was not really a lot of crime in Philadelphia. Meera's mother acted as if the crime in Mumbai didn't count.

"Maimai," Meera said. "It wasn't me. And things happen. Things happen everywhere. And I am at work."

"Yes, yes. I will go away now that I know nothing is wrong. I only had to know that you were safe."

"I am safe."

"Yes, yes. And you are ill. You should leave work and spend the day in bed."

"I've got too much work to do."

"Yes, yes."

And then the phone went dead. Just like that.

Meera began to boot up her computer. A woman in a garbage bag. There must be something on the news. Hadn't there been a picture of this woman? That would not necessarily have stopped Maimai. She would think the picture was distorted, or just plain wrong.

There was movement in the doorway, just outside her vision. Meera looked up. Rita was standing there, but she didn't come in this time. She didn't knock, either. This was fortunate for Meera's head.

"Miss Agerwal?" Rita said.

"I am sorry," Meera said. "I think I feel less well than I thought I did."

"You don't look well," Rita said. "But there's something out here we thought you'd better see."

"What is it?"

"We don't know."

Fine. Wonderful. Exactly what she needed. Meera made herself stand up.

When she got into the bullpen, what she saw was all the girls standing around—nothing. They were just standing in a little circle and staring at the floor.

Meera went up to them and looked at the floor herself. There was something on the carpet, a jagged-edged splotch about three inches across, brownish red and thick looking.

"It's sticky," one of the girls said, pointing a toe at it. "It's sort of like paste."

"Karen almost fell in it," one of the other girls said.

Meera made herself get down in a crouch to look at it. Her headache had suddenly receded. Her fever and chills had reduced itself to chills alone. It wasn't just that it was three inches across. It was thick, thick enough so that it had not been completely absorbed by the carpet. It was *deep*.

Meera made herself stand up. "It looks like hot chocolate. Have any of you been drinking hot chocolate?"

"No, we haven't," Rita said. "And that wasn't here when we left last night, either. Somebody would have noticed."

"Maybe it was one of the cleaning staff then," Meera said.

"It doesn't look like hot chocolate to me," one of the girls said.

"I think somebody threw up," said another one.

Meera put a hand against a desk to steady herself. "Call maintenance and get it cleaned up," she said. "We can't stand around staring at it all day. Tell them they're probably going to need some carpet shampoo."

"Yes, Miss Agerwal."
"Yes, Miss Agerwal."
"Yes, Miss Agerwal."

Meera went back into her office and shut the door behind her.

Now that she wasn't staring at the thing, the regular sick was coming back. She felt shaky and unsure of her ability to stand. That might be the flu. She went to her desk and sat down again. The computer was up and running. She got on the Internet and typed in the web address of the only local news station she could think of.

She didn't know if she should call Cary Alder about this, or not.

2

There were times when Sister Margaret Mary longed for the days before the convent reforms of Vatican II—even though she hadn't been alive back then, and even though she didn't think she could have survived in a wimple. In the old days, the convent had been a threshold. No newspapers or magazines had crossed its threshold. Radios and televisions existed, but hidden away out of sight except for emergencies. The Maryknolls were considered very progressive because they had allowed their sisters to listen to FDR's fireside chats. A very old nun who had been at the motherhouse when Margaret Mary was a novice had told the story of being a novice herself on the day the mother superior had appeared in recreation with a television set and they had all sat down to listen to the news of the Kennedy assassination.

These days you had to work very hard to keep a lid on all the media, but there was no way to avoid it entirely. Sister Margaret Mary did what she could by insisting that no sister look at anything until after morning Mass, and no sister spend more than half an hour a day on the Internet. Sisters had to spend more time than that on computers, of course. Here, like everywhere else, everything was done on computers. Grades. Papers. Forms to be filled out and sent to the archdiocese and the superintendent of schools and the health department. It saved paper and storage space, but it gave Sister Margaret Mary eyestrain.

Sister Margaret Mary was polishing the brass candy bowl on the long coffee table in the convent's front parlor when Sisters Rosalie and Jacob came running in from outside, worked up beyond recognition and completely out of breath. There were a lot of sisters in this convent, but still not enough to cover all the bases. Everybody pitched in to do housework on the days when school was not in session. Sister Margaret Mary put down the chamois cloth and looked up to see what the fuss was about. Sisters Rosalie and Jacob were very young, and they were also very flustered.

"Sisters," Margaret Mary said. "Decorum."

The wimple might have been a pain to negotiate, but an old-fashioned habit did slow everything down.

Sister Jacob was waving a copy of the *Philadelphia Inquirer* in the air. "We've got to call the police," she said. "Right this minute."

"The police?"

"Sister, we really do have to call the police," Rosalie said. "This woman is unconscious and she didn't have any identification on her and we know who she is. Well, we sort of know who she is. I mean, somebody here must—"

Sister Margaret Mary got up and took the newspaper out of Sister Jacob's hand. The relevant headline was easy to spot. It appeared over the masthead in a banner with a picture on one side and the words DO YOU KNOW THIS WOMAN? across the top of the page. Sister Margaret Mary stared at the picture for a moment. Then she began to read the text. She had to turn to an inside page to finish it.

"She does look familiar, doesn't she?" she said.

Sister Peter came into the parlor, carrying a vase of wildflowers. She was not running. "What's all this?" she asked, putting the vase down on the mantel of the fireplace.

"We have to call the police," Sister Jacob announced again.

Margaret Mary passed the paper to Sister Peter. "Remember all the noise last night? The sirens and all the rest of it?"

"I remember thinking somebody had been murdered," Sister Peter said. "Was somebody?"

"Not exactly. As far as I can figure out from the story, a garbage bag fell out of the back of a truck and there was a woman in it, but she wasn't dead. Look at the picture on the front."

Sister Peter looked. "Oh," she said.

"She lives in the parish," Sister Rosalie said. "I've seen her a dozen times. And I've seen her in church at Forty Hours' Devotion."

"I've seen her at Mass," Sister Jacob said. "The four o'clock English Mass. She's a daily communicant."

Margaret Mary nodded. "I've seen her too. I've never talked to her."

"I've never talked to her either," Rosalie said. "But Father Alvarez must have. If she's a daily communicant, she must go to confession at least sometimes. He must have talked to her at least in confession."

"He can't go running around telling people what he heard in confession," Jacob said.

"Of course he can't," Rosalie said. "I just meant that if she comes to confession, he probably knows who she is. What her name is. I know she doesn't have to tell him her name in confession, but still, if you go then you have a relationship with the priest and a lot of people do tell their names in confession and talk to the priest just like they'd talk to anybody."

"She was in a garbage bag," Jacob said. "They put her in a garbage bag and dumped her on the street. Nobody knows who she is. We've got to call the police and tell them what we know."

Margaret Mary sat down in the big armchair next to the fireplace. Then she reached out and took the paper from Sister Peter. "All right," she said. "First things first. Let's get everybody else in here and see if any of us knows her name, or where she lives, or who she knows. I've seen her, but I can't remember ever seeing her with anybody."

"I can't either," Sister Peter said. "But they're right. I see her around all the time. Forty Hours' Devotion. Stations of the Cross on Good Friday."

"Let's show this around and see what we come up with," Margaret Mary said. "Then we can show it to Father Alvarez, if he hasn't seen it already. He's head of the parish. He's got to be the one to decide who to call." She looked at the paper again. "There has to be a number in here to call to give information. They always do that."

Sister Peter looked at Rosalie and Jacob. "Why don't the two of you go round up the troops and bring them here. And don't run everywhere. Decorum, like Sister Superior said."

Rosalie and Jacob looked at each other. Then they rushed out of the room together, full-tilt boogie.

Sisters Margaret Mary and Peter looked at each other and shook their heads. Margaret Mary deposited the paper on the coffee table. "Tell me I'm not crazy to think we were better trained in our day."

"We're just getting old, that's all," Sister Peter said. "I'm just grateful we're getting the vocations. Right now, I want you to pay attention to this. You didn't read that article very well."

"I didn't? What did I miss?"

"It's not what you missed. It's what you mistook. Go back and look at it if you don't believe me. She didn't fall off a truck. She fell out of the back of a black van."

Sister Margaret Mary sat bolt upright. "What?"

"A black van, Sister. It's right there."

"The same black van? Could it possibly be the same black van?"

"I only saw your black van for a second," Sister Peter said. "And I didn't see the van she fell out of and neither did you. But I think you'd better mention it."

Sister Margaret Mary thought she would have done better to get the license plate last night, but she hadn't thought of it.

3

The call came in at nine thirty. Tibor Kasparian knew who it was as soon as he heard it ring. He almost thought about not answering. His kitchen table was piled high with the endless paperwork that was the inevitable result of dealing with one government agency after another. The entire world was going digital and paperless, but government agencies would never leave it at that. Once you got on a computer and filled out the forms online, you had to print them all out and submit them again in "hard copy." Tibor remembered when "hard copy" meant a newspaper story about something serious, like a world war. He also remembered when a world war was the worst thing he was worried about.

He picked up after five rings and then answered, reflexively, in Armenian. Then he cleared his throat and tried again.

"I am here, Russell. You are out of your schedule."

Russell was breathing heavily. He was a young man, but ever since he'd gone to prison he seemed to be always out of breath.

"They all know Tommy was here yesterday. They think something's up."

"Is it?"

"I don't know. He tried to call me yesterday."

I should have gone to the Ararat, Tibor thought. It would never occur to Russ to call him at the Ararat. Russ might call his cell phone, but probably not. Tibor didn't understand why, but prisons hated the very idea of cell phones. Prisoners were not allowed to have them, and calling out to them caused all kinds of problems.

Tibor got his coffee from where he had left it on the kitchen table and took it over to his living room couch. The apartment was enormous, but it was still an open floor plan. He got some books off the couch and sat down.

"What did he call you about?" he asked. "What did he have to say?"

"I don't know," Russ said. "He called after lockdown. We aren't allowed to get calls then."

"What time was it?"

"I don't know that either. They didn't come and tell me about it. They just notified me this morning. I suppose I could have asked them. I didn't. I'm sorry."

"I'm sorry, Russell. I don't know why I asked that. I don't think it matters."

"They would have asked him if it was some kind of an emergency. I guess it wasn't."

One of the books he had moved out of the way was a James Patterson novel he couldn't remember buying. The other was Augustine's *Confessions*.

"Tibor?" Russ said. "What happened last night?"

"Tcha," Tibor said.

"It could just be him following up after yesterday," Russ said. "But I don't believe it. Lockdown is at ten. If he called later than that and from home, there had to be something up. If Donna'd found out about it, she'd have gone berserk."

"Tcha," Tibor said again. Then he sucked in enough air to inflate a balloon and tried to give a concise summary of the something that had happened. The news would have gotten to Russ eventually, even if Tommy had not called. It would have been in a newspaper or on a television program or on the Internet. It would just have taken longer.

Russ listened to the whole thing without asking questions. Then he said, "Jesus."

"It was not as bad as it sounds," Tibor said. "I'm just very tired and not speaking well. The woman was not dead. It was not a murder."

"Is she dead now?"

"I don't know."

"It's the kind of thing where somebody ends up dead," Russ said.

"Why wasn't it you who went out and looked at her? Why did you send Tommy?"

"I didn't send Tommy, Russell. It was a fast thing. One moment we were walking on the sidewalk and then there were the sounds of a car coming too fast. Tommy pushed me out of the way and the car hit a lamp pole. I am speaking badly again."

"So, who was this woman? Who is she? The woman in the garbage bag."

"I don't know."

"You don't know her name or anything?"

"Nobody knows anything," Tibor said. "I called Krekor, and he came. Tommy called 911. Then we all stood around while other people came and people went and people stood around. She didn't have a handbag. The police looked through her pockets and her clothes and the bag and did not find any identification. Nobody knows who she is."

"A white woman? A black woman? An Asian?"

"Does it matter?"

"It does for purposes of identification."

"From what I could see, she was a white woman. She could have been Spanish. The place where we were was on the edge of a Spanish neighborhood."

"I can't stay on the phone much longer. They only give us three to five minutes."

"It was an accident, Russell. It had nothing to do with us. It was an accident we were there. I don't think you have to worry about Tommy being in trouble."

"Jesus," Russell said again. Then he sighed. "When I got here, I thought it was me. Because of the way things were. The way they happened. I thought I was the only one, cut off from everything and everybody, cut off from all connections. But it isn't just me. Everybody here is like that. Almost everybody."

"I think that is normal, Russell."

"There's nothing normal about it. It's insane, trying to live like that. I don't mean being locked up. I mean not knowing what's going on, not knowing what's happening to—people. There are guys in here, they don't have anybody. No wives. No girlfriends. No children. I mean, they have them, but they don't really have them. There's no real connection. Even their mothers don't come to visit."

"It is a sad thing, Russell, yes."

"I was never like that."

"No, Russell, you were not."

"I don't want to wake up three months from now and find out Tommy's in juvie and nobody told me anything about it. They haven't shut down any of those places. We're still running for-profit juvenile detention centers in the Commonwealth of Pennsylvania."

"Russell—"

"Never mind," Russell said. "I've got to get off. But I meant what I said. I don't want to wake up three months from now and find out God knows what has been going on and nobody's told me about it. Don't do that to me, Tibor. No matter what you think of the rest of it. Don't do that to me—"

"I would not—"

Russ Donahue was off the line. There was nothing but dead air in Tibor's ear.

THREE

1

Gregor Demarkian had always thought that life in the District of Columbia changed people more than life in other places did. It had changed him, when he was with the FBI. He had come to the Bureau thinking he knew something about corruption. He had spent an inordinate amount of time taking courses in the then-new field of forensic accounting, and he had been a witness to the politics of Philadelphia all of his life. Then he'd run into his very first congressman on the take, and he'd never felt the same way about arithmetic again.

The District of Columbia had changed John Jackman, too. At the moment, this was most obvious in the way the man held himself. He looked as if nothing had ever made him feel insecure, ever. He looked as if he had emerged from the womb in complete control of his world and the universe it was in. This was not true, but Gregor was not going to remind him of it.

The meeting turned out to be in Jackman's constituent office in downtown Philadelphia. It was a small suite of rooms on the ground floor of a building near Independence Hall. It didn't look as if it were used much. Jackman himself was standing next to a window that looked out on a street that ran along the side of the building. The other man—the Philadelphia commissioner of police, Gregor supposed—was sitting in an armchair near the desk.

"You have the oddest look on your face," Jackman said, as Gregor walked in.

"I was thinking of what it was like when I first joined the FBI," Gregor said. "Did you know that in those days, if you wanted to be a special agent, you had to be a lawyer or an accountant? I don't think they do that anymore."

"Which were you?" Jackman asked.

"I was an accountant," Gregor said. "And no, I couldn't do your taxes. I can't even do my own."

The other man had stood up. He was enormous in both height and bulk. The black skin on his head shone as if he'd polished it.

"Gregor Demarkian," John Jackman said. "This is Michael Washington."

Michael Washington held out his hand. Gregor shook it.

"You're an accountant?" Michael Washington said. "I thought John said something about serial killers."

"The Behavioral Sciences Unit," Gregor said. "I spent the last ten years of my career setting that up and running it. You had to be a lawyer or an accountant to get hired. That didn't mean they used you as a lawyer or an accountant."

"I was telling Mike that the BSU is practically the only part of the FBI that deals with murders," John said.

"They don't call it the BSU anymore," Gregor said. "I think the initials got to them. But, yes, murder is almost always a state crime. The BSU was founded to deal with the reality that serial killers often operate in more than one state. Some of them operate in four or five states. It helps to have something that can connect it all up."

Michael Washington looked slightly confused, but he didn't ask any more questions. Instead, he sat back down.

John Jackman waved Gregor to one of the other chairs and came away from the window to sit at the desk.

"I told Mike here that you weren't going to hold a grudge against the Philadelphia police for arresting Russ Donahue, but he wanted to be sure," John said. "And I wanted to be sure that we could look into all parts of this situation without letting the cat out of the bag. We need someone who can investigate something without letting anyone know what he's really investigating."

"You need to investigate a murder without letting anyone know you're investigating a murder," Gregor said.

"It's not a murder," Mike Washington said. "At least not yet."

"And murder or assault, that part of it is secondary," John said.

"All right," Gregor said. "Let's say it's an assault. What assault?"

"The woman dumped in the garbage bag last night," John said.

Gregor shook his head. "You realize I wasn't actually there. Tibor and Tommy were on the scene accidentally and Tibor called me to come hold his hand. I didn't see the incident. I have no idea what went on."

"That doesn't matter," Mike Washington said. "The thing with the garbage bag is an accident, really. If it wasn't for the Aldergold, we wouldn't have thought to connect up the two. But now we've got this thing, and we can't let it go."

"Do you know who Cary Alder is?" John Jackman asked.

"Sure," Gregor said. "It's hard to miss him. Alder Properties. Great big high-rise monstrosities all tricked out in gold paint."

"Right," John said. "Except there's a lot more to Alder Properties than that. They own more than a dozen buildings in Philadelphia, and most of them are not high end. The company was started by Alder's father, and it was started the way a lot of these things are. You buy the building you're living in. You put some of the money you make from that aside and buy another building. If you're good at it and you're ambitious, you get bigger and bigger buildings in better and better neighborhoods, and eventually you get Alder Tower."

"And you think Cary Alder has something to do with the woman in the garbage bag?"

"We don't know," Michael Washington said.

"We think Cary Alder is bribing the mayor and half the building inspectors in the city," John said, "but there's nothing all that odd about that. At least half these guys do it. They see it as part of the price of doing business. What has me here is that we're pretty sure he's also paying off his congressman, and nobody knows why."

Gregor considered this. "That really is a job for the FBI."

"They're on it," John said.

"Then I don't know what I'm doing here."

"We were kind of hoping you could consult on the case of the woman in the garbage bag," Michael Washington said. "And, you know, keep your eyes open. For whatever it is. We don't know what it is. We just know it isn't drugs."

John Jackman reached into the pocket of his jacket and came out with a gold coin the size of an Olympic medal. "Ever seen one of those?"

Gregor took the coin. "No. What is it?"

"It's Aldergold," John Jackman said. "There are half a dozen places in this city, owned and operated by Alder Properties, where those things are the only legal tender. You can't go up to the bar and take out your wallet. You have to have those. And you use them just like cash. But first you have to get them. Not everybody can get them. You have to rent one of Alder's more expensive apartments, or be one of Alder's big customers in that place he's got in Atlantic City. There are probably a couple of other ways, or Alder could just give them to you. But the point is, they aren't easy to get, and not everybody can get them."

"And this has something to do with the woman in the garbage bag, how?" Gregor asked.

Michael Washington shifted his bulk in the chair.

"When they got her to the hospital and started to go through the things she had on her," he said, "she didn't have a wallet, she didn't have money, she didn't have identification, she didn't have anything. But she did have fifteen of those."

2

They wanted to get him out of the building without being seen by reporters, although Gregor didn't see why that should be an issue. No one knew he was there, and no one knew the police commissioner and the senator cared one way or the other about the woman in the garbage bag.

"You're something of a public figure," John Jackman said by way of explanation.

It wasn't much of an explanation, but Gregor let it ride and installed himself in the reception room to make some phone calls. He hadn't asked about the elephant in the middle of the room, and for the moment he didn't want to. At some point, though, he was going to have to know what was going on with the mayor. It was the mayor he would have expected to find at this meeting, whether Michael Washington was there or not. Instead, the mayor was nowhere to be seen, and anytime anyone mentioned him they made little coughing noises, as if they were strangling.

Gregor called Bennis first.

"I'm filling out forms," she said, when she picked up. "There are a lot of forms."

"Is Ed still there?"

"No, he left almost as soon as he got here. He showed me where the little Xs were that mean we're supposed to sign, and where the little check marks were that mean we're supposed to initial. I'm leaving all the signing and initialing until you get here. We both have to do those."

"Where's Javier?"

"Sitting here with Pickles and a coloring book and a plate of those Armenian almond cookies Lida makes that I like. Lida and Hannah were here. I told you they were coming. They dropped off boxes. I put the chocolate chip up in a cabinet where Javier can't get to it."

"Javier isn't supposed to have chocolate chip cookies?"

"Javier can have them all he wants, but chocolate is a poison for dogs. And Javier feeds Pickles everything. I think Pickles got more breakfast than I did. She certainly got more bacon."

"Ah," Gregor said. "Listen, do you want me to bring something home? I don't know what we're doing about dinner, unless you mean to get the Ararat to send something in again. Or you want to go out. And I don't know when I'm going to get back to you."

"We'll be fine. I'll think of something. We do have food in this house."

"I know. Don't mind me."

"Is it at least something interesting, what you're doing?"

"It's about that woman Tibor and Tommy found yesterday."

"Really."

"I'd better tell you about this when I get home," Gregor said. "Let me get off and see if I can find out what's going on. Or not."

"I have cold cuts for lunch."

"I'll remember that."

Gregor closed down. The building around him was very quiet. The rooms that comprised John's offices were even quieter. He opened the contacts list on his phone and scrolled through it. When he found what he was looking for, he considered for one last time and then punched it in.

Drew Tackerby picked up himself. Gregor had called his private cell phone, not anything connected to Drew's office.

"It's Gregor Demarkian," Gregor said.

"Gregor Demarkian on my private line," Drew said. "Why do I think I'm going to regret this?"

Drew had a desk job now. It had taken him five years longer

than it had Gregor to get out of the field, but Drew had not been as determined as Gregor to *get* out. Greg couldn't remember what Drew's title was these days.

"I'll admit," Gregor said. "I was a little afraid you'd retired."

"End of the year. What is it you want me to do?"

"Get me some information. I don't think it's top secret, classified information."

"Information about what?"

"I want to know if the Bureau is investigating my congressman."

"For what?"

"I don't know," Gregor said. "As far as I can tell at the moment, nobody here seems to know. Which doesn't make a lot of sense to me. In my day, the Bureau didn't open investigations into United States congressmen willy-nilly."

"In J. Edgar's day," Drew started.

"I know," Gregor said. "But we're past all that, and there's something about this that just feels all wrong. Whatever it is that's going on has to do with a local guy, a real estate developer, named Cary Alder."

"Bingo," Drew said. "You just said the magic words."

"Cary Alder?"

"He's not as local as you think," Drew said. "He operates in Pennsylvania, New Jersey, and Florida. Which means what he does crosses state lines, so the Bureau can investigate him."

"So you're investigating him. For what?"

"You want a list? Bank fraud, including international bank fraud. That's a good one. Bribery. The guy's absolutely bribing a couple of mayors. Unfortunately, he's more intelligent at it than a lot of people are. We aren't going to get lucky and find a freezer full of money in anybody's basement."

"So you're going to arrest him?"

"Not right away," Drew said. "Here's the thing. Bank fraud and bribery? All these guys do it to one extent or another. We follow what they're doing until we hit something we can really nail them for, which is harder than you'd think. In Cary Alder's case, something else looks like it's going on, but it's not clear what. And the problem with that is that the whatever it is might not even be illegal. People hide parts of their lives for lots of different reasons, not all of them connected with the criminal justice system."

"That's what they're saying up here," Gregor said. "This is the part that sounds all wrong to me."

"I can put you in touch with the guy who's in charge of that investigation," Drew said. "He won't mind talking to you. Especially if you're investigating Alder yourself for some reason. Are you?"

"I don't know."

"You sound just as coherent as the rest of us," Drew said. "But let me have Judson Tallirico call you. He might not be able to get back to you until this evening, but it's like I said. He'll be glad to talk to you. And I'll run in to him around here sometime today."

"I take it Virginia hasn't had the ice storm to end all ice storms."

"Nothing close."

"All right," Gregor said. "Have him call me at this number around nine o'clock tonight, if that's possible. I ought to be completely free and clear by then."

Gregor hung up. John's offices were still quiet. The building around them was still quiet.

Everything was quiet, except that somebody had dumped a woman in a garbage bag on an iced-over city street.

3

When Michael Washington reappeared, he was alone and carrying a large, black zip folder. He looked sweaty and tired, as if the smallest amount of exertion wore him out.

Gregor stood up and took the zip folder. It weighed a ton.

"It's everything we have on Alder," Washington said. "The good, the bad, and the inexplicable."

"I think it's interesting you're willing to say there's something good about Alder."

Washington shrugged. "I'm not one of those people who has some vision in the sky about perfection and thinks everything else is crap. It would be nice if every building with low-cost housing in it looked like the Bellagio and ran like the Waldorf Astoria, but they don't. It would be nicer if public housing was fit habitation for children, but it isn't. We have a million people in this city who have to live somewhere. It seems like almost all the people willing to provide them with a place to stay are more like Cary Alder than they are like Saint Michael the Archangel."

"So you don't really want to arrest Alder?"

"Oh, we want to arrest him, all right. His operations are getting more out of hand by the minute and the secret thing is driving us all nuts. And then there's the servants' entrance thing. That got up everybody's nose."

"What's the servants' entrance thing?"

"It was when John was still mayor," Washington said. "He got the idea from New York. Always a bad sign to me, the idea comes from New York. Anyway, we've got height restrictions on new construction and a lot of the developers don't like it. The lower they have to stay, the fewer the apartments they can build on the same lot. Luxury apartments, you know. Anyway, there was this thing in New York where they'd give you permission to build a higher high-rise if you included a certain percentage of 'affordable' apartments in the same building. Affordable. Jesus. Two thousand dollars for a postage stamp."

"Are we that expensive here?"

"No," Washington said. "I think that's why John thought he could get away with it. He could make the guys provide actually affordable apartments, if you see what I mean."

"For poor people."

"That was the idea," Washington said. "So John put the idea out there to a couple of guys who had applications in to build, but most of them weren't interested. I was an old man before I realized most people are a lot more interested in status than they are in money. Oh, not people like Cary Alder. I mean the people they sell and rent to. This really *isn't* New York. In New York, just being in Manhattan is enough to give you a shine. Here, you've got to have visible signs of exclusivity. The developers were all worried that nobody would buy a luxury apartment in a building that also had affordable apartments in it."

"Except for Cary Alder."

"Yeah. John should have known better. He's a smart man, and he's been around. But he didn't. The shoe didn't drop until the building opened. When it did, it turned out that Alder had built those affordable apartments, but to get to them you had to go to a separate entrance. They were totally sealed off from the rest of the building. You couldn't go in the front door. You had to go around to the back. The separate entrance wasn't even on the same street. You wouldn't even have the same address as the rich part of the building. And the front entrance had a doorman. The back entrance didn't."

"Seriously," Gregor said. "It sounds like some Thirties movie. And people put up with this?"

"The people who took the apartments didn't have a choice," Washington said. "They were placed there by the social services departments. John had a world-class hissy fit, but there wasn't anything he could do. It was, though, the last building that got built that way in Philadelphia. John tried to impose conditions that would eliminate the backdoor thing, but under those conditions nobody was willing to bite."

"Because the people in the luxury apartments are more interested in status than money," Gregor said.

"And they don't want to know that the poor people even exist," Washington said. "But it's more complicated than that, at least for me. My father had a three-story stacker out in Lansdowne. We lived in the top floor and rented out the two floors beneath us. We rented to people more or less as poor as we were ourselves. You may not believe this, Mr. Demarkian, but it's expensive to rent to poor people. Most poor people are fine, you know, but even the good ones have money problems and can't pay the rent. The others will kill you. They break things. They get hyped up on alcohol and drugs and wreck the place. There are domestic disputes and the cops get called. The rent on those other two apartments paid our mortgage. It got hard sometimes to make that mortgage payment."

"All right," Gregor said. "I can see that."

"You can see it, but you've got to think it through," Washington said. "It can be hard to make enough money to keep a place running when you're renting affordable apartments. That's why the services in those places are so bad. Some cities put up all kinds of regulations demanding that every building have this service or that service, and then it gets to be impossible to run those kinds of buildings and make them pay at all. Then you lose small owner-occupied buildings, which is too bad, because conditions are better for everybody when the owner lives there, too. If you jack up the regulations high enough, you start to lose the corporate-operated ones, too. And every building you lose, every rental unit that disappears from the market, means another guy out on the street in the winter weather. And not just guys."

"I take it there isn't enough public housing to carry them," Gregor said.

"No sane person wants to live in public housing if they can help it," Washington said. "And no sane person wants to bring up children there. But it's more than that. Undocumented immigrants can't get into public housing."

"At all?"

"If there's a member of the family that's here legally, or a citizen, that person can get into public housing and bring some of the undocumented family with them. That happens sometimes. But this is a city with a big undocumented population. ICE has practically taken up residence downtown. We had a raid in North Philadelphia that cleared out eight hundred people in a single day. And maybe those people shouldn't be here and we can take up that argument another day, but a lot of those people are children. And I don't want to see children sleeping in the parks when it's seventeen below."

"So you put up with Cary Alder," Gregor said.

"So I won't say there's nothing good to say about Cary Alder," Washington corrected. "He serves a purpose. Until we can find a way to provide better housing to more people, people like him are going to be necessary to keep people off the streets. And I'm not looking at a world where we're going to find a way to provide better housing any time soon."

"Are you sure you want me to find out what the man is doing?"

Michael Washington sighed. The air came up out of the middle of him in a gigantic wave, so that he inflated and deflated like a bellows.

"Yes," he said. "Because I'm with John. There's something going on there that's weirder than a grade-B horror movie plot, and I don't like the way it makes me feel."

FOUR

1

It was Tommy Moradanyan who convinced Bennis to take Javier to McDonald's instead of the Ararat for lunch, and talked her out of taking him to Taco Bell.

"I think people like you and my mom are way too hinky about Taco Bell," he said, as they walked Javier through the streets to the restaurant. "I mean, I know, it's Tex-Mex and not real Mexican, blah blah blah, but a lot of the Latino kids at school like eating there, and there's even this video by Jennifer Lopez or maybe that woman in Black-Eyed Peas where she and her girlfriends go through the drive-through. But McDonald's will be good. Under the circumstances."

"What are the circumstances?" Bennis asked.

"You know yesterday when I got to St. Catherine's first and I had to wait for all the rest of you? Well, I introduced Javier to Pickles, and Javier cracked up and started singing the Big Mac song."

"Pickles!" Javier said.

They had reached the big glass doors of McDonald's. Javier was looking at the building very solemnly. Bennis wondered if it confused him. It didn't look like the McDonald's buildings in commercials. It was wedged into a city street, not freestanding on a highway. The only arches it had were abstract and symbolic.

"Big Mac," Javier said, sounding confident.

Tommy held open the doors and shooed them inside. "Go sit in a booth. There are booths empty. I saw them through the windows. Do you mind if I get Javier a Big Mac on top of his Happy Meal?"

"Why not just get him a meal with a Big Mac in it?"

"Grown-up meals don't have toys in them," Tommy said. "I almost said 'adult' meals. But 'adult' means sex, right? Everything that's adult is about sex."

Tommy was right about the booths. Bennis grabbed one next to a window looking out on the street, opened her bag, and pulled out a sheaf of random bills. It had to be fifteen years since she'd been in a McDonald's. She seemed to remember that she and Gregor had driven down to South Carolina on a vacation, and they'd gone through a drive-through on the way. She felt unbelievably inadequate. Kids ate at McDonald's. They carried backpacks and watched anime and played in the Little League. Or they didn't. She just didn't know. She knew nothing about children or their lives. And here she was, taking responsibility for a child.

"Spend what you want," she told Tommy. "Just get me a hamburger and maybe a Diet Coke. Do they have bottled water here?"

"Probably," Tommy said. "But there's no point to it. I'll get you a Quarter Pounder without cheese with a Diet Coke. I'll get him a cheeseburger Happy Meal and a Big Mac and just a regular Coke."

Javier had slid into the booth bench across the table from Bennis. "Happy Meal," he repeated. "Excellent!"

Bennis was startled. "That's new," she said.

"I think it's my fault," Tommy said. "I'll be right back."

Tommy disappeared. Bennis shrugged off her black wool jacket. Javier looked solemn, but now Bennis thought he looked a little odd. She really did know nothing about children, and, what was worse, the only ideas she had about them came from the children on Cavanaugh Street, and Tommy when he was younger. She had bought clothes for Javier without thinking, the same kind of clothes Tommy wore, the same kind of clothes she saw on children when she went back to visit on the Main Line. Javier was wearing a Baxter State parka, a pair of new jeans, a white button-down shirt, and a blue cotton Vineyard Vines crewneck sweater with the little pink whale logo on the right shoulder.

He could have come right from school at Bryn Mawr Country Day.

Tommy came reeling back, loaded down with bags. He dumped the bags on the table and took off again. Javier's eyes followed him as he moved through the room.

Then he said, "Tom," and nodded.

"That's right," Bennis said. "That's Tom. And I've got to stop calling him Tommy, or I'll still be doing that twenty years from now when he's getting a Nobel Prize or something."

When Tommy came back, he was carrying two large and one small containers of soda. He put them down on the table and slid in next to Javier. Then he shrugged off his own parka and started tugging at Javier's.

"You've got to take that off when you're inside," he told the boy. "Either that, or you burn up. Now." He picked up the smallest bag. "This is the Happy Meal."

He handed it over. Javier took the bag and opened it. Then he put his hand in the bag and came out with a tiny car in a little plastic bag. He ripped the bag open and looked immensely satisfied.

Tommy handed Bennis a cardboard box. Bennis opened it to find a hamburger without any cheese on it. Tommy took out another box and handed it to Javier.

"Big Mac," he said.

Javier opened the box and looked inside. Then he put the box down on the table and took out the thing inside. To Bennis, it looked sort of like a layer cake, except with hamburger. Hamburgers.

Tommy took out three more boxes. They all contained Big Macs, and they were all for himself.

"I don't understand how you two can eat like that," Bennis said, watching Javier make his way through the Big Mac. "Javier ate enough breakfast to feed the Fourth Army this morning, I'm not kidding. The Melajians sent it over as a favor."

"Well, you're supposed to put some weight on him, aren't you? He's been deprived."

"We think so," Bennis said. "Still. I think I'm surprised that he'd be so enthusiastic about unfamiliar food."

"Maybe it's not unfamiliar food," Tommy said. "This isn't the Middle Ages. There are McDonald's places everywhere these days. Especially if Mr. Demarkian is right and he comes from somewhere near the Mexican border. I went to Tijuana once. The only way you know you're in another country is you have to go through a check-point."

"I suppose," Bennis said.

Javier had retrieved his French fries from the small bag and was playing with the little car, but he was also eating through his Big Mac. There were also apple slices in another little bag, but Javier paid no attention to those.

"It would be so much better if we knew something about him," Bennis said. "Where he came from. What he went through to get over the border. What happened to his family? We don't even know if he came over the border. We don't know anything. And then sometimes I worry we shouldn't even try."

"With Mr. Demarkian around?"

"I see what you mean," Bennis said. "But what if there's a reason for all this secrecy? What if it protects him in some way we don't understand? I have this vision of us getting to the bottom of things the way Gregor likes to do, and then when we get there, we've put him in terrible danger and can't get him out. I don't know. I'm glad he's here. I am. I like him. But I had no idea what I was getting into when Tibor asked us to do this."

"I was just thinking," Tommy said. "Tijuana, you know? We went there on vacation. Mom and me and the squirt and, of course—"

"Russ."

"I don't think you should worry too much. From where I sit, it doesn't look like anybody knows much about anything. It's got to be awful, the places he used to be. It had to be awful enough to make it worth it to send him here."

"I wish I could speak Spanish."

"Pickles," Javier said.

They both looked over at him and he was holding one in his fingers. He'd taken a bite out of it, and the expression on his face was absolutely clear.

Yuck.

2

The problem with keeping two sets of books is that you have to keep track of both of them, and the one for show is always more trouble than the one you keep out of sight.

Bob Borden was waiting at her office door when Clare McAfee came back from picking up lunch. He was bouncing around from one foot to the other as if the floor underneath him was electrified. Clare didn't usually go out to pick up food for lunch. She called for delivery, or had her secretary go. Today she was stressed out and annoyed and claustrophobic. She thought air and exercise would do her good. She walked all the way to the Vilna Deli and picked up a hot pastrami sandwich the size of a bowling ball.

Bob straightened up when he saw her coming, but he didn't stop wriggling around. Clare was carrying a large sack in one hand and a tall coffee in the other. She'd bought the coffee at Starbucks. The containers of coffee at the Vilna were too small.

"Ms. McAfee!" Bob said, sounding anguished and overwrought.

Clare wondered if the bank was about to collapse beneath both their feet, he was that upset. She brushed by him and went to her desk. It was her secretary's lunch hour, too. If it hadn't been, Bob would have been sent packing until he was called for.

Clare put her coffee and her lunch down on her desktop and then went around her desk to sit down. Bob had come in behind her. He was still half hopping from foot to foot.

Clare opened the bag and took out her sandwich. It was wrapped in shiny silver paper.

"Yes?" she said.

Bob suddenly stopped moving. Then he came right up to the edge of the desk and took a deep breath. "It's the oddest thing," he said.

"What is?"

"All I can think is that it has to be a system failure," he said. "The alert system. You know what I mean?"

"I take it the alert system alerted you to something," Clare said, trying to be patient. "What was it it alerted you to?"

"But that's just it! It alerted me to something that isn't there. I don't understand it. I don't understand how it can happen. There has to be a glitch in the system someplace and if there's one glitch in the system there could be thousands and the whole thing could be going to hell. I don't know what we'd do."

"Try starting from the beginning," Clare said.

"Right." Bob took another deep breath. "It was right before lunch. I was trying to clear up some bookkeeping stuff and the alert system sent me one of those messages that ping, you know what I mean. It pops up on the screen. And this one told me that we had a nonperforming loan. We'd made this loan to Mallard and Mallard, the architects, you know them. They do those houses in colors, little town houses—"

"I'm familiar with Mallard and Mallard."

"Right," Bob said. "It said Mallard and Mallard had a loan for one point six million dollars and it was now officially nonperforming. Which means, what? No payments for at least ninety days, right? So I clicked on the alert and it took me to a page that said Mallard and Mallard had taken out a loan on May twenty-seventh of last year to buy some property in Merion Township. It was supposed to be phase one of a larger mortgage loan so that they could build eight town houses on the property. There's nothing wrong with that, is there? We do lots of those loans. And in the middle of all this, I looked it up. We've done lots of those loans for Mallard and Mallard. The only weird thing this time is that there haven't been any payments in forever."

The books for show are always more trouble than the books you hide. Clare's throat felt very sore. She took a long sip of coffee and wished she hadn't.

"So," she said. "Did you call Mallard and Mallard?"

"No," Bob said. "I thought I'd better talk to you first."

"Why?"

"Because I checked it all out," Bob said, getting agitated again. "I thought I ought to do that before I did anything else. I looked through all the stuff the alert system sent out, but then I went directly to our Mallard and Mallard file and looked at that. We do a lot of business with them. And guess what? They've got five separate construction loans out with us right this minute, and every one of them is performing just fine."

"All right," Clare said. "That's not so impossible, then. There's some glitch in the system. We should just correct the alert system so that—"

"No, no. You don't understand. Mallard and Mallard have five loans, but none of them is the loan the alert system is talking about. They don't have a construction loan for any project in Merion Township."

"Well, then—" Clare said.

"*Nobody* has a construction loan out for a project in Merion Township. Well, for that project. I checked. I did global searches all over the place. We haven't made any such loan to anybody. I thought I was losing my mind. That's when I did some calling around. And you know what?"

"What?"

"Mallard and Mallard have no such project going in Merion Township, and neither does anybody else. Most of the land described in the file the alert gave me is a parking lot to a big box store and it's not for sale and isn't going to be. There is no such project anywhere, being pursued by anyone."

"It must be a mistake." Clare put her head in her hands. Count to ten in English. Count to ten in Russian. Try to think.

"The alert system couldn't have just generated this itself," Bob said plaintively. "It's too detailed and complete. Somebody must have put that file in the system deliberately. And gone to a lot of trouble doing it. We must have been hacked. It must be some kind of cyberterrorism."

Think. "Cyberterrorism meant to do what?" Clare asked.

Bob went still. "I don't know," he admitted.

Think. "It's not like a data breach," Clare said. "The only people this could hurt are Mallard and Mallard. Do you think somebody is trying to ruin the credit of Mallard and Mallard?"

"I don't know," Bob said.

Clare knew that if she had any sense, she would find Cary Alder today and kill him with her bare hands. Instead, she sat still at her desk, working very hard to appear totally and deeply calm. Then she came to the only decision she had left.

"Get all your stuff and bring it in here," she said. "Let's bring all this alert stuff up on this computer and see what we've got. I want to see it for myself."

3

Cary Alder's father had been a frugal and deliberative man. He rented all his best apartments out at the highest price he could get for them. He installed his family in a decent but modest place, with just enough space so that they didn't feel cramped. In those days, Alder Properties didn't have buildings with rooftop swimming pools and ground-floor day spas. Cary's father wouldn't have known what to do with them anyway.

Cary was a very different human being, and not just because his father had sent him to all the right places for school. He had learned that having control of high-end places got you things the low-end places never could, even if the low-end places made you lots of money. He liked the rooftop swimming pools and the ground-floor day spas. He especially liked owning things that were both very expensive and of absolutely no use. Well, absolutely no real use. You could say his sterling silver napkin folder had a use; it was just a use most people wouldn't see the point of.

He did understand the need to be seen as a hardworking person. All the really rich people these days prided themselves on how hard they worked and how little time they had to relax. Cary found this, quite frankly, bat crazy, but he put his time in and made himself looked as harassed with responsibilities as possible. It was a kind of status symbol. Today the weather was so awful and the moods of everybody at the office were so depressive, he just couldn't stand it anymore. He came home early, and he had every intention of staying home until the night started and there was something serious to do.

Home was the thousand-square-foot penthouse on top of the best building he owned in the city. It had four bedrooms, seven bathrooms, its own movie theater and its own lap pool. It also had a game room with a pool table and a bar as long as the one in the Alder Palace VIP room. He had wanted to put in a bowling alley, but one of his people had convinced him that the damned thing would make too much noise.

It was two thirty in the afternoon when he let himself into his own living room. He sank himself into a large old-fashioned armchair and called the houseboy to ask for a glass of scotch. This apartment was his private retreat. Nobody was invited here. Cary made a mystery of that, a little eccentric quirk that was supposed to become part of his legend. What he really wanted was a place where he could drink blended whiskey without evoking the pitying stares of people who thought he ought to know better.

The whiskey came. He took a long drag of it, then got the remote for the television that occupied almost one entire wall of the room. At this time of day, there would be nothing on but soap operas, which he didn't like. He still needed the noise. He hated being by himself with no sounds anywhere. He found a country music station and put that on. He had never understood what most people were attracted to in music, any kind of music, but at least it was noise.

No matter what anybody thought, Cary Alder wasn't a complete idiot. He had figured out long ago that practically every phone he owned and every space he inhabited was likely to be bugged. It would be royally stupid if he wasn't being bugged. The financial stuff alone ought to give some agency somewhere grounds to get a warrant. The issue became what to do after that.

There was a landline right next to him on a round occasional table. The table was thick and sturdy and nothing like an antique.

He dialed his number and waited. The line rang and rang until it was finally picked up.

"¿Sí?"

"It's Cary Alder. I thought I'd check up on our projects."

The man on the other end of the line coughed. When he started speaking again, there was no indication that he had ever said a single word in Spanish in his life.

"Our projects are the same as they were yesterday," the man said. "Things don't move as fast as you want them to."

"Nothing ever does."

"You need pills," the man said. "Something to calm you down. Everything is going according to plan. Everything is on schedule. We're not due to move into the next phase of any of this for at least another two weeks."

"Two weeks? All of them are moving into the next phase in the next two weeks?"

"North Carolina," the man said. "North Carolina moves into the next phase in the next two weeks. Georgia doesn't move for at least another month. Mississippi isn't going anywhere until May. We've had a few problems with permits and other government bull-crap in Mississippi."

"Figures," Cary said.

"People are people," the man said. "You can't blame them for being people. We'll be all right."

"Have you talked to Mr. Green Jeans?"

"Just last night. You had him all agitated about something or the other. He wasn't being very coherent. I tried to call him back today, but I haven't been able to get in touch."

"Seriously? Not even on his cell phone?"

"Not nowhere no how," the man said. "Don't worry about it. He's probably got a household emergency. I'll track him down."

Cary took another long pull of scotch. "I know you will. I don't know what's wrong with me today. I've been jumpy since I got up."

"I think you ought to consider spending some money to save yourself some trouble," the man said. "Sometimes it makes sense spending the cash for copper pipes instead of the crappy stuff. They don't break as much. You don't have to replace them as often."

"They get ripped out of the basements by junkies," Cary said. "You wouldn't believe it. They go down into the basements and just take the pipes. You can get a ton of money for copper pipes if you know where to sell them. And they don't do anything sane. They don't turn off the water or anything like that. The next thing you know, the basements are waist-deep in water and somebody has to come out to get rid of it and it's not worth it."

"I can't do anything about junkies," the man said. "You have something you want from me? I've got a few things to do."

"No," Cary said. "I was just checking in."

"Pills," the man said. "When you get like this, you take a pill and go to bed. I'm going to get off this damned phone and get some work done."

"Listen," Cary said. "About North Carolina."

"What about it?"

"You sure you have the mix right this time? We don't want to make the same mistakes over and over again."

"That was five years ago," the man said. "You learn things from experience."

"I know."

"Just stop this," the man said. "We're on track. We're well organized. We've got the right mix. Go play with yourself and leave me alone."

The phone clicked decisively. The connection was broken. Cary finished his scotch in one long gulp.

He wondered if there really were people out there bugging his phones, and what they thought of conversations about Mr. Green Jeans.

of decades. Why would she be living there if she was some kind of Anglo?"

"We have no idea," Horowitz said.

"We also have no idea what she was doing in a giant-sized leaf bag," Morabito said. "We're assuming somebody was trying to kill her, but then why not just kill her and dump the body in an alley? Where did they think they were taking her? What was the point?"

"If she woke up, we could maybe just ask her," Morabito said. "But we're not expecting her to wake up."

They were interrupted by the appearance of a policewoman, tall and blond like she'd just emerged from a television cop show.

"Hey you two," she said. "There's a woman who's just come in. You'd better listen to her."

2

The woman that the uniformed policewoman brought in was middle-aged, stocky, red-haired, and uncomfortable. Her gray suit was too cheap, too shiny, and too tight. It was also shorter than she was comfortable with, although it was not short. She came in clutching a black purse large enough to be Captain America's shield and tugging at the hem of her skirt.

"These are detectives Horowitz and Morabito," the policewoman said, obviously trying to sound encouraging.

"This is Gregor Demarkian," Horowitz said.

The middle-aged woman flushed. "Oh," she said.

The policewoman brought over a chair and shooed her into it. "Maybe you should have had this meeting in the conference room," she said. "The chairs in here are ridiculous."

"Now, now," Morabito said. "Miss . . . ah . . . Mrs. . . . ah—"

"Mrs. Denning," the woman said, flushing again. "Patty Denning."

"Mrs. Denning isn't a suspect," Morabito said. Then he paused. "Is she?"

The policewoman gave them all the fish-eye. "I'll go arrange for some coffee," she said. Then she turned on her heel and left.

Gregor turned his attention to Patty Denning. She was still clutching her pocketbook to her chest as if she were trying to protect herself from a stabbing, and her tugs at her skirt hem had become frantic.

"Now, Mrs. Denning," Horowitz said, "if you could tell us—"

"I know who Gregor Demarkian is," Patty Denning burst out. "I read about you in the papers. And that's it. It's the papers."

"What's it?" Gregor asked.

Patty Denning clutched and tugged, clutched and tugged. "There was a picture of a woman in the paper this morning. Except I didn't see it in the real paper. I don't have the time to read the real paper anymore, and it's expensive, and I can read the same paper online while I'm at work. Not that Miss Agerwal is happy with that, I can tell you, but we all do it. And she can't be out in the bullpen prowling around every minute of every day."

"Maybe we ought to start from the beginning," Horowitz suggested.

Now Patty Denning looked bewildered. "The beginning?"

"You saw the picture in the paper," Horowitz said. "I take it that was the picture of the woman from the incident last night. The woman we can't identify."

"That's right," Patty Denning brightened. "And of course, I recognized her. We see her at least once a month, and sometimes we see her more often than that, because there's always something, and I think she's stopped talking to her super altogether, which drives Miss Agerwal out of her mind, but practically everything drives Miss Agerwal out of her mind—"

"Wait," Horowitz said. "You said 'we' see her. Who's 'we'?"

"Oh." This time Patty Denning took a deep, deep breath. "Oh,

I see. Yes. My name is Patty Denning and I work as a clerk in the main offices of Alder Properties in the rental processing department. Alder Properties rents a lot of apartments. Hundreds of them. And the supers in those departments collect the rent checks and send them to us, and we process them. Record them, you know, put all the information in the computer. Keep track of who's on time and who's late and who's not paying at all."

"And the woman in the picture works there, too?" Morabito suggested.

Patty Denning shook her head. "No, she rents an apartment. I know I said the tenants give their checks to the supers, and almost all of them do, but they don't have to do it that way. They can bring their checks right in to us and we'll give them a receipt for them. We don't encourage it, you know, because if everybody did that it would be chaos, but some people do. Miss Warkowski did. She did it every single month going on two years now."

"Miss Warkowski is the name of the woman in the picture?" Gregor asked.

"Exactly," Patty Denning said. "Marta Warkowski. She was having some trouble with her super, I don't know what it was, but for some reason she didn't trust him. She thought he wouldn't hand in her rent check to us and then she'd get evicted. So, she brought in the check and we gave her a receipt."

"Was Alder Properties trying to get her evicted?" Gregor asked.

Patty Denning shook her head. "You never want to evict someone who doesn't cause any trouble and always pays her rent on time unless there's some other reason, like you want to convert the building to luxury condos or sell it. And nothing like that is going to happen in that neighborhood, at least any time soon. One of the girls in the office said that Miss Warkowski's family had had that apartment since all the way back in the Forties. Can you imagine? She grew up there."

"Is there a reason why the super would want her evicted, even if the company didn't?" Gregor asked.

"I'm not sure," Patty Denning said. "It's a very large apartment, three bedrooms. Miss Agerwal said that Mr. Hernandez thinks that if you're going to have a large apartment you should have a large family to live in it, and if you're by yourself you should have a small one. It might be about that."

"Who is Miss Agerwal?" Morabito asked.

"She's the head of the department," Patty Denning said. "She's from India. But she doesn't wear saris, or anything like that. And that's why I'm here, you see. When I saw the picture, I called everybody over to look, because I didn't want to make a mistake. And we all recognized her right off, in spite of the fact that that picture was so awful. It really was awful. We all thought she looked dead."

"She's in a coma," Horowitz said, "but last we heard, she was alive and hanging in there."

"Well, good," Patty Denning said. "It was a terrible thing, wasn't it, stuffed in a black plastic garbage bag like that. You don't like thinking about someone you know being treated like that. And what could it have been about? I suppose she must have some money, to go on renting that place month after month now that she's retired. But if she had any real money, she wouldn't live there in the first place."

"So your office sent you down here—" Morabito started.

Patty Denning's shake of the head was vigorous. "No, no. Miss Agerwal didn't want anybody to talk to the police. She didn't think the office should get involved at all. Did I tell you she's from India? I don't think she understands how the police work here. We tried to tell her you'd find out eventually and then everything would get crazy, but she wouldn't listen. We tried to tell her you'd send someone down to the office, but she wouldn't listen to that, either. She practically threatened to fire anybody who tried to get in touch with you."

"Ah," Gregor said.

"I just couldn't stand sitting there thinking about it," Patty

Denning said. "I don't think Miss Warkowski has any family living. All the family she ever talked about were dead. I didn't know what it would mean, with her being in the hospital like that. So, I said I was feeling bad and had to go home early. I didn't know if it would work, but Miss Agerwal has the flu so there wasn't as much lecturing as there usually is. She's always lecturing about how Americans don't work very hard and they want all these special privileges. But I think she had a headache today. She didn't say much of anything."

"There's just one more question," Gregor said. "Do you happen to have the exact address of this apartment Miss Warkowski has been living in all her life?"

3

It was a classic example of the problems with cases of attempted murder. Since Marta Warkowski was still alive, they needed permissions. It took so long to get them, it was already getting dark by the time they arrived in front of the four-story tenement where Warkowski was supposed to live, and the young woman sent by Alder Properties to let them in was already furious.

"You don't want to be a woman alone on a street like this even in broad daylight," she said, as Gregor climbed out of the back of the unmarked car. Her voice was high and her accent was the singsong of a native Hindi speaker. Gregor thought she might also have a cold or the flu. She would have been beautiful if she hadn't been so implacably angry.

Gregor straightened himself up on the sidewalk and looked around. It took him a minute, but he realized he almost recognized this neighborhood. It was the part of St. Catherine's Parish that spread out from the church in the other direction from Cavanaugh Street. As a neighborhood, it looked to Gregor not much more dangerous than dozens of others. It didn't give off the menace of some of the places in North Philadelphia. It wasn't as placid as some of the neighborhoods on the Main Line. It was just a street that should have been crammed full of people. Instead, it was deserted.

"They can spot a cop car three blocks away," Morabito said. "Even the unmarked ones."

Horowitz ignored him. "Are you Ms. Agerwal?" he asked the young woman.

"I am Meera Agerwal," she said. "And it's *Miss* Agerwal. I'm going to need to see some identification."

Horowitz and Morabito brought out their shields and cards. Meera Agerwal turned to Gregor.

"I take it you're the other one," she said. "I'm going to need to see some identification from you."

"Mr. Demarkian is acting as a consultant on this case for the Philadelphia—"

Gregor already had his passport out. Meera Agerwal looked at the picture there, then at his face, then back at the picture again.

"It's ridiculous, what goes on in this city," she said. "If you're the police, you should go right in. You shouldn't have to drag me all the way down here. I could be killed."

"I don't know," Morabito said innocently. "It looks pretty deserted to me."

Meera Agerwal gave him a withering glance. "It's deserted because the police are here. That's what these people are all about. They're like criminals everywhere. They hate the police."

She whirled around and marched up the four steps of the stoop, expecting them to follow her.

They did follow her, with Gregor bringing up the rear, holding back a little so that he could look around at the buildings and the cars. The cars were all old and dilapidated. The buildings were also old, but most of them had been decently kept up, and there were no vacant lots in his direct line of sight. That didn't mean the neighborhood was a good one, but it did mean it was a better one than most. That answered one question. Even if the neighborhood had changed significantly over the years, even if it had become Spanish and Marta Warkowski was not, it made sense for the woman to want to hold on to her apartment here. Three bedrooms, Patty Denning had said. It would be hard to find an apartment that large in all of Philadelphia. To find one in a stable neighborhood would be a kind of miracle.

Meera Agerwal and the two detectives had disappeared into the building. Gregor hurried a little to catch up. He found himself in a cramped little foyer with a bank of mailboxes built into one wall. None of the mailboxes looked as if it had been jimmied or forced.

Meera Agerwal was marching up the stairs right in front of him. "You'd better get ready. It's a climb. It should be Hernandez taking you up here, not me. My God, I don't know what it is with these people. You can never get them to do anything. And when you really need them, they disappear."

"And Hernandez is?" Gregor asked.

"The superintendent," Meera said. "He's got an apartment on the ground floor in the back. He's not there, of course. He's not next door, either. And he's not in any of the bars that I could see. And yes. I tried to call him. I'm not an idiot."

"Alder Properties owns the building next door?" Gregor asked.

They'd reached the second floor. Meera Agerwal was out of breath. "Alder Properties owns a total of four buildings on this street," she said. "They're all apartment houses, and they're all fully rented. Of course, the rentals are all problematic. The rents are always late or short or I don't know what, and you have to watch the supers, because they steal. We tell people moving in that they should always get a receipt from the super when they give him their rent. Of course, half the time they're not paying their rent and they don't have a receipt because they didn't hand in any money, so they just lie. It's supposed to be profitable running buildings down here, and if Cary Alder says it is, I'll believe him. It's his money. But, my God."

They had started up another flight of stairs. Gregor was beginning to get a little fatigued himself. Morabito and Horowitz had just clammed up.

"I take it Marta Warkowski wasn't like that," Gregor said. "She paid her rent on time."

"Marta Warkowski is a pain in the ass and a bitch," Meera Agerwal said. "There's more ways to be a pain in the ass and a bitch besides not paying your rent. And just you watch. She's going to be a bitch about this, too. We're going to have to watch our rear ends every second. If she comes out of that hospital alive, she's going to expect to move right back into this apartment."

"It is her apartment," Gregor pointed out. "Shouldn't she move back into it?"

"She could be in that hospital for months," Meera Agerwal said. "And the rent could go unpaid all that time. But we'd better not move her out of it and somebody else in. She knows the law. She knows all the agencies, too. She'd crucify us as soon as she woke up."

"I see," Gregor said.

Meera Agerwal shrugged. "There was no need for her to come down to our office every month. I'm not an idiot. I am aware of the problem. I would have double-checked to make sure her rent checks were being passed along. And what she expected us to do about the handymen, I don't know. We hire handymen. They fix things. As long as they fix things, who cares who they are?"

"Isn't it the supers who fix things?" Gregor asked.

"Of course it is," Meera Agerwal said, "but we keep these places up. There's no point having trouble with the city or the housing people. The supers take extra people on when they have to. Why should that make a difference? And Marta was in housing court every time you turned around. There was always something wrong."

"Is she in housing court now?" Gregor asked. "Does she have a case in proceedings?"

"Not as far as I know," Meera Agerwal said. "Not at this exact minute. Trust me, though. She'd have gotten there. Mr. Alder hates going to housing court. I hate it. Every time you do it, you have to unearth all the records and make copies and waste an entire week documenting things people ought to be able to look up on their own computers."

They had reached the third floor. Meera Agerwal led them to the front of the building. In the other direction, toward the back, there was a series of doors. Here, there was only one.

Meera Agerwal got a set of keys out of her purse. "Here it is," she said. "It's the biggest apartment in the building. It's the biggest apartment in any of the buildings we own on this street. That's because it's never been partitioned. You can only partition an apartment when it's empty, when somebody moves out. Marta has never moved out. Marta's parents never moved out. It's like they're all ghosts haunting the place."

Meera had the key in the lock. Horowitz stepped forward and put his hand on it. "Why don't you stand back and let me open that," he said. "Just in case."

"Just in case of what?" Meera demanded.

Horowitz first tried turning the doorknob, but the door was definitely locked. Then he braced himself, turned the key, and turned the doorknob again.

The door swung open onto a large and overly furnished living room. There were pictures in frames on every surface. There were antimacassars on the backs of the couch and all the chairs.

There was the body of a man with the back of his head blown off lying on the living room rug.

PART TWO

PART TWO

ONE

1

The body on the floor of Marta Warkowski's apartment belonged
to Miguel Hernandez, the superintendent for this building and the
building next door. That much they learned from Meera Agerwal
immediately.

"I don't understand what he's doing in here," Meera Agerwal
kept saying. "He's not supposed to be in here ever. Not even to fix
things. He's got handymen he can use to fix things without coming
in here. We have a consent decree with the housing court."

Horowitz got on his phone to call the usual suspects: ambulance and medical examiner's office; forensics and photographers; a
couple of mobile units who would blow their sirens coming in and
then deal with crowd control. If there was any crowd control to deal
with. People *were* coming out of the other apartments, slowly and
furtively, to see what was going on. Still, "furtive" was the operative
word. Nobody wanted to get too close to the police, or make herself too visible. And "her" was the right pronoun, too. The building
seemed to be full of women.

Morabito was trying to usher Meera Agerwal back into the hall without touching her. The woman would not stop talking.

"Mr. Alder is going to have a raging fit," she said. "You have no idea what kind of trouble we had over that consent decree. God, the woman was just such a bitch. And completely irrational. And down at the office all the time. We couldn't get rid of her."

Gregor moved around the living room, carefully touching nothing. It was a large, old-fashioned apartment from the days when families lived in apartments more often than they lived in houses. Before Alder Properties came in and started cutting up the apartments into smaller units, there had probably been six or seven places like this scattered over the four floors. Gregor remembered such apartments from his own childhood. The people who lived in them were considered "rich" in the neighborhood. Not-rich people lived in smaller places, or railroad flats.

Over on one side of the room there was a television console that had been covered by a large fringed shawl. On top of that there was a new flat-screen television, not very large, but very modern looking. On either side of the television set there were more pictures, in frames like the other pictures in the room, and mostly black-and-white. All the photographs were posed, the kind of thing that came from school photo sessions or a photographer's studio visited to commemorate a special occasion, like First Holy Communion or confirmation. The children were all dressed to the gills in stiffly starched clothes. Their hair was so perfect it might have been fired in a kiln.

Gregor found the gun on the floor about a yard away from the console, lying half under a straight-backed chair that looked as if it had never been sat in. He motioned to Horowitz. The detective came over, looked down to where Gregor was pointing, and blew a raspberry.

"Well, that settles that," Horowitz said.

"Maybe," Gregor said. "Assuming it's the murder weapon. But even if it is, it raises a number of questions."

"Like what?"

"What's it doing over here when the body is over there?" Gregor asked. "This isn't a huge room, but it's big enough so that a shot couldn't have been fired from here and made that mess over there. Whoever shot Mr. Hernandez had to have been standing almost right up against him. So why is the gun over here?"

"Maybe it isn't the murder weapon," Horowitz said. "Maybe it's Marta Warkowski's gun."

"And Marta Warkowski didn't shoot Hernandez?"

"I don't think that's likely," Horowitz said. "Do you? Marta Warkowski ended up in the garbage bag. There had to be a third person who did both."

"There had to be a third person," Gregor agreed. "I wonder if it is Marta Warkowski's gun. Would she have had a gun? What do you think that is, a .38?"

"I'm not touching it until forensics gets here."

"I'm not touching it, either," Gregor said. "But it looks like a .38. You can buy those fairly easily on the street. They aren't even expensive. You do have to ask yourself, though, how she would have found somebody to sell one to her."

Horowitz looked incredulous. "For God's sake, Mr. Demarkian. I've had people waltz right up to me on the street and offer me one. Not only .38s, you know, but other guns. Bigger guns. They're everywhere."

"I believe they're everywhere," Gregor said. "I don't know if I believe that somebody would have gone up to a middle-aged white woman like Marta Warkowski and offered her one. I wish the woman was awake and talking."

"So do I."

"I wish I knew if she was a woman who fit this room," Gregor said. "You have no idea how many women I've known in my life who did fit this room. There are—parameters to behavior."

"Anybody can do anything," Horowitz said. "People act out of character all the time. People get upset or they go crazy or they get hysterical."

"True," Gregor said, thinking that didn't answer any of the questions he had.

He moved away from the gun and across the living room. At one end there was a narrow hallway. He moved down that, looking to the right and the left, still touching nothing. Two of the doors were shut, but the door to the bathroom was open, as was the door to a largish bedroom. The bathroom was pristine. Every white ceramic surface shone. The light from the ceiling fixture glowed. The fan purred in the background.

"She wouldn't have just left the light on," Gregor said. "She would have been worried about her electric bill. Even if Patty Denning's impression was right and she had 'enough' money to live on, whatever that means, she would have been brought up to worry about the electric bill."

He drifted the rest of the way down the hall and stood in the door of the largish bedroom. It contained a four-poster bed that was covered with a white-patterned bedspread with fringe on it. Next to the bed was a small night table that was also covered with a white-patterned something with fringe on it. It looked to be part of a set with the bedspread. On top of the nightstand was a lamp. Its shade was also white and patterned and had a fringe.

"I wonder if Marta Warkowski was married," he said.

Horowitz had come up behind him. "We'd better go. That's the cavalry arriving on the street."

"It makes a difference if she was married or not," Gregor said. "Look at this room."

"What the hell is wrong with this room?"

"These things"—Gregor gestured at the bedspread and the night table and the lampshade—"these are the kinds of things women get as wedding presents. Or at wedding showers. If Marta Warkowski was married, that would be one thing. But I can't see it. Didn't someone say that Marta had lived here all her life?"

"What of it?"

"She wouldn't have stayed here with a husband," Gregor said. "They'd have rented their own place. Which means these things would have been given to her mother. And they're in wonderful shape. Which means her mother barely used them."

"You are making absolutely no sense," Horowitz said, "and we've got to get back out there. That's the EMTs out there."

Gregor took a last look at the bedroom, and turned to head out into the fray.

2

If a body is dead, you can leave it in place for a very long time. Gregor knew this was considered to be a good thing. He even knew why. It was just that he'd never really liked it. There was something inside him that wanted dead bodies to be valorized: in open coffins, the centerpiece at a wake; in churches in front of the altar. He always wondered what people had done before forensics became so complicated, and such a production. Did they leave dead bodies lying there when there was nothing much you could learn from them outside a coroner's office?

It didn't help that forensics now sent so many people, it was hard to get them into small spaces. This living room was not that small, but it was a tight fit for half a dozen people in hazmat suits along with EMTs, photographers, uniformed police, and an evidence clerk. Gregor let himself be pushed relentlessly into the hallway along with Meera Agerwal. There was nothing that was going to go on in that room right now that he had to see firsthand. Usually, it was well past this stage when he was called in on a case at all. If there were things they wanted him to know, they would send him a report.

Or tell him.

Or something.

He turned to watch two more people come upstairs. They were both official. Except for the various official people, the building seemed to be deserted. The doors were all tightly closed. Nobody had come out to check on what was happening.

Gregor felt a hand on his arm and looked around to find Meera Agerwal scowling at him. She was a very tiny woman. Gregor hadn't noticed that before.

"You're supposed to be someone famous," she told him. "That's supposed to matter to me."

"I don't think I'd call myself famous," Gregor said cautiously.

Meera Agerwal wasn't listening. "Look at all this fuss," she said. "Just look at it. For a man who would be eating out of garbage cans if it wasn't for Cary Alder. You can find a dozen like him actually eating out of garbage cans if you go down to the street. Those that don't run away as soon as they hear somebody coming, that is. Most of them run away. Dirty and ragged and living in their own filth. And for that they send in the police!"

Now Gregor was interested. "Do you mean to say Miguel Hernandez was a homeless person before he came to work here?"

"Homeless," Meera Agerwal said. "How am I supposed to know if he was homeless? I should be hiring and firing all the staff here myself. At least that way I could find people who could be trusted to do their jobs. But no, no. Mr. Alder has to do all that himself. He has to pick his staff personally. It's total crap. It's completely ridiculous. He doesn't know what he's doing."

There was a soft cough just to their side. Gregor turned to find a tall, massively obese man moving up to them, rubbing the palms of his hands against his shirt and looking close to panicked.

"*Por favor*," he said.

"Speak English," Meera Agerwal snapped. "For God's sake, how many times do people have to tell you?" She turned back to

Gregor. "They're all like this. All of them. Dirty and stupid and so lazy you don't know how they get up enough energy to breathe. And we have to hire them. That's Mr. Alder, too. You can't hire a decent worker for a neighborhood like this. The neighborhood won't put up with it."

Gregor looked back to the man and tried to sound encouraging. "Can I help you?" he asked. "Do you live here?"

The big man rocked from side to side. "*Sí*," he said. "*Sí*. I am—" He started speaking rapidly in Spanish, then stopped himself and tried again in English. "I am work here. For *Señor* Hernandez."

"You work here as what?" Gregor asked. "What's your name?"

This took a few seconds for the big man to sort out. Meera Agerwal nearly exploded.

"Oh, for God's sake," she said. "At least Hernandez could speak English. Even I can speak English, and it isn't like I was brought up knowing it. What is wrong with these people?"

The big man concentrated on Gregor. "I am Juan Morales," he said. "I am work for *Señor* Hernandez. I fix."

"You fix what?" Gregor asked him. "Plumbing? That kind of thing?"

"*Sí*. Plumbing. Steps. Doors. Walls. With wood. Lightbulbs. Carpet." He considered for a moment. "Steam clean?" he said finally, as if he weren't sure.

"He's one of the handymen," Meera Agerwal said. "I told you people before. Hernandez has handymen. Two or three. Maybe four. They do the scut work. Badly."

"*Por favor*," Juan Morales said again. "*Señor* Hernandez?" He looked toward the door of the apartment.

"*Señor* Hernandez is dead," Gregor said. "I am very sorry."

"*Sí. Gracias.*" Juan Morales shook his head. "I do?" he ventured.

"Unbelievable," Meera Agerwal said. Then she raised her voice as far as Gregor thought it could go. "I've already talked to Mr. Alder about it! There will be instructions later! Wait for instructions!"

"I wonder why it is that everybody, no matter where they're from, thinks people who don't speak their language will understand them better if they shout," Gregor said.

"I speak four languages," Meera Agerwal said, "and I only shout at stupid people. Don't give me that sanctimonious horse manure. He's got to wait for instructions. That's it."

"¿Señor?" Juan Morales touched Gregor's sleeve and looked to the door of Marta Warkowski's apartment. "¿La policía?"

"That's right," Gregor told him. "The police are in there. They're going to be in there for a while. I don't think they'll let you in to do any work for a while yet. It might even be a couple of days."

Juan Morales considered this. "¿La señora?"

"Miss Warkowski is in the hospital," Gregor said. "She's very ill. She won't need to get back into the apartment right away."

Juan Morales considered this, too. He nodded. "Sí," he said.

A moment later, he was gone, melting away into the empty hallways as if he had the power to make himself invisible.

Meera Agerwal looked like she was ready to spit. "It's unbelievable. There isn't a handyman in these two buildings that hasn't been with us for at least six years. Six years! How does he live here six years and not know the language?"

"Do you know him?" Gregor asked her.

"Of course I don't know him. Why would I? Mr. Alder hires the supers and the supers hire the handymen. But you can bet Mr. Alder has them all checked out. As much as he wants to."

"Which means what?"

"Which means what it says," Meera Agerwal said. "I can't help it if you don't know what's going on around here. And now I've got this. This is going to be a mess."

"This is already a mess," Gregor said.

"I don't suppose that vile old woman killed him. That would solve all of my problems. Both of them gone in one fell swoop."

3

It was two hours before the ambulance took away the body and Horowitz and Morabito were free. By the time he saw them coming downstairs to where he had parked himself on the second-floor landing, he was half convinced that this was the end of his involvement in their case. It was hard to work it out. The willingness of the city of Philadelphia to pay for his services was predicated on the possibility that Marta Warkowski was in some way connected to Cary Alder. Who knew what was going on now?

Meera Agerwal disappeared as soon as she was told she could go. That took longer than it should have, but nobody was paying attention to her. The hallways remained as empty as they had been when they first arrived. Uniformed patrolmen went from door to door, knocking, and got virtually nowhere. Every once in a while, somebody opened up. When they did, they were struck deaf and dumb, or insisted that they spoke no English. If there were any children in this building, they had disappeared absolutely.

When Horowitz finally came up to Gregor on the landing, he looked exhausted.

"Listen," he said, when he saw the way Gregor was staring at him. "You should see Morabito. He's worse."

Gregor got up and stretched his legs. "Did you make any progress? I assume it will take a while to check whatever fingerprints are on that gun."

Morabito came over to them both. "Let's get out of here," he said. "It feels like a mausoleum."

The three of them went steadily down the stairs, past clutches of forensics people on their way out to cars and vans. They came out the front door to find that the street was no longer empty, but that what it was full of had nothing to do with the normal life of the neighborhood. There were dozens of police cars and vans, some with their bubble lights flashing. There were other vans, too, from the television stations. Those had disgorged cameras, complicated electrical equipment, and dozens of people, all of them training their attention on the door of the apartment house where the murder had taken place. What was not on the street was any sign of anyone who might actually live on it. It was too cold a day for people to be hanging out in doorways and on benches, but there would usually have been somebody.

"Know what we did?" Morabito asked. "We've got two patrolmen who speak Spanish on the scene here. We sent them to do a second round of knocking on doors. They might as well have been speaking Martian."

"I keep telling you, you can't blame them," Horowitz said. "They're afraid of being deported."

"And they wouldn't have to be afraid of being deported if they hadn't broken the law to begin with," Morabito said. "And don't bother to give me the lecture. I've heard it before."

"Morabito here has a bee in his bonnet about people breaking the law," Horowitz said. "As if that's the issue."

Gregor decided he'd better get past this, fast. At least for now.

He gave the two men a quick rundown of his conversation with Juan Morales. "He was willing to talk to me," he said, "chances are good he'll be willing to talk to you. And he's not the only one. From what Miss Agerwal said, there's at least one more handyman attached to these two buildings. I don't know how their employment works. I suppose they aren't around here all the time. Even so, my guess is that if they don't live in one of these two buildings, they probably live in one of the others owned by Alder Properties, on this street or close. And they'd know things about how the buildings run, what kind of security there is, even garbage collection and maintenance. Things that might help."

"Juan Morales," Morabito said. "It's like saying John Smith."

"Did the medical examiner's people say anything useful?" Gregor asked.

Horowitz shook his head. "Not really. At one point one of them said something about if the shot didn't kill him, he'd be a walking miracle. I guess that's about right. That was one hell of a hole in his skull."

"We should get something straightened out," Morabito said. "I got to admit, I wasn't really in love with the idea of you coming in and consulting, whatever that is. There we were, in the middle of everything, and suddenly you're coming in."

"You should have said something," Gregor said. "I don't usually take cases where the main detectives don't want me. It's hard to get anything done in that situation."

"Yeah, yeah," Horowitz said. "But the point is, we changed our minds. The city's already paying you, right? So if they're already paying you, we might as well use you. And there are aspects to this case where we could use you."

"That's nice to know," Gregor said cautiously.

"He just means we could blame it on you if it all went horribly wrong," Morabito said. "And those people," he glanced up at the news vans, "already know you're here. You know they do."

"Just in case they didn't, we told them," Horowitz said.

Gregor shook his head. "Tell me one thing," he said, "you didn't happen to find any of that Alder money on the body?"

"Aldergold," Horowitz corrected. "And no, we didn't, but we weren't looking especially. That Aldergold they found on the woman in the garbage bag—"

"Marta Warkowski," Morabito said.

"We don't actually know she's Marta Warkowski yet," Horowitz said. "We're going to have to get somebody down there to confirm the identification."

"There were pictures of her up there," Morabito said. "In frames."

"I saw them," Horowitz said. "Like I was saying. The Aldergold always bothered me because it didn't fit anything. There's a whole bunch of other things going on, and if the Aldergold wasn't there, it wouldn't matter to any of them. There's no connection."

"She lives in an apartment in a building owned by Alder Properties," Gregor said.

"Lots of people do," Horowitz said. "They don't have pockets full of Aldergold. Hell, even the people who live in those expensive high-rises don't always have the stuff. It's some kind of weird status thing. I can't even figure out why she'd want to steal the stuff, if that's how she got it. They'd take one look at her in the Cleopatra Bar and boot her right out the door."

"Would they?" Gregor asked. "Even if she had the Aldergold on her?"

"The clothes she was wearing were ancient," Horowitz said. "And I'm no good at that kind of thing, but my best guess is they came out of Walmart."

"She would have looked pretty out of place," Morabito said.

"And this guy upstairs," Horowitz said. "There has to be a connection. It's her apartment we found him in. Hell, maybe she even killed him. In fact, the best guess is that she did kill him. What does he have to do with Aldergold?"

"If she killed him," Gregor said, "how did she end up in the garbage bag?"

"Got to be a third person involved in this," Morabito said. "I've been trying to tell Horowitz that for an hour."

"Obviously there has to be a third person involved in this," Horowitz said. "I was never arguing that point."

Gregor was beginning to think they argued every point.

Some of the police vans were packing up and beginning to gun their motors. The news vans were galvanized into activity, the reporters and the cameramen starting to press forward, closer and closer to the scene of action.

Gregor galvanized himself into action.

"We'd better get out of here," he said. "We're about to get caught."

TWO

1

Tommy Moradanyan could hear his mother moving around in the kitchen—banging around, as he thought of it. There was a while after Russ had first been arrested when banging around was the only way she moved. She went from room to room and place to place picking things up and smashing them down again, as if she could hammer reality back into the shape she wanted it to be. There had been less of that for a time. Then Tommy had gone up to visit Russ, and the thing had happened on the street, and now here she was again.

Tommy didn't really blame her. He wanted to hammer reality back into that same shape. He wanted to wake up one morning and find Russ in the kitchen, complaining that all his papers had gone missing overnight. He wanted to look up into the stands while he was playing basketball and see Russ halfway to the rafters, staring at him as if he were the only player on the team. Most of all, he wanted adults to make sense to him again—and he didn't think that was ever going to happen.

He checked his face in the bathroom mirror one more time, just in case he needed to shave. He didn't. He'd shaved just last week, and he'd done it long before he should have. If you shaved little gray patches on your cheeks, all it did was make you bleed. It also made you look like an idiot.

He went out to the kitchen. His sister, Charlotte, was sitting at the table, calmly eating Cheerios from a Disney princess bowl. Charlie had a whole collection of Disney princess bowls. This one was Rapunzel, from *Tangled*, Tommy's favorite one. If Charlie had to grow up to be a Disney princess, Tommy wanted her to be just like Rapunzel from *Tangled*.

His mother was putting away plates and bowls. If she didn't calm down, she was going to break some of them.

"Hey," Tommy said.

Then he came into the room and sat down at the table himself. Charlie gave him a great big smile and said, "Hi!" His mother stopped what she was doing and turned to look at him.

"The police called," she said. "They want you to come down to some station or the other and make a formal statement. I wrote down the address."

"Cool," Tommy said. It seemed safe.

"I don't think you should go down there by yourself," his mother said. "I think you should have a lawyer with you. I should go with you."

"And bring Charlie?"

"I called Bennis and Gregor. Gregor's going to be in the same place later this morning. He can sit in with you."

"You do understand I'm not in any trouble," Tommy said. "I didn't do anything wrong. Nobody thinks I did anything wrong. Father Tibor and I were just standing there on a corner when that van came by and dumped that woman in the street. And it was a good thing, because if nobody had been there to see it, the woman would have been left out there forever, and maybe she would have died."

Donna Moradanyan took three eggs and a big brick of cheddar

cheese and put them on the counter. Then she reached for the frying pan in the dish rack.

"I got another phone call. Last night."

"From the police?"

"No," Donna said. "From Russ." Tommy felt the air in the room get thick, like the ether people thought filled up outer space before they knew better. He was almost afraid to move. No wonder his mother was banging around. He was lucky she wasn't exploding.

"I thought you didn't talk to Russ," he said carefully.

"I don't. He leaves messages on the machine. He saw you on television."

"Great."

"You're a minor. They're supposed to keep your identity confidential. But you were in some picture. He knew who you were as soon as he saw you."

"Did he have something to say?"

"Only that you shouldn't talk to the police alone, and that it's against the law for them to question you without a parent or a guardian present. He's still a lawyer, no matter what he's done."

"He is that."

Donna got a bowl down from the overhead cabinet next to the sink and started breaking eggs into it. "And there were some other things."

"You could stop him from calling if you wanted to," Tommy said. "I'm sure there's some way to put your number on some kind of list of numbers he isn't allowed to contact. You don't have to listen to him lecture you about—"

"I wish I knew what it was about," Donna said. "It sounds so crazy, I nearly go insane myself, except it's not crazy. It's not schizophrenia or delusions or any of that kind of thing. America's going to have a civil war, there's going to be blood in the streets, we have to protect ourselves or we'll all be dead or worse. What is all that supposed to mean?"

"He's spending too much time on the Internet."

"Last night, he wanted us to go to France," Donna said. "He said we should pack up and go to France because the French would never back down. The French would always insist on being French, so when everything blows up, they'll fight. And then he started apologizing to me. He kept saying that he knew we needed money, a lot of money, without money we would never be safe, and he was sorry he'd done it all the wrong way, he should have been more careful. More careful! At what? Tommy, we have money, we're not short on money, we never were. Things got tight, yes, because Russ liked to pay for everything himself, he pushed himself into corners trying not to use any of my income, but that's not the same thing. And if there was the kind of civil war he's talking about, you'd have to be Bill Gates to be safe from it. It just doesn't make any sense."

"I think we all got the part where it doesn't make any sense."

"Then I think about you," Donna said. "There's your biological father. He's an irresponsible jerk. Then there's Russ, who's gone, I don't know, something. I keep telling myself you have plenty of role models. Gregor. Father Tibor. Even Ed George. But I can't see my way to the end of it."

"You should make that omelet and I should eat it." Tommy pointed at the bowl. "Then I can go down to this police station and make my statement. Then I can go over to the Demarkians and hang out with Javier."

"He killed two people," Donna said. "He shot Gregor in the face."

"And I still love him and so do you."

"I don't want you to."

"I don't want me to, either," Tommy said. "But here it is, and I don't see what we're supposed to do about it. Father Tibor offered to loan me the money for the bus the next time I want to go up to see him."

"Okay," Donna said. "I guess that's better than hitchhiking."

"Yeah, well. I wasn't really all that happy with the hitchhiking. It can get kind of weird."

"What?"

"Omelet," Tommy said.

2

Sister Margaret Mary had never felt at home anywhere until she entered the convent, but once she did she found she was at home in convents everywhere. She loved the silence, the lack of that endless white noise that filled every place else people were gathered—televisions, radios, YouTube videos, vacuous conversations about nothing in particular. She loved the absolute respect for individual space. Nuns and religious sisters did not speak unless they absolutely had to. They did not intrude into another sister's silence except in cases of emergency. It worked, what they were taught in the novitiate. If you could learn to practice silence, silence inside yourself as well as silence in public speech, you could sometimes hear the soft, still voice of God.

Sister Margaret Mary did not feel at home out in the neighborhoods, no matter what neighborhood she was in, but there were times she had to be there. Years and years ago, nuns had maintained a practice of never going out alone. Marching along side by side together, in full habits with long veils and their hands tucked up under their demi-capes, they were almost as untouchable as they were back at the house. Their veils were mounted on headdresses that kept the fabric well back away from their faces. They still had demi-capes, but nobody ever thought to fold their hands up under them. Pope John XXIII had said the religious should go out and meet the world. Sister Margaret Mary understood the point. She even agreed with it. She just wasn't all that happy to carry it out.

Today she was making a round of the parish. This was important. The success of the school depended on good relations with the people of the community, and this was a difficult community to maintain good relations with. There were issues here that could not be spoken about directly, and yet had to be clearly understood. ICE. Child Protective Services. The police. So many of these people had come from countries that were shot through with force and violence. Gangs patrolled the streets. What little police presence there was being paid off by the gangs. Army squadrons marched in formation to no obvious purpose. Sometimes they stopped and snatched children right out of their own houses—the boys to fight in the hills, the girls for reasons no one would talk about.

The situation here was better. Sister Margaret Mary was sure of that. Still, the situation here wasn't really good.

The first place she stopped was a bodega just a block and a half from the church. It had a name, but she didn't understand enough Spanish to understand which of the words on the sign it was. She went through the plate-glass door into the overheated, crowded space. There were dozens of packets of Latin American junk food on all the counters. There were glass cases of soda against the walls. There were straw dolls in garish colors hanging from the ceiling on strings.

The woman behind the glass counter was heavyset and exhausted. Everything about her was gray except her hair. That had been dyed a blond so platinum, it was almost white.

"*Hola,*" Sister Margaret Mary said.

The woman grunted something that might have been *hola*, too, but might also have been a curse word. Twenty or thirty years ago, the people in this neighborhood all came from either Mexico or Puerto Rico. They spoke a form of Spanish Sister Margaret Mary still would not have understood, but would have heard enough of, often enough, to sort of get. These people came from Central America. Their dialects were so strange, they made no sense to Sister Margaret Mary at all.

Sister Margaret Mary pulled her bag off her shoulder and put it down on the counter. She reached in and brought out a packet marked "Jessinia." Sister Margaret Mary had no idea if that was correctly spelled or not. She had not been able to get the woman to say.

She opened up the packet and revealed a set of six church candles, each with a cross embossed on its side.

"I'm sorry it took me so long to get here today," she said. "There's been all that fuss because of the trouble down the block. I talked to Isidra Allende this morning, and she told me there are still police all over the building. And the apartment is still blocked off. And, of course, it's the woman who lives in the apartment who was the one they found on the road the other night. The papers are saying all kinds of things."

Jessinia picked up the candles.

"*Gracias,*" she said, staring straight over Sister Margaret Mary's shoulder toward the front of the store.

"Oh, that's no problem," Sister Margaret Mary said. "We just got six boxes of them shipped out from the motherhouse. I think it's a lovely custom, putting prayer candles in children's rooms. It's such a simple way to remind them that God is watching over them. We forget that God is watching over us."

Nothing. Jessinia's face was impassive. Her eyes were staring into the distance. She could have been the only person in the room.

"Well," Sister Margaret Mary said. "Are you sure you have everything you need? We have new holders, too. Some of them are very pretty. We have Our Lady of Guadalupe. And the Sacred Heart. We even have some with the Miraculous Medal."

Nothing. Not a sound. Maybe she should bring some of the holders the next time she came around. She could bring a selection. Jessinia had a granddaughter in the Cadette Scouts. Sister Margaret Mary could ask her.

"Well," Sister Margaret Mary said.

Then she gave up. When she walked along the streets and listened to the people around her, they were always animated and always talking. When she tried to talk to them herself, they were made of stone.

She went back onto the street and headed up the block. She had prayer cards for the woman who ran the fruit stand, whose name she had never been able to establish. The prayer cards were all of Our Lady of Guadalupe. She had a catalog of First Holy Communion dresses to drop off at the tiny dress shop that usually specialized in tight dresses with short skirts and lots of glitter. Some of the women were collecting a fund to make sure all the girls taking First Holy Communion had traditional white dresses and veils.

There was a lot to do, and they were making at least some progress. A year ago, she wouldn't have been able to make even this much contact.

Even so, she was moving much more slowly than she had been when she left the convent this morning. It was like trying to push a pebble up a hill with her nose. There was movement, but there was not significant movement.

She was coming around the corner on her way to the fruit stand, not paying attention to her surroundings, not even practicing inner silence, when she saw the van. For a few seconds, she didn't recognize it for what it was. She had put a call in to Gregor Demarkian yesterday, to tell him about the van that had been driving through the streets in front of the school the night Marta Warkowski was dumped, but he hadn't gotten back to her. That wasn't surprising, since the murder had happened since then.

And this van made no sense. Why would the people who dumped Marta Warkowski bring their van back into this neighborhood? It wasn't just Sister Margaret Mary who had seen it that night. Father Kasparian and the boy had seen it, too. And wouldn't the police have already checked out all the black vans in the vicinity? Wasn't that the first thing they would do?

She stood for a few seconds on the sidewalk, staring at it. She knew nothing about vans. She knew nothing about cars, either. Make. Model.

She got up closer to it, then went around the back. Its license plate was from New Jersey. That wasn't unusual in Philadelphia. She reached into her bag and came up with the tiny notebook she always intended to use in the neighborhood, but never used at all. She wrote down the license plate number and then—not sure what information would be needed—wrote down everything else. The van was a Ford. It had once been sold by Willie's World of Wheels in Newark.

For the first and the last time in her life, Sister Margaret Mary wished that nuns were allowed to carry smart phones.

3

Marta Warkowski was in a room.

She did not think it was a room she was familiar with. She could not see it, because she could not force her eyes to open. Sometimes she could force her arms to move, or her legs, but not very often or very far. Sometimes she thought she only imagined she could make things move. The room smelled funny. Most of the time it was quiet, and empty. Every once in a while, people would crowd in and talk.

"It was very helpful," a woman's voice said at one point. "She has been here before. That means we have records. Records tell us a lot about what we need to know."

"Do they tell us anything we need to know?" a man's voice asked.

The woman was moving back and forth, very quickly. "I don't know what you need to know. They give us her medical history. That makes a great deal of difference to anything we do for her . . ."

"Was there anything unusual in that medical history?"

The woman seemed to be moving around something on wheels. "You ought to be glad you're on official business. There are HIPPA laws these days. There are rules about who we can give out that kind of information to."

"*Is* there anything unusual about her medical history?" This was a man's voice, too, but not the same man who had been talking before.

The woman picked up Marta's arm. Marta knew it was the woman because of the smoothness of the hands. Then Marta felt the cold metal of the stethoscope and the plastic cuff encircling her biceps. The woman was taking her blood pressure.

"It's not her medical history that's unusual, if you ask me," the woman said. "She doesn't have type two diabetes, which is atypical for someone of her age and ethnicity. And weight. But that's the kind of thing that happens. She's not in very good shape, and she's not in very good health, but no, nothing too far out of the ordinary."

"That's not much help." First man again.

"We did go down and check all the records as soon as you got us an identification," the woman said. "It's the other things that give me pause."

"You mean that she doesn't have a driver's license?" Second man again.

"She does have a state ID," the woman said. "I agree it's not very common these days for someone to be without a driver's license, especially if they were born here and there are no difficulties with documentation. But that isn't it. It's the money."

"There are difficulties about money?" Second man yet again.

"No, no," the woman said. "That's the point. She's seventy-two years old. She's got Medicare and nothing else. No gap insurance. Nothing. And even so, there are no problems with money."

The blood pressure cuff hurt. It began to deflate and hurt less. Marta felt herself relax. She hadn't realized she was tense.

"We get hundreds of patients in the same position every month," the woman said. "We get thousands every year. And we know how it works. They come in. They get treated. They get a bill. It's like the

126

bill never happened. Unless it's a very large bill, we eventually just stop asking."

"What happens if it's a very large bill?" The first man was back.

"Well," the woman said, "if the patient is dying, we'll make a claim against the estate. If the patient isn't dying, we'll get more aggressive about the billing, but we really aren't trying to ruin people or force them out of their homes or any of that kind of thing. What we want is for them to meet with a social worker. There are a lot of resources out there to help pay your medical bills if you know how to navigate the system. The biggest mistake most people make is that they don't navigate anything. They get paralyzed and freeze up and don't do anything."

"And she didn't do that?" First man again. "She worked with the social workers?"

"Nope," the woman said. "She just paid her bills."

There was an oddly long pause. Then the second man said, "I don't understand what you mean."

"I mean just what I said," the woman said. "She just paid her bills. Every one of them. Within thirty days. Like she was paying off her cable bill. It takes insurance companies longer to pay than that."

"I take it they were relatively small bills?" the first man said.

"It depends on what you mean by small," the woman said. "About eight years ago, she broke her left leg falling down stairs in an ice storm. We kept her overnight for observation even though it wasn't that serious a problem. The notes say everybody was worried about her general physical condition. Like I said. Not in very good condition."

"And?" One word. Not enough to tell which man.

"And," the woman said, "her part of the bill was just under five thousand dollars, and she paid it. In thirty days. Just like everything else. Just like the time she had a bill for a hundred and seventy-four dollars when she came in for a blood test."

"Ah," the second man said. "She must have been spending down her savings."

"Maybe," the woman said, "but it must be one hell of a savings account. Four years ago she got rushed in here with a bad gallbladder that had gone so toxic, they thought she was going to die. She was here for two weeks. The bill was five solid pages long, and that wouldn't include separate bills from the surgeons and all the other support people. The bill was over twenty-six thousand dollars."

"And she paid it?" the first man said. "In thirty days?"

"You got it," the woman said. "No social workers. No negotiations. Nothing. And we do negotiate. We expect people to negotiate. This is a Catholic hospital. We have a dozen or more funds set up to help people with things like this. But there's absolutely nothing in the records. She was here. She went home. She paid her bill."

"Well," the first man said. "It's hard to know what to make of all that."

"I explained all this to your Mr. Demarkian," the woman said. "I sent him down to talk to the people in administration. I know I should have all the access to all the information. I'm the case manager. But the more I looked into this, the stranger it got. Do you know what else I checked into?"

"What?" One word again. Marta wanted to scream.

"When she went home from the gallbladder thing, she had a home health aide," the woman said. "For three more solid weeks. Used the best agency we deal with. I called them just to find out."

"And?" One word. One word. One word.

"Another sixteen thousand dollars, paid on time and in full," the woman said. "If I was you people, and Mr. Demarkian, that's the kind of thing I'd look into. If you think there has to be something strange enough to explain what happened to this woman, I'd start there."

Marta could feel herself falling into sleep again. She fell in and out, in and out, without rhyme or reason. What had happened to her? She could hear Hernandez coming down the stairs, but they were the wrong stairs. She could hear the sleet pinging against the windows, but there were no windows on the staircase.

The woman and the men were still talking, but they were too far away from her now to matter.

THREE

1

Gregor Demarkian had spent most of the night sitting up reading through papers on Cary Alder, and even though those papers were extensive and detailed, they hadn't done much good. He could, if he wanted to, get even more detailed papers. The Bureau would bring him in as a consultant if John Jackman asked him to. That way, he could go look at the banking and transaction files in the raw. At the moment, he didn't see how that would help. It hadn't taken him long to understand what was getting everybody from the city of Philadelphia to the federal government in a twist. The weird thing was that the Alder files were entirely straightforward, with one vital omission. If that omission hadn't existed, he would have understood immediately what was going on. But then, if that omission hadn't existed, everybody else would have understood exactly what was going on immediately, too, and he wouldn't be there.

It made no sense to bring Gregor Demarkian onto the case to follow hidden sources of cash or streams of revenue. There were people who spent their lives doing that. It only made sense to bring

Gregor Demarkian on if what it looked like was happening wasn't what was actually happening. That could be a mistake. Maybe everybody was seeing complications where they didn't exist.

The other question was whether or not the Cary Alder problem was related to the cases of Marta Warkowski and Miguel Hernandez. The simple fact that these two people had lived in an Alder Properties building didn't establish the connection. Alder Properties owned a lot of building. It owned a lot of buildings in bad neighborhoods, and that meant it was home to a fair number of crimes. If it hadn't been for that Aldergold, it wouldn't have occurred to John Jackman or Michael Washington that there was any connection to be made.

Gregor found it hard to admit he had no idea where this was going, but he had no idea where this was going.

Now he went around the back of the church and up the small flight of steps to Father Tibor's apartment door. He had Pickles on a leash, in a red, white, and blue sweater, a red, white, and blue cap, and red, white, and blue booties. Tommy Moradanyan was right on both counts. You felt like a damn fool walking around the streets with Pickles dressed up this way—and Pickles absolutely loved it. She pranced around like a diva model appearing before the paparazzi.

Tibor came to the door as soon as Gregor rang the bell. Pickles greeted him ecstatically and then raced inside in search of a food bowl. The food bowl was there, full and waiting. So was the gigantic dog bed set up in front of the gas fire.

Gregor unbuttoned his coat. "Tommy Moradanyan has a point," he said. "I feel like an idiot."

"I have been thinking about the dog," Tibor said. "I think there is a real bond. Between Pickles and Javier."

"That's why Bennis is being careful to take Javier out every day without her," Gregor said. "I understand the concept of therapy dogs, but stores and restaurants aren't always accommodating. And we did think you'd probably want her back eventually."

131

"Well, yes, Krekor. That's what I've been thinking about. I think maybe it would be best if you and Bennis kept Pickles with you. For Javier."

"Permanently?"

"As permanently as possible." Tibor had started to fuss around the big open space, setting up the machine that made Armenian coffee, setting out one of the tiny, ceramic cups. "We do not know, do we, how long Javier will stay?"

"No," Gregor said. He sat down on the long leather couch and leaned over to free Pickles from her leash. "We don't know what's going on at the moment. I know Bennis hopes it will be a long time."

"And you?"

"I'll admit the kid's been growing on me."

"There are a lot of rescue dogs out there," Tibor said. "There are a lot of dogs and cats and even children who have been neglected or abandoned. Or both. Or worse. I've been thinking about that."

"About neglected dogs?"

"About abandoned everything," Tibor said.

The coffee machine made a sound between a cough and a burp. Tibor brought the small cup to it and filled up. The coffee came out looking like sludge. Tibor brought the full cup to Gregor and put it down on the side table.

"It's new, I think," he said. "At least, new here. Or maybe I'm wrong. When that thing happened, with Russ. Paying judges to give children longer sentences so they have to stay in juvenile hall. Paying lawyers to do bad work on their cases. Private prisons. Sometimes I think that before Russ did what he did, I was . . . too sentimental."

"That's a word for it."

"You wouldn't think somebody with my history could be sentimental," Tibor said. "I don't know. I just think there's too much of it now. And I was thinking Javier and Pickles are very close. They were close right from the first time they saw each other. Two abandoned persons. I was thinking that if Bennis wouldn't mind it, Pickles could stay with Javier and keep Javier calmed down."

"What about you? I thought you and Pickles were bonded, too."

"Yes, yes, Krekor. I know. But there are other abandoned dogs who need a home. I even know of one. And it has been a long time since I lost everything."

"All right," Gregor said. "I'll talk to her about it."

"I will talk to her about it, too," Tibor said. Then he picked up his own tiny cup of Armenian coffee and came to sit down in the overstuffed chair opposite Gregor. Pickles had taken up residence in the dog bed and curled up for a nap.

"So," he said. "Have you come to grill me about the woman in the garbage bag?"

"Not really," Gregor said. "I'm told you have a date at the police station to make a formal statement. And, for what it's worth, it wasn't really a garbage bag. It was two of those enormous leaf and lawn bags you can get at Costco or Walmart."

"It's still metaphorical. A real person, like that. Like trash."

"They got fingerprints off the bags. Of course, some of them are going to be Tommy Moradanyan's, since he says he handled the bag when he went to see what it was. Did you handle the bag at all?"

Tibor shook his head. "When the van came down the street, it was making an awful noise. Tommy pushed me back toward the buildings. I think he wanted me out of the way of any possible accident. Then the van skidded and—fishtailed? And the back of the van hit the pole of the streetlamp. Then the doors popped open and the garbage bag came bouncing out. Then the van got traction and took off."

"With its back doors still open?"

Tibor nodded. "And flapping. Flapping and banging."

"And nothing else fell out and onto the street."

133

"No, no. The police would have seen it. Tommy would have seen it."

"Did you by any chance see anything *through* those back doors? Anything inside the van?"

"No, Krekor, I'm sorry. It happened very fast and it was very frightening."

Gregor took a sip of the Armenian coffee and decided he couldn't go on with that without killing himself.

"Well, there's one thing I do know, even if it isn't doing me any good."

"What's that?"

"That van couldn't have gone very far without stopping," Gregor said. "It couldn't have been moving at the pace you say it was with its back doors flapping open through the streets of Philadelphia in the middle of an ice storm without being spotted by a cop or a maintenance crew or something. They'd have hunted it down or taken enough digital video to be able to identify it later. Most people on the street would have tried to get a picture of it. The driver must have pulled off within a block or two to fix the doors. If he hadn't, he wouldn't have been able to disappear."

2

It was not a long walk from Cavanaugh Street to St. Catherine's School and the convent and the church that went with it. Gregor and Bennis had made that walk in both directions on the night they picked up Javier. In spite of the short distance, though, it required negotiating not one but three distinct neighborhoods. Cavanaugh Street was Armenian, and had been all Gregor's life. He had grown up there when it had been poor and Armenian and most of its residents had come directly from the old country. Now it was rich and Armenian. Its residents were attached to it because they knew it. It was home. The Ohanians had run the grocery store forever. The

Melajians had run the Ararat Restaurant forever. There was a little hole-in-the-wall store that sold religious articles only members of the Armenian church would recognize, including catechisms imported from Armenia itself and written in the Armenian language. Nobody on Cavanaugh Street would ever refer to that cup of sludge Tibor had just served him as "Turkish" coffee. Nobody on Cavanaugh Street would ever refer to "Turkish" anything, except the Armenian Genocide.

The other two neighborhoods were newer, at least in terms of population, part of the shifting population of every American city. Groups moved in and then moved out again. People immigrated and then took off for the suburbs at the first opportunity.

These days the first neighborhood next to Gregor's own was Somali. It was a small patch of ground with a smaller population, but Gregor knew from what he was told by local law enforcement that the young men who inhabited it caused more than their share of trouble. They came from a country where women were veiled and monitored, and any women who were not veiled and monitored were fair game. Women who wandered through accidentally were likely to get hit on or worse. Bennis had once come close to breaking the wrist of a boy not more than twelve years old when he'd put out his hand to grab her breast when she was walking by. Bennis had considered calling a cop and having the kid arrested for assault. Gregor would have backed her up. In the end, she had decided not to. She was never sure why.

The next neighborhood after that was the fiefdom of people from a small nation in the Pacific. Gregor had never quite gotten them straightened out, but he loved being in their territory and he loved being around them. Every other storefront seemed to offer food. The food was undeniably exotic but also completely wonderful. They fried everything, which was definitely Gregor's idea of a good time. There were also stores that sold clothes that seemed to consist of large sheets of fabric in bright colors. You could also get cloth like that to use as tablecloths or curtains. The only time Gregor had ever seen anyone angry in the neighborhood was when some boys stole some fruit from a fruit stand. The man who owned the fruit stand had chased them halfway down the block, threatening them with coconuts.

St. Catherine's Parish was more familiar, one of a dozen or so Spanish neighborhoods in the city. Gregor came there on and off when he wanted to trade Armenian food for tacos or to bring home a quart of chili for dinner. They'd have to do that more often now that Javier was with them.

Detectives Horowitz and Morabito were standing in the doorway to the building directly next to the school—the convent, Gregor assumed. Two nuns were standing with them. One of them was Sister Margaret Mary.

"You people must be freezing," Gregor said as he came up to them.

"Come right in," Sister Margaret Mary said. "Our parlor is a public space."

She opened the door behind them and shooed them all in. "I have Sister Peter here with us because she was with me when I saw the van the first night. Not that she noticed it particularly."

"I thought Sister Superior was exaggerating," Sister Peter said, as they came through to the stiffly formal parlor. "It was a very busy night, what with the foster parents and the Daisy Scouts and everything up in the air to get school started for the new year. That's one of the things we didn't think of when we started this whole project. If we're going to run this by ourselves, we're going to have to do all the work ourselves."

Sister Margaret Mary sat down in the single large wing chair. Another nun, tall and very young, stuck her head in. Sister Margaret Mary nodded at her.

"Sister Evangelina will bring in the coffee things," Sister Margaret Mary said. "I don't know if you realize, but when nuns first came to the United States to open parochial schools, they staffed every school with sisters exclusively. It was the only way we made Catholic education affordable to the people of the parish. Nuns don't have to be paid much, you see. Then when sisters started leaving the orders, we responded to that by putting one or two nuns into every school to serve as principals and vice principals, and hiring lay teachers for the rest. Unfortunately, that was very expensive. So, our order has turned that around. We gave up control of most of our schools. We now operate only three, of which this is one. But we staff them all ourselves."

"Which lets you charge cheaper tuition," Gregor said.

"It does once you finish arguing with the cardinal archbishop."

Gregor had met the cardinal archbishop of Philadelphia. He let it go.

"So," Sister Margaret Mary said. "The van. A big, black, shiny new van. Or at least it looked new. I've told you before. It just kept coming through the neighborhood. It must have passed the school half a dozen times that night."

"Sister was worried it had something to do with ICE," Sister Peter said.

Sister Margaret Mary drummed on the arm of her chair. "We have to be very careful here. These people are never safe, even if they're in the country legally. A lot of them live in households where some of the members are undocumented. Then there's the fact that we're all mandated reporters. We're supposed to call Child Protective Services if we're even vaguely suspicious that there might be abuse or neglect in the home. But there's a cultural disconnect. These people don't have the same norms for the raising and disciplining of children that we do. They do things we find odd or disturbing that are perfectly normal to them. They've learned to isolate themselves as much as possible from us and from all official—well, official anything. And I saw this van, and I kept seeing this van, and it was all wrong. We don't have vehicles like that around here. It was too new, or at least it looked too new. It looked too expensive, too. So, I started to worry that it had something to do with the ICE raids that have been going on the last few weeks."

"But it didn't," Detective Morabito said.

"Apparently not," Sister Margaret Mary said. "At least, it never stopped here, or anywhere else in the neighborhood I could see. And then, like I told you before, I sort of half forgot about it. And then there was poor Miss Warkowski. And then there was this morning."

"This morning is when Sister found the van," Detective Horowitz said.

"I don't really know it's the same van," Sister Margaret Mary said. "It's just that it seems likely. Black vans everywhere, when we haven't had any before this. It was just sitting there on the street, two blocks down and around the corner."

"Do we know if it's still there?" Gregor asked.

"Surprisingly enough, it is," Morabito said.

"I should have waited next to it," Sister Margaret Mary said, "but it just didn't occur to me. I took down all the information I could and ran right back here to call the police. And I had a cell phone on me, too. Just a flip phone, very basic, but I probably could have found a way to call if I'd kept my head."

"When we got here, we were convinced it would have disappeared," Horowitz said, "but it hadn't. We've got a couple of patrolmen waiting there in case anybody tries to pick it up. We haven't heard anything, so we don't think anybody has."

"I did write down the license number," Sister Margaret Mary said. "A New Jersey license plate number. It seemed like the least I had to do."

"We called in to request a warrant," Morabito said. "If we have any luck, the guy we sent to get it will be waiting for us when we reach the van. And so will the van."

"A New Jersey plate," Gregor said.

None of the three men had ever sat down. They were all half pacing and half fidgeting. Gregor didn't blame any of them, even himself.

3

The van was parked at the curb like any other vehicle. It already had one parking ticket on it. If it had been left where it was, it would eventually have been towed, stuffed in an impound yard, and ignored. The city of Philadelphia had multiple impound yards full of cars that nobody wanted and nobody would claim. Gregor was willing to bet that most of those vehicles were not as shiny and new looking as this one was. Cars broke down. They became eligible for repo. Husbands stole them from wives and wives stole them from husbands and girlfriends who were just not going to take it anymore stole them from boyfriends. Cars became the hostages the city would pay to keep.

The man with the warrant hadn't arrived when Gregor and the two detectives pulled up, all on foot, because Gregor was going to be damned if he was going to get into a car to drive a distance that short. There were other cars there, though, blocking off the space. One was a patrol car with its siren silent but its bubble lights flashing. One of the uniforms attached to it was standing near the license plate. The other was standing near the driver's door.

"We had our hopes up, but we didn't get lucky," that uniform said, a small Spanish woman whose gun looked too large for the slenderness of her hips. "We kept hoping that somebody would just come up and try to get into the thing, but nothing happened."

"We have had an audience," the other uniform said. He was both Anglo and pudgy. He looked like he was going to fail his next physical. "Bunch of kids standing around trying to see what we were doing."

"Which has been nothing," the first uniform said.

At that moment, another car pulled up and a man got out of the passenger's side, holding an envelope. "Warrant," he said, handing the envelope to Morabito.

Morabito took the envelope and opened up. "Did we get everything?"

"Everything," the man who'd brought the warrant said. "We went to old Judge Horhsam. If the Supreme Court wasn't restraining him, he'd hand you the farm."

"Good," Horowitz said.

Gregor walked around the van one more time. Sister Margaret Mary had been accurate. It was big. Very big. It was black. It was shiny. It looked like it ought to have a logo on it and be hauling equipment.

Gregor came back to Horowitz and Morabito. "We probably ought to have the forensics boys out here," he said. "At least the driver's door and the back doors ought to be fingerprinted."

Morabito reached into his pocket and came up with a packet of latex gloves. "Wear these," he said, handing them over to Gregor. "They'll do all the basic stuff down at the garage once we haul it in. Right now, I just want to make sure there isn't a dead body in there."

Gregor took the gloves out of the packet and put them on. Then he went to the driver's door and opened it. The cab smelled nothing like a dead body, but it did smell like smoke. Gregor looked into the ashtray and saw that it was dusted with ash, but there was nothing actually in it. No cigarette butts. No cigar stubs. Certainly, no keys or loose change.

Gregor stepped back out and closed the door again.

"Nothing?" Morabito asked him.

"Nothing immediately visible," Gregor said. "I was half afraid I'd look in there and there'd be some kid's soccer gear. Do you remember what I told you when I called you last night?"

"The guy couldn't drive through the streets of Philadelphia with his back doors flapping open," Morabito said. "Yeah, I got that. That was smart."

"Thank you," Gregor said. "My point was that if he couldn't do that, he didn't. So either he pulled over somewhere close, got out, and shut the doors. Or he had somewhere close where he could pull in out of sight. My best guess would be the latter. Which leaves us with a new question."

The guy who'd brought the warrant was intrigued. "What's that?" he asked.

"If the guy's got somewhere close he can stash this thing," Gregor said, "what's it doing here now? Why not just leave it where he put it? Why risk taking it out of wherever he put it, driving it around looking for a parking space, parking the thing, and then getting out in full view of the city?"

"Maybe he's one of their own," Horowitz said. "Maybe he doesn't expect anybody to turn him in. Or mention it at all."

"Neighborhoods aren't hermetically sealed," Gregor said. "Most of the people in them may be your people, but chances are good that outside people will be going through on and off. And outside people will talk."

"We can send a bunch of uniforms around to ask again," Morabito said. "We could put out a notice in case there are outside people who want to come forward."

"Good idea," Gregor said. "We have to start with a few assumptions. Marta Warkowski is, from what everybody tells me, a large, heavy woman. She wasn't in good shape, but she also wasn't frail or elderly or incapacitated. She couldn't have been stuffed into those plastic bags unless she was stone-cold out, and she probably couldn't have been rendered unconscious in the open. So, she was—hit?"

"Yeah," Horowitz said. "With a blunt instrument."

"She was hit," Gregor said. "The best scenario for her attacker would have been to hit her when she was already in the back of the van, but I'm not sure how he would have talked her into getting into the back of the van. Whatever. She was hit, already in the back of the van or out of it. She was stuffed into the plastic bags. Again, either already in the back of the van or out of it. I would say it was most likely she was both hit and put in the bags while she was not in the van, and then later pushed in. That would go a long way to explaining the accident. We're agreed it must have been an accident, her falling out the back?"

"I don't see how anybody could do that on purpose." Horowitz said.

"Or would want to," Morabito said.

"She can't have been pushed very far into the back," Gregor said. "She had to be in a position to be leaning against those doors. Otherwise, she wouldn't have popped them. So he pushes her into the back of the van and closes up. Either he doesn't know she's still alive, or he doesn't care. He figures she'll be dead soon enough."

"I heard you lecture once at the main library," Horowitz said. "You said over and over again never to assume that the perpetrator was male or female."

"And I meant it," Gregor said. "But in this case, no woman on her own was going to lift Marta Warkowski into this van. A woman might get her into the bags once she was in the van. She'd have to be a particularly strong and athletic woman."

Gregor walked to the back doors and looked up at them. "I take it you two tried the doors when you got here," he told the two uniforms. "This wasn't left here unlocked."

"No," the young woman said. "Tight as a drum. If it had been open, we could have fudged a little. We could have said we were worried about theft or something and gone in."

Gregor nodded. "And there were no signs of the keys?"

"If the keys had been in that van, it wouldn't be here," the young woman said. "That's how cars get stolen. You wouldn't believe how many people leave their keys in their cars and then they're shocked to find out their cars have disappeared."

Gregor nodded again. "Well," he said, "we'd better force it and go in and find what we're meant to find."

"What we're meant to find?" Morabito asked.

"Exactly," Gregor said. "Officer?"

The young Spanish woman retreated to the patrol car and came back carrying a small lever. Gregor expected the male officers to offer to wield it for her, but they didn't. She marched up to the van's back doors, wedged the thin end of the lever in the crack between the two thin door handles, and slammed the heel of her left hand against the lever's thick end.

The pop the door made coming open was impressive. It sounded like a firecracker, or worse.

The doors swung outward. They started to swing inward again, but the officer caught them.

Gregor and Horowitz and Morabito crowded in to see what was there.

The back of the van was clean and empty, with one exception. The carpet on the floor was pristine. It must have been vacuumed. The walls of the van were as shiny and polished as its outside was. There were no dents.

What they had been meant to find was right there in the middle of the emptiness.

It was a three-foot-long tire iron, one half of it clotted with blood and hair, the other half covered with bloody fingerprints.

FOUR

1

Meera Agerwal called in and told the girls in the office she was taking the rest of the day off. The flu had come back to hit her again. Her muscles ached. Her head pounded. Her body temperature was as high as the hot season in Mumbai.

This was true, although it had nothing to do with why she was going home. The afternoon was beyond insane. She didn't usually go down to the properties, and especially not to the properties like that one. Her work could be done safely from her desk. Lateness warnings could be sent overnight mail. Eviction notices could be sent registered mail. There were a dozen people who could deliver the more serious legal documents if they had to be delivered. She had been to this particular building only once before.

The flu symptoms were making everything worse. There were two kinds of people who came to the United States from India. There were people like her brother, with degrees in tech, who wanted to take up residence in California or Colorado or Boston and just plain stay there. They brought wives and children and later brothers and sisters and parents. The extended families opened businesses. When they got a little ahead, they built temples and founded benevolent societies. Meera had to admit that this seemed to work for a lot of them. Their children did well in school and went to universities whose names were known at home. The second generation became doctors and university professors. Everywhere you looked, somebody was collecting money for a start-up.

Meera belonged to the second kind, the kind that knew it would never work for them. They came to make money until they had enough to go home and start a life for themselves. They got engaged to another Hindu of good family before they left. They did not get married until they were ready to go back to Mumbai and settle down. They did not Indian themselves up and make a display of their ethnicity. Meera owned two saris. She wore them to weddings and funerals.

It would be terrible, she thought, to die in this place.

She'd heard many things about America before she had come. What she had found had been stranger and more alien than she could ever imagine. The whole premise of the place was wrong. All men were *not* created equal—and what's more, most Americans knew it. It made them completely crazy. In Mumbai, the truth was openly acknowledged. Karma itself meant that all human beings were born different, some better, some worse. You could tell who belonged to which group just by looking at them, and if they were wearing a proper caste mark you could situate them absolutely. There was one American saying Meera liked: *A place for everything and everything in its place.* That was exactly right. That was exactly what it was like with people, too.

In Mumbai, Meera wouldn't think for a moment that she would have to worry about being involved in the murder of a man like Hernandez. He was a man without caste. She would not have been expected to know him. If she had known him, she would only have known him as an underling or a servant. She would not touch him because he was so obviously unclean.

She didn't know what to think about that scene back there. The body lying on the floor. The blood and skin and bone everywhere, on all the closer surfaces. In Mumbai, there were places where the lower castes went to defecate in the open. The river and its beaches were filthy. The air was foul. That had been less disturbing to her than this thing.

There was a Hindu restaurant about three blocks from her apartment, an actual Hindu restaurant, vegetarian, that followed all the dietary rules. Most of the restaurants that called themselves "Indian" in the United States were actually Muslim, and no Muslim was a *real* Indian. Muslims were conquerors and collaborators with conquerors. They also ate meat.

She picked up two containers of chana dal, spiced enough to do a serious assault on her clogged sinuses. Then she walked the rest of the way to her apartment staring straight ahead. There was another thing about Americans. They all wanted to make eye contact with you. They all wanted to make your acquaintance.

When she got into the apartment, she went into the kitchen and put the two containers and her purse on the counter. Then she went back to the foyer and locked up. Her head was clear enough this time so that she forgot nothing. She did all the locks. She did all the bolts. Then she went back to the kitchen and started tea.

Here was the problem: Americans documented everything. If you went to the bank and cashed a check. If you went to the ATM and took out money. Your vital statistics and your picture went on your driver's license, and you had to show it if you wanted to use a credit card or buy a pack of cigarettes at the convenience store. Even an eighty-year-old woman who looked her age had to show her driver's license to buy alcohol or cigarettes. The pharmacy wanted a driver's license before they filled your prescription. Every cell phone call you made was logged and could be traced. Every landline call you made was logged and could be traced, too. If you were ever in trouble, the police went into all these systems and found you.

Meera had taken her money out in the first six months after she arrived. It could be traced, too, but it would have to be traced back years, and she thought that was relatively safe. Nobody could use it to prove that she had taken the money out to buy what she was about to buy today. How would she have known then that she would even need it?

The water boiled and she poured it. Then she went to the counter next to the sink and took the middle metal canister from the line of them she had against the wall. The canisters all contained necessary foodstuffs. Flour. Sugar. The middle canister held red lentils.

She put the canister with the red lentils on the table. She got a clean bowl from the cabinet and put that on the table, too. Then she sat down, took the tea leaves out of the teacup, and opened up the canister with the lentils in it.

The canister was half full. She made red lentils often. They were easy.

She poured the contents into the bowl. Then she reached down and tugged against the red paper liner with the tip of her fingernail. Her fingernails were very long, meant to look like a Bollywood movie star she had had a crush on when she was in secondary school.

The liner came off, but the tug was hard. Under the liner was money: three thousand dollars in twenties, tens, and fives.

This was not the only cash Meera had hidden away. She had some at the bottom of a tin she kept in her desk in the office. That tin also had family pictures in it and a false bottom. She had some in her locker in the gym where she worked out twice a week. The locker was not very secure, but it was hers and lockable as long as she kept up her membership and she had found a way to stash the money in the bottom of it.

All in all, she had ten thousand dollars stashed away in places she could get to easily if she needed it. Even the gym was open twenty-four hours a day. None of that cash was anywhere she would have to sign for it or would be likely to be seen getting it.

Now she counted out five hundred dollars and set it aside. Taking actual money with her was always a risk. You could get robbed on the street at any moment. She'd had her purse snatched on a bus once on a perfectly placid Sunday afternoon.

She folded up the cash and then pulled her necklace up so she could get to the little pouch on the end of it. Necklaces could be snatched, too, but this one wouldn't be. It was made of steel and not breakable, and the clasp had been welded shut.

She put the five hundred dollars in the pouch and the pouch back under her blouse. Then she looked back into the canister and smoothed out the rest of the money so that it wouldn't give itself away by being lumpy.

She had extra canister liners in a drawer near the cooktop. She took one the right size and pulled the backing off it. Then she put the liner down in the can and tamped the edges down until they were tight. She was careful putting the lentils back in the canister. She didn't want them to go everywhere. Then she closed up the canister and put it back in the row.

She took the new backing and the old liner and put them down the garbage disposal. Even the police would not find this. A drug-crazed hoodlum from the street wouldn't even look.

She got up and put her purse over her shoulder. Her tea was only half finished. It was the police she had to worry about now. Now that they knew who Marta Warkowski was, they would find somebody to tell them that she had been in the office, or near it, the night she was assaulted. They would ask questions. She had not had that patch of blood cleaned up with any thoroughness. They would find it.

Meera was really too sick to go out in cold weather. Her head was fuzzy. Her mind was not alert enough so that she could be sure she wouldn't walk right into a mugging.

But she couldn't help it.

She needed another gun.

2

When Bennis Hannaford got to Donna Moradanyan's house, she had Javier and Tommy in tow, and Tommy was carrying the bags.

"We should have dropped some of this stuff at my place," she said, as Tommy dumped the whole pile on his mother's kitchen table. "I went a little nuts in Ohanian's."

"Javier likes loukoumia," Tommy said.

Javier looked through the bags and came up with a package wrapped in waxed paper. "Loukoumia," he said.

Tommy took it away from him. "That's for here," he said. "The other package is for your house. Meet my sister, Charlie."

Charlie was sitting in a high chair, drinking something out of a sippy cup. She had been playing with a wooden jigsaw puzzle with large pieces when they came in, but she had stopped to watch what was going on. Now she looked at Javier and said, "Hi!"

Javier said, "*Hola.*"

Bennis grabbed a chair and sat down. "I'm exhausted," she said. "We've been pretty much everywhere. And we sat down online and ordered Javier's backpack. Red, with 'JHD' on it. I didn't know what else to do for initials."

"She got it from L.L.Bean," Tommy said. "I told her she shouldn't get him anything more expensive than anybody else was going to have. She didn't think the other stuff was strong enough."

"You ought to be glad she didn't get it from Vineyard Vines," Donna said dryly.

"She got everything else from Vineyard Vines," Tommy said. "The kid's going to look like he belongs to the British royal family."

"Lida came in when we were getting the loukoumia," Bennis said. "Javier took one look at her and lit up like a Christmas tree. Then he called her '*Señora* Cookies.' Then Lida lit up like a Christmas tree. I think the shakeout is going to be Lida and Hannah over at my house tomorrow with more boxes of cookies. And old Mrs.

Ohanian gave him loukoumia from the case. And Linda Melajian put marshmallows *and* whipped cream in his hot chocolate. I think one of my principal worries has been put to rest. I think the street is going to adopt him."

Tommy lifted Charlie out of her high chair. "I think Javier and I are going to take Charlie into the living room and read her some books," he said. "You two can do whatever it is that you do."

He grabbed Javier's hand and shuffled the three of them off down the hall. Bennis watched Donna watch them go, a peculiar look on her face.

Donna turned back to the table. "It's me, of course," she said. "Charlie's really too big for that high chair now, or any high chair. She's too big to be carried everywhere, too. And she doesn't like it. She's very independent."

"She's very beautiful," Bennis said. "Look, Donna, you know I love you more than I ever loved any of my own sisters. And I was very happy when you came back. But maybe you shouldn't have."

Donna had a cup of coffee in front of her. She tasted it and made a face. "He isn't even Armenian," she said. "I kept thinking that this isn't my home. Okay, I didn't grow up here. I grew up in the suburbs. But I came here as soon as I was finished with college. And I had Tommy here. And for God's sake, Bennis, I married Russ here, right in Father Tibor's church. I keep asking myself why I have to lose my home because Russ turned out to be—turned out to be—"

"Crazy?"

"Is that what he is?" Donna asked. "He still calls here, you know. I never answer the phone straight out. I let him leave messages on the machine. Maybe I should get rid of the machine, but if I did, one day I'd pick up and there he'd be."

"You could—"

"I know. Tommy told me that, too. And Tibor. And Gregor. I could talk to the prison and they'd forbid him from making the calls. You know what the funny thing is? I think if I just told him, straight out, he'd stop making the calls all on his own. This whole thing is so odd. He's so different, but in a lot of ways he's so much the same. And he's not a bully. And he's not a stalker. And he always takes no for an answer."

"Do you want to hear from him?" Bennis asked. "Gregor could probably arrange something."

"I want to hear something else from him," Donna said. "It's always the same thing, now. It has been, ever since—ever since he shot Gregor in the face. It probably was before that, but I don't think he used to talk about it. At least he didn't talk about it all the time."

"About how we're about to be in a civil war," Bennis said.

"The whole world is coming apart and we're going to start shooting at each other in the streets. The whole thing is going to collapse into violence and there's going to be blood everywhere and we have to protect ourselves. We have to get together as many resources as possible and hide ourselves because when it starts they'll come after the women first, me, and—and Charlie. They'll do things to Charlie I can't even say out loud, but he says them—"

"Donna."

"I know," Donna said. "I know. I think that what keeps me going, the reason I don't cut off contact, is that I'm pretty sure he means it. He isn't putting on an act. He really believes all these things he's saying. And he's scared to death. It's like one day he looked up and all the world was ugly and violent and mean. All the people except us were evil and—I don't know I don't know I don't know. It's like reality just morphed around him and now he's living in a world I don't recognize."

"And Tommy?"

Donna shrugged. "Tommy says he wishes I'd decorated the house for Christmas. He doesn't mean inside, you know. We do have a little tree up and we did stockings and the rest of it last week. I just couldn't get all that enthusiastic. No, he meant the house. The outside of the house."

"We all miss it," Bennis said. "You do know that, right? It used to be one of the hallmarks of Cavanaugh Street."

"Bennis, I just can't."

"I know," Bennis said. "We all understand. I'm sure Tommy understands, too."

"I wish I understood," Donna said. "I don't think Cavanaugh Street is what Russ keeps describing the world as. I don't think it ever was that way and I don't think it is that way now. But it's the oddest thing. Sometimes when I'm sitting by myself in the living room, it feels to me as if the world really is like that, right across the street from us, right around the corner. Maybe Russ is crazy, but maybe he isn't. Maybe he sees things I don't. That we don't. Maybe the world out there really is getting to be what he says it is. Then I think that if I decorate the house, if I wrap the place up in silver tinfoil and put bows on it, it would be like a beacon. All those people out there would see it. And then—"

"Donna."

"I know," Donna said again. She began to look through the packages on the table, putting aside each one old Mrs. Ohanian had marked with a "D": the loukoumia; two kinds of cheese; spice packs; mint leaves; a big pack of lamb hunks for stew.

"I start cooking sometimes and I stop in the middle of it and I can't understand why I'm doing it," Donna said. "We have to eat, but it seems too much, making things, using the recipes I got from the Very Old Ladies. It doesn't seem to matter anymore, putting in the effort to make us a family."

"Well, if you don't want to make the effort, come over to our house next week, after school starts," Bennis said. "I've got Javier, and I'm putting in the effort. I'm just not very good at it, and you know how I cook. I tried yaprak sarma right before Christmas, and Gregor thought I was trying to poison him. But I want to put together a dinner thing, with lots of people from the neighborhood, a sort of coming out party for Javier as he starts school. It's too bad we don't have much in the way of kids that age around here now."

"It's New Year's Eve in three days," Donna said. "It hardly seems possible."

To Bennis, Donna hardly seemed possible, but everything she could think of to do about it seemed even less possible, and on this day on Cavanaugh Street, nothing was getting fixed.

3

The best thing about upper management was that, if you told them something was going wrong with the tech, they believed you. They didn't know what you were talking about. They didn't want to know what you were talking about. They assumed that all the computers in the world were both zombies and maniacs, busily humming along making all life miserable.

It wasn't hard to get out from under the mess that had been caused by that unpaid bill. It wasn't even hard to fix the system to the point where the accounts were no longer sending off warning signals. Middle management wasn't much more comfortable with the tech than upper management was, and Clare McAfee knew better than to actually talk to any of the techies who knew anything. A few of the lower-level techies knew less than she did. They were okay.

Clare herself was not okay. The day of putting out fires had been miserable, and she had spent her evening almost haunted by her memories of home. Not that Lithuania had ever felt like home to her when she was living there. Home should be a comfortable place, and a refuge. At best, Lithuania had been familiar. It was occupied territory, run by a foreign power, hostile to its own history. There were beautiful buildings in her country, but she was never allowed to go into any of them. She lived with her parents in a big cement-block building in a bigger collection of cement-block buildings. She went to school in another cement-block building. She looked at pictures of Stalin and statues of Lenin and tried to memorize tables of mathematical facts so that she could pass her examinations and go on to another cement-block building that would not be a cement-block building full of factory work. She did what she could to put one foot in front of the other. She did what she could to wait it out.

Of course, the United States didn't feel like home to Clare, either. She'd been taught a formal English based on British school standards. Nothing was formal here. She had learned elaborate rituals of politeness that had no place in Philadelphia and probably had even less place in the smaller towns and cities outside it. People thought she was "cute."

Then there was the money. She hadn't realized what it would mean that you were expected to do for yourself, no matter what happened. You didn't have to be a political liability to end up on the street here.

Clare wasn't really worried about ending up on the street. She wasn't even worried about going to jail, although she was sure she could be sentenced to decades for all her side businesses. What bothered her was the possibility that she could be deported. She'd looked it up when she started. Back in the 1920s and 1930s, the American government had stripped a whole little cabal of people of their citizenship and sent them back to their home countries—Italian mobsters and members of the Mafia, mostly. Then they had stopped doing that and hadn't done it since. Now there was this latest administration. Nobody knew what was coming next.

Everybody at the bank who did direct business with Cary Alder had Aldergold. The bank's top brass was not entirely comfortable with this, but it wasn't unusual for the management of international banks to have social dealings with their biggest customers. By now, nobody thought it was suspicious that Clare would have lunch with Cary Alder in one of Cary Alder's special places. It could look suspicious eventually if she wasn't careful.

Clare went to the bar at the Alder Palace. It was on the very top of the building, encased in darkened glass. It had a waterfall and a lagoon. It had taken Clare most of the morning to find out that this was where he would be, and to convince him to sit still until she got there.

She handed a piece of Aldergold to the man at the desk when she walked in. He called another man, who walked her across the wide room to the booth where Cary was sitting. The place was nearly empty. All the places that required Aldergold were always nearly empty. That was part of the point. There were no crowds. There was no waiting. There was no crush. There were just these spaces that belonged only to those of our own.

Cary looked up when Clare came to the booth. He looked at the man who had brought her and said, "The young lady is going to want a Bloody Mary." Then he looked at Clare and said, "You should sit down. You sounded frantic on the phone."

He did not stand up. Clare let it go. She sat down on the other side of the booth and folded her hands on its polished wood surface. A moment later, a Bloody Mary arrived, as if out of nowhere.

"It can't be a coincidence," Clare said. "You can't just be accidentally hiring only men."

"What of it?"

"It's illegal in this country, isn't it? They taught us that when I first came to the bank. You are not allowed to discriminate on the basis of sex."

"You didn't come here to talk to me about discrimination on the basis of sex."

"I came here to try to pound some sense into your head," Clare said. "You can't do what you just did, Cary. We can set things up fifteen different ways and we can both make a lot of money, but the requirement is that you fulfill your part of the bargain. There can't be any red flags. And you can't disappear into thin air when there are red flags. Where have you been for the last twenty-four hours?"

155

"Believe it or not, I've been home."

"Not answering the phone," Clare said. "Do you want to know how many times I called? The mess at the bank would have been bad enough on its own, but then I started watching the news and looking at the websites and what did I see? That woman. The one you said you'd taken care of."

"I know."

"So now I've got a mess at the bank and a murder investigation. The police in this country are not idiots. And they're thorough. And now they say they've brought in that man, that Gregor Demarkian. God only knows where this is about to get to."

Cary Alder shifted suddenly in his seat. "She's not dead," he said.

"Somebody's dead," Clare said. "It was on the news."

"She's only in the hospital. She's in a coma."

"Cary, what are you doing? You're acting drugged. I almost had to invent an entire computer-hacking conspiracy to get myself out of that mess. And you. I was getting you out of it, too. Don't think if this thing comes apart I'm going to sit tight with my mouth shut. If something is going wrong here, if we need to reconsider our positions and regroup, you'd better tell me now. The more time I have to cover our asses, the more likely I'll be able to cover our asses. Don't put me in a position where I'm scrambling to get out from under the Feds."

"Okay."

"*Cary.*"

"I already arranged for the partial payment this morning. It should have been through to your desk before you came over here."

"The whole partial payment."

"All of it."

"Right now."

"Already taken care of."

Clare felt as if she were about to throw up. The room around her was cavernous but also too close. She had spent the last couple of days trying to talk herself out of the obvious. There was exactly one thing that could kill the two of them absolutely, without a hope in hell of either of them being able to dig their way out.

"Just tell me one thing," she said. "Just tell me you haven't run out of money."

FIVE

1

The call from John Jackman came while Gregor was sitting in the squad room, drinking bad coffee with Horowitz and Morabito and watching the avalanche of information come pouring over their heads like snow in a movie about a Swiss disaster. It would have been helpful if some of this information had been organized. It would have been more than helpful if any of this information had been sorted. Worse yet, the forensics were going to "take time," as usual. He could stare at that tire iron for six months and know in his heart it had been used to smash Marta Warkowski over the head. He couldn't do anything about it until people in lab coats checked all the blood and hair.

There was one thing Gregor could do, and he did it.

"You need to do a house by house, lot by lot, block by block in a radius of at least six blocks of the place we found this thing," he told Morabito and Horowitz. He felt a little like an idiot. Usually by the time he was called in to consult on a case, the police were well past this stage of the investigation. All he had to worry about were the reports they'd already filed.

"There's no way on earth this guy went driving around the city with his rear doors flapping in the wind without getting noticed," Gregor said. "There had to be a place to park that van close to where Marta Warkowski was dropped. Someplace it could be parked, out of sight, and left with some security."

"It could just have been some kind of vacant lot," Horowitz said. "There aren't a lot of garages and things out there."

"A vacant lot would be too open," Gregor said. "If it's just sitting where anybody could see it, either the police would have stumbled over it or it would have been stolen. There has to be something else. An alley we've overlooked. Maybe one of those weird little places some people put their garbage before they put it out."

"It won't tell us who the van belonged to," Morabito said. "New Jersey plates."

Gregor's phone went off. He looked at it to see John Jackman on the caller ID. John didn't show up as himself, but as "Lamb Chop," the old puppet from the Shari Lewis show. Gregor didn't want to think about it.

Gregor picked up. "Give me a second," he said. "I'll be right with you." He looked at Morabito and Horowitz. "Private call."

One of the policewomen motioned to him. He followed her out of the squad room and across the hall. There was a small interview room. None of the chairs looked comfortable.

"That is two-way glass," she said, pointing to the window along one wall, "but nobody's looking. You should be all right here."

"Thanks." Gregor went back to Lamb Chop. "You've got spectacular timing, John. This whole thing has blown completely up."

"I've been hearing about it," John said. "I take it you now have an actual murder on your hands."

"Is there a point to this? We're waiting for forensics to bring back a ton of information it's going to take them a week to get to. We've got a body in the morgue with the back of its head blown off. I've got a bunch of leads on Marta Warkowski from the hospital I haven't been able to look into yet. This entire mess has to be connected somehow and I don't know how as yet. I don't know what you expect me to be doing here."

John cleared his throat. "There are—things happening. On the Cary Alder front."

If Gregor Demarkian had ever smoked cigarettes, he would have smoked one now. "What kind of things happening?"

"The FBI and the SEC are going to be ready to move on the bank fraud within the next week. They'd rather do it sooner. We'd rather get some handle on the other thing first. Did you have a chance to look at the material on the other thing?"

"I looked at it."

"And?"

"And what, John? I'm not a forensic accountant. At least not anymore. You've had forensic accountants looking at that material for months. At the raw material, not just the summaries. You know what you're looking at. I know what you're looking at. I can't tell you any more than they have. Accept the evidence of your own eyes and get on with it."

"A coyote operation," John said cautiously.

"A coyote operation," Gregor agreed. "Assuming the information you provided me with is complete and without bias, there's no other possible interpretation. He's moving people from south of the border all the way up here, or at least some of them. My guess is that if you could look hard enough, you'd find that he's staffing almost all his properties with illegal immigrants. John, this isn't even all that odd. A lot of these guys do it. It looks like Alder is doing a lot of it personally, and most of them don't expose themselves that way, but what the hell. He's supposed to be something of a nut anyway. He's bringing them into the country. He's probably putting them to work."

"A modern form of slavery," John said. "They can't leave. They can't control their employment. Or their living conditions."

"I'm not arguing with you."

"I'd like to see him arrested for that," John said.

"And maybe you won't get that," Gregor told him. "From the material you gave me, he doesn't seem to be doing a lot of it. There aren't a lot of people involved, at least in the operations you've been able to tie directly to him. And he's hidden the money trail perfectly. If you were expecting me to stumble across whatever it is he's doing with the cash that has to be flowing into this, I'm going to have to disappoint you. If the professionals aren't going to do it for you, I'm not going to be that much help."

"You sometimes have interesting ideas."

"I'm not a clairvoyant," Gregor said. "John, you lose some. If you're going to get this guy on bank fraud, you'll at least be able to get him into a prison and keep him there. Maybe you ought to accept the fact that you're going to have to leave it at that."

"I hate leaving it at that," Jackman said. "I hate this whole immigration thing from one end to the other. I don't care if you're for more immigrants coming in or against it. The way this is set up, the people on the absolute bottom are getting killed. Worse than killed."

"I know, John."

"I'm sorry I dumped this on you," John said. "I thought I'd just take one more chance that somebody could have some insight. It's bad enough when these guys are evil. It's worse when they're smart."

"Maybe it will turn out he was involved in the murder of Hernandez," Gregor said.

"Was he?"

"'Involved' is an elastic word," Gregor said. "For what it's worth, it doesn't seem like his style, exactly. Especially the hit on Hernandez. I can see someone like Cary Alder ordering a hit on Hernandez, or even killing the man himself, but I don't think he would have done it in Marta Warkowski's living room. I can't even see him going down to that building in person. He'd be far too public."

"Cary Alder is always far too public," John said. "It's enough to make you nuts."

2

Gregor Demarkian found Detective Morabito sitting on a bench in front of the station house when he walked out to "get some air." The air was cold and he didn't really want any of it, but the pressures inside were more than he was willing to put up with any longer. Besides, there was nothing to do. There were a million questions, but before forensics came back with information, there was no way to definitively answer any of them. Some of them might never be answered at all.

Detective Morabito was smoking a cigarette. It surprised Gregor more than a little. The police could no longer smoke around crime scenes. That was a sensible precaution and Gregor approved of it. The police could no longer smoke indoors in public places, either. That was true of everyone. A public bench fit into none of these categories, but Gregor thought there was some kind of rule that meant Morabito wasn't supposed to smoke anywhere at all.

The neighborhood was not of the kind Gregor had been thinking of. It was not residential. It was not coherent. Storefronts stretched out along the street, each with a little concrete parking lot in front of it. The places had names that were entirely generic and without character. Zippy Tires. Dollar Bonanza. Modern Pawn.

Gregor went to sit down next to Morabito, who was in the middle of throwing one cigarette butt to the ground and lighting a new stick. Morabito looked up, and shrugged, and went on lighting.

"If you shoot off your mouth, I'll have HR down on me in a second," he said. "Smoking cigarettes. One more thing I'm not supposed to do anymore, even on my own time."

"Technically, you're not on your own time," Gregor pointed out. "Although I see what you mean."

"Do you? I thought there was supposed to be a difference between having a job and being owned by somebody. Anybody. Even the city of Philadelphia. I do what you want on your time and then I go home and it's my time and it shouldn't be any of your business. Smoking cigarettes. Drinking beer. Putting stuff up on the Internet you don't like the sound of. When I was in school, they had this thing in the textbook called the panopticon. It was a kind of prison—"

"I know what a panopticon is," Gregor said. "It's a prison that's designed so that the prison administration can see everything the prisoners do, every minute of every day."

"Right. Well, that's what it's like these days. They own you, these people. Every little scrapping piece of you. Breathe the wrong way and you're out on the street, rooting through garbage cans. But your kids aren't. Your kids are in their schools, being taught that everything you are and everything you do and everything you believe is evil. And if they're boys, they're being taught that they're evil, too."

It had been a long time since Gregor had smelled cigarette smoke. Bennis had given up the habit years ago. Tibor had given up the habit before Gregor had ever met him, when he first came from Armenia and found out that American cigarettes were almost as expensive as liquor.

"Do you live in the city?" Gregor asked.

Morabito shook his head. "Little township right on the edge. Lancaster, they call it. Little houses. Little lawns. Hundreds of people, all of them just like me. All of them fed up."

"About workplace rules?"

"About everything," Morabito said. "You ever wonder why we do it, any of us? Work hard and play by the rules. Righty-roo. Except that if you play by the rules, you're a sucker, and we all know it. I got admitted to Penn, did you know that?"

"No," Gregor said. "I went to Penn. It's a hard get. Did you go?"

"Even after all the financial aid and all that crap, I'd've had to

163

borrow forty thousand dollars just to get myself through, and that wouldn't have included money to live on. My father and I sat down and did the math and decided we couldn't do that. You have to pay that stuff back. You make a promise. So I went to community college instead. Now there's this woman running for president who wants to 'forgive' all the college loans. Do you know what that means? She wants to just make them go away. If you're somebody like me, if you wouldn't make promises you couldn't keep, you can just suck it up. If you're some irresponsible dick head who just didn't give a damn if you could ever make good, you're fine. You'll go to Penn for free on the rest of us. You'll probably end up head of HR somewhere telling guys like me we can't smoke a cigarette in our own living rooms and you'll take our kids away from us if we don't raise them your way."

Morabito's second cigarette was burned nearly to the butt. He threw it into the gutter and got out another one. Gregor could feel the waves of anger coming off him like heat. He hadn't noticed the anger before. He thought it must have been there.

There was a very slight wind. The smoke from Morabito's cigarette twisted in it, slightly. Morabito was staring out across the street at Bob's BBQ, but not seeing it.

"I know I'm not supposed to say it," Morabito said, "but I will say it, and if you turn me in you can go to hell. There's a lot going wrong in the world today, but you know what isn't going wrong? ICE. ICE picking up all the illegals and shipping them back where they came from. You want to hear about playing by the rules? Those people don't give a flying damn."

"Some of them are children."

"And all of them come from hellholes where the gangs grab twelve-year-olds and put them to work on the street," Morabito said. "Don't you think I know that? And if I had kids in one of those places, I'd want to get them up here as fast as I could. But they're not the only ones. My wife's family is from Kosovo. It took

164

us *five years* to get her cousin into the country. She couldn't just walk across the border somewhere. By the time she got here, she was a wreck. She'll probably always be a wreck. And why? Because the illegals break the rules and overwhelm the system and then expect to get away with it and we let them. And if you complain that people like my wife's cousin should come first because they did the right thing—well, then you're a racist bigot who doesn't belong in the police department."

"We bring a fair number of people from Armenia to my neighborhood," Gregor said. "I don't think it's just Kosovo—"

"It's not," Morabito said. He stood up. The cigarette was only half smoked. The city around them felt empty and inorganic. A man was being pushed out the door of one of the pawnshops across the street. He looked drunk.

"I don't care anymore," Morabito said. "I keep thinking about that woman who started all this. Nice woman, probably. No evidence otherwise. Lived in the same place all her life. Went to Mass every single day from what people have told us. Where does she end up? In a garbage bag. It's one of those metaphors. That's where we're all ending up, the people like me. In garbage bags."

"Maybe she'll come out of her coma and be able to tell us what happened to her," Gregor said. "There's a part of me that really hopes that will be our solution. It's always easier when you know exactly what happened."

"Maybe the guy who put her in the garbage bag will turn out to be the guy we found dead in her apartment," Morabito said. "Then we can all listen to lectures about how illegals don't commit crimes, it's white guys like me you have to worry about. I could have gone to Penn. I could be telling guys like you how to run your lives. I wasn't enough of an asshole."

"Well," Gregor said.

"Never mind," Morabito said. "Let's go find out who killed that illegal piece of shit. Let's pretend we care. It's all coming apart anyway."

Morabito took off, back into the building. Gregor twisted around to watch him go.

The lecture was so much like the lectures Gregor had heard from Russ, or heard other people say they had heard from Russ, it was shocking.

3

Gregor did not start out going in any particular direction. He was just getting away from the hothouse, getting into the air. He remembered this phase of things from his own days in law enforcement. Everything had gone wrong but nothing had gone particularly right. There were conjectures but no real facts. People were spinning every piece of gossip and stray observation. Gregor sometimes wondered what it had been like in the days *before* modern forensics, when this was all detectives had had. He wouldn't have liked to see the rates for false arrest, or worse.

He was still getting used to the fact that these neighborhoods around Cavanaugh Street were so close together and yet so very . . . diverse. He really hated the word "diverse." It felt like a piece of jargon, a sanitized phrase meant to conceal as much as it revealed. "Diverse" sounded like one of those old UN posters of happy children of different colors holding hands. These neighborhoods were little monocultural enclaves, sealed off from each other, always potentially hostile.

He reached St. Catherine's Parish in no time at all. Coming at it from the direction of the station house, he reached St. Catherine's Church first. It was a tall brick building with a tower that looked like it ought to contain bells. Gregor didn't think it did. He couldn't remember ever hearing bells while he was in this neighborhood. There were no bells at the Armenian church on Cavanaugh Street, either. When that church had to be rebuilt, they had offered

Father Tibor a bell tower. Father Tibor had been astonished. What would he use it for?

Gregor was just coming up to the tall steps when the church's double front doors opened and people began trickling out. There weren't many of them, and all of them were older women. They might be older Spanish women, but they were the older women of his own childhood—short, heavyset, dressed entirely in black.

In a moment they were followed out by a small man in Mass robes and then another man with a candle on a tall pole. On further observation, the second man was not a man at all but a boy about Tommy Moradanyan's age, looking disgruntled and uncomfortable.

The small man—the priest—shook a few hands, said a few words, then came down the stairs toward Gregor.

"It's Mr. Demarkian, isn't it?" he said. "I saw your picture in the paper. I've been expecting you. Well, you or the detectives. We did have a couple of uniformed patrolmen in yesterday."

The boy with the candle seemed to mutter something under his breath. Then he turned and hightailed it into the church. The priest turned around to watch him go.

"Their grandmothers insist," the priest said. "If they're here assisting at Mass, they're not out there doing God only knows what. I'm Henry Alvarez. Father Alvarez. I'm the priest at St. Catherine's these days."

"It's good to meet you," Gregor said. "Do you mind if I ask you a question? Do the people here really have that much to worry about from the police? And I'm not even the police."

Henry Alvarez had made it to the bottom of the steps. "It's ICE they worry about mostly. And nobody knows what ICE is going to do anymore. Now, to answer the question you're not going to ask but you're going to think about anyway. No, I don't have a Spanish accent. I was born in Queens. My father was born in Queens. My grandfather was born in Queens. We all sound more like Jimmy Cagney than a movie version of a Spanish immigrant."

"But you speak Spanish," Gregor said.

"I have to," Henry Alvarez said. "Most people in this neighborhood do speak English, but they're more comfortable in Spanish, and some things you have to be comfortable when you say them. And not enough people here speak English as a first language for us to celebrate Mass in English only. Except for the four o'clock. The four o'clock Mass on weekdays I celebrate in English."

"The one Marta Warkowski attended," Gregor said.

Henry Alvarez nodded. "Every single day, Monday through Friday. She was an old-fashioned daily communicant. They exist in every Catholic country, no matter what the home language. Saturdays and Sundays, we have no Masses in English. She came to the noon Mass on Saturdays and the seven A.M. on Sundays. I think the point of the seven A.M. on Sundays was to avoid the kiss of peace as far as possible. I don't think she would have been comfortable with that even if this was still a Polish parish. She wasn't a touchy person, Marta."

"And Hernandez? Was he a touchy person?"

"At the kiss of peace? I wouldn't know. I don't think he ever came to Mass if he could help it, and he could help it most of the time."

The two men were now standing at the bottom of the church steps. Maybe because Gregor was not identifiable as law enforcement, the street was not empty. Teenage boys were sitting on steps, calling out to girls as they passed. The doors of bodegas were opening and closing. A food stand on the corner was serving a growing line of customers who each came away from the counter holding something wrapped in a tortilla.

"It must be lunchtime," Gregor said. "I should get myself a taco. Or six."

Alvarez laughed. "They're very good tacos. Not Taco Bell. I can't tell you much about Marta Warkowski, you know. She came to Mass, but she never really talked to me. Or to anyone in the neighborhood, as far as I know. A couple of times I made a point of getting out ahead of her so I could shake her hand after Mass. She was perfectly polite, but she didn't stop to talk."

"She must have talked to some people," Gregor said. "She must have done some shopping, if nothing else."

"She did grocery shopping once a week," Alvarez said. "Or at least, once a week she left the neighborhood on foot and came back in a cab, and when she came back in the cab, she had grocery bags. Wednesday afternoons. Some of the women in the Sodality told me about it. They resented it, I think, that she didn't shop locally. They took it as part and parcel."

"Of what?"

"Of the fact that she didn't belong here," Alvarez said. "That she wasn't one of them. That she was a stranger and an outsider and wanted to stay that way. Not that she ever could have been anything else, of course. They wouldn't have trusted her. She didn't belong here."

"She did belong here once," Gregor said.

"Oh, yes," Alvarez said. "And once upon a time her grandparents moved in here and pushed out the Irish who were here before them. Things change. I'm sure she resented it. I would resent it. There's a push these days back in New York, the Columbia campus has started to take over Harlem. Harlem resents it. And I couldn't tell you what to do about it."

"Nothing anybody tries to do about it seems to work," Gregor said.

"And nothing ever will," Alvarez said. "But a lot of people out at Penn will yell and scream about racism and a lot of other unbelievable crap and make everything worse. People aren't wrong to resent it when their homes are yanked out from under them. Everybody wants a home, a place he can go and just relax, just not think twice about what he's doing or saying or going to find around the next corner. You don't have to hate other people to want to spend some of your time with your own. I think it must be very hard to have to live in a place where you are entirely alien."

"And Marta Warkowski was entirely alien?"

"Entirely," Alvarez said. "And don't give me a lecture about how she should have moved out years ago. Assuming she had the money to do that—and she actually might have—she couldn't have gone any-place that would have been more home to her than that apartment. Born and brought up there. Made her first communion and confir-mation from there. Buried her parents and at least one sibling from there. Anywhere else would have been an outpost in the wilderness."

"And Hernandez?"

Alvarez shrugged. "Classic case of culture clash," he said. "To Hernandez, Marta Warkowski was insane. She had that enormous apartment to herself, and he was constantly looking for places to put new families, large families who needed the room. He'd see these families stuffed into tiny little places, three and four to the room. Miserable conditions, and dangerous conditions, too, and not just in the usual fire hazard sort of way. The people who own these buildings pay off building inspectors right and left, but there's a limit. There's always a danger they're going to get caught and hauled up in front of the authorities. Then the families are out on the streets. The landlords have empty apartments. And sure as hell, excuse the expression, somebody is going to pick up the phone and call ICE. So every time Hernandez had a new family he wanted to place, he'd bug her to move out to a smaller apartment and she'd haul Alder Properties into housing court."

"That must have been expensive."

"Like I said, there's a chance she could afford it. Oh, not that she had endless money, but that she'd managed to function. I think she may have been one of those people. Never got into debt, not even with a credit card. Never overspent. Put aside in savings every week of her working life and didn't touch it until she retired and was careful about touching it then. So, housing court. Which makes what happened to Hernandez even stranger."

"Why?"

"Because among the other judgments Marta Warkowski managed to get from the courts was a restraining order that said Hernandez couldn't enter her apartment. Ever. Not even to make repairs. Hernandez was livid about the whole thing. He couldn't stop talking about it for weeks. I can't imagine that Marta asked him in that night. Which leaves us with how he ended up there, dead."

"Did you see the black van that night?" Gregor asked him. "The one the sisters are talking about?"

"I didn't see any black van at all. Not then and not later. If I had, I'd have thought what Sister Margaret Mary did. I'd have thought it was ICE. But I'll tell you what I did see."

"What?"

"Marta Warkowski," Alvarez said. "She left church after the four o'clock at about four forty-five. She went back to her building. I saw her go. But just about five o'clock, I saw her come out again. I remember because it was really unusual. She mostly didn't go out after dark, except for Mass, and then just because it's dark by four thirty in the winter and she had no choice. But she went out that night and started off in that direction."

"Did you see her come back?"

"No. I don't know if you remember, but the weather was awful. I wasn't hanging around outside any longer than I needed to. I never saw her again until her picture showed up in the paper after she was dumped on the street. I have been out to the hospital a couple of times. I may not really have known her, but I am her priest."

"I wonder where she went," Gregor said.

"So do I," Alvarez said. "I wonder what Hernandez was doing in that apartment. It doesn't seem possible that that man could be dead and that woman could be in a coma over an apartment in a barely habitable building, but here we are, and I don't see anything else."

"I don't see anything else either," Gregor said.

Then his cell phone began to buzz and vibrate in his pocket.

PART THREE

ONE

1

The man at the front at the Aldermine Cavern was holding a plain white envelope for Gregor behind the desk. He handed it over when Gregor presented himself. Then, when Gregor opened it, he took it back. Gregor had been able to feel the round hard metal of the Aldergold piece inside it. The man behind the desk took it out and put it down out of sight.

"It's just a formality, Mr. Demarkian," he said. "Mr. Alder was quite explicit about what we were to do with you. Why don't you come along with me?"

The Aldermine Cavern was not actually underground, but it was built to feel like it was. There were no windows that looked out on the street or any other scene of the outside. The walls were covered in dark green fabric that gave off the impression of moss. The floor was carpeted in brown. There were tiny white runner lights along the pathways that wound between the heavy wooden furniture. It could have been midnight or noon.

The young man brought Gregor far into the room, then stopped at a deep, solid-mahogany booth in what might have been a back corner. Gregor couldn't tell.

The man in the booth looked up when Gregor arrived, but made no effort to stand. Gregor eased his way onto the bench on the other side of the booth table.

"Mr. Demarkian," Cary Alder said.

"Mr. Alder."

Cary Alder looked at the young man who was standing by, waiting patiently. "Maybe you should get Mr. Demarkian something to drink. Scotch, isn't it? Some kind of unblended scotch would be good."

"Ginger ale," Gregor said.

"You must be joking. You're not going to tell me you're on duty. The police department isn't actually employing you."

"The police department is employing me," Gregor said, "but I'm playing hooky, or I wouldn't have answered your text without bringing them with me. But I not only don't drink in the daytime, I don't want to. So if you want to get me something, ginger ale."

"You can't tell it's daytime in here."

"You can't tell the world hasn't ended in here."

"Get Mr. Demarkian a ginger ale," Cary Alder said. "It's a damned waste, but everything's been a damned waste for days."

The young man murmured something unintelligible and disappeared. Cary Alder watched him go.

"He's gay, of course," Alder said abruptly. "All the people we hire to work up front in Aldergold venues are gay. Gay men, that's it. They're impeccably groomed, they know how to dress, and if they don't know how to behave when we get them it takes them a week to learn. Are you going to give me a lecture on what a bigot I am, stereotyping the hell out of people? Or are you going to have a fit that I'm operating against the law because I'm not an equal opportunity employer?"

"I'm going to find out what it is you got me out here for," Gregor said. "I do wonder if your employees know what your hiring policy is."

"Of course they do. They're like everybody else. They like an advantage if they can get it. We don't even bother to advertise openings anymore. The boys find me other boys. There are always more in the pipeline, so to speak."

Another young man showed up at the side of the booth. He had a tall glass of ginger ale on ice and a small square of linen napkin. He put them both down and disappeared.

Cary Alder watched him go, too. Then he turned his attention to Gregor.

"Let's be real here," he said. "This is something of a preemptive strike. I figure we're in the midst of one of two scenarios. Either you found a pile of Aldergold pieces on Marta Warkowski when you brought her to the hospital. Then I've got to expect you to show up here, or my office, or God knows where, to ask about it. Or you didn't find them, and there's somebody out there holding on to them who will end up being my problem sooner rather than later."

"Because Aldergold can only be spent here," Gregor said, "and nobody can get any unless you give it to them."

Cary Alder took a long pull at his drink. Gregor would be willing to bet it actually was scotch, middle of the afternoon or not.

"Let's not let this get out of hand," Alder said. "For all the legends about Aldergold, it's a very simple promotion based on a very simple premise. If you are an Alder Properties client in any of our high-end operations—gated communities out in Bucks County and on the Main Line, apartments in the two most expensive buildings we run in the city, a guest at our main resort in Palm Beach—we give you a few pieces of Aldergold on a regular schedule. You can use those to come in here, or in any of the other five venues we have that will only admit you if you have them. I don't have to give them to you directly."

"And it's that desirable, coming in here?"

"It's like the first-class VIP lounge at the airport," Cary Alder said, "but more restrictive. Not everybody can get in here. It's never crowded. You never have to wait for service. All the people you meet will be—like you. Or like you'd like to think you are."

"Rich."

"Rich, yes," Alder said, "but a certain kind of rich. It's the same principle here as it is with the neighborhood where Marta Warkowski lived. Still lives, I suppose. She's not dead, last I heard."

"She's not dead," Gregor agreed.

"People like to be with their own," Alder said. "It's a pile of crap, all that diversity stuff. People don't want to live in the middle of a bunch of diversity. They want to live alongside people just like them, and they want to be able to police it, or to have somebody police it. This is our place. These people are our own people. And don't tell me rich people are more like that than poor people. It isn't true. All people are exactly the same way."

"Are they? What about Atlantic City—you operate there, don't you? Do you run Aldergold venues there?"

"No," Cary Alder said. "But that's because I don't run casinos. We do have buildings in Atlantic City, but they're just standard issue middle-class and lower-middle-class apartment buildings. The kind of places you live if you're dealing blackjack or tending bar."

"That seems a little odd," Gregor admitted. "I'd think casinos were right up your alley."

"There's no way to get into gambling without getting into trouble," Cary Alder said. "Jersey. Las Vegas. It doesn't matter. You always have to be mobbed up, and no sane person wants to deal with any of those people. And then there's no guarantee you're going to make any money."

"At gambling?"

"At gambling," Cary Alder said. "I know casinos are supposed to be a license to print money, but have you got any idea how many of them go belly up every year? Hell, the Mashantucket Pequots are practically making a hobby of it up in Connecticut. So, no. I don't run casinos, and I don't hand out Aldergold to gamblers. I like guys who work in the financial industry. Hedge funds. Stock brokerages. There's more of that in Philadelphia than you'd think."

Gregor thought about Bennis and Bennis's family. He was sure he had a pretty good idea of how much of that kind of thing was in Philadelphia.

"I don't think you got me out here to talk about who you give Aldergold to," Gregor said. "Except for Marta Warkowski. And yes, we did find the Aldergold on her. Fifteen pieces. I'm told that's quite a lot."

"Do you know about the building downtown, the one where we included fifteen units of affordable housing? We got a deal from the city on the land-use regulations. If we included the affordable housing, we got easements. And we needed the easements."

"If this is the place where the people in the affordable housing had to use a separate entrance in the back—"

"That's the one," Cary Alder said. "I don't know what the crap the mayor was expecting, but the kind of people who pay one and a half million for an apartment aren't going to want to share a lobby with a bunch of file clerks. They're not going to do it."

"And that has what to do with Marta Warkowski? She didn't live in an expensive building. She lived in her old neighborhood."

"I know," Cary Alder said, "but she was not your usual afford-able-housing tenant. Not by a long shot. And everything connects. The affordable housing is our bread and butter, but the high-end housing is the serious money. And the kind of people who live in the high-end housing don't like certain kinds of publicity. Which is where Marta came in. Marta was loud. She had money—not the kind of money to live in one of our high-end buildings, but enough to do what she wanted to do and operate the way she wanted to operate. She'd already taken us to housing court half a dozen times. She'd taken us to regular court twice. And now I've got this building going up, tens of millions of dollars already on the line, inspectors and bankers and everybody but the tooth fairy on my ass, and she was about to blow the whole thing up."

"Marta Warkowski," Gregor said incredulously.

"I'm going to have something to eat," Cary Alder said. "I'll have them bring a grazing spread. You should eat something."

2

A grazing spread turned out to be the kind of food that made Gregor Demarkian a little nuts. It was food he ought to be familiar with—hummus, melitzanosalata, manti—that was rendered completely alien because it was made of . . . stuff. The hummus had cilantro in it. The melitzanosalata had sprigs of something sticking out of it. As for the manti—my God, Gregor asked himself, what could you possibly do to mess up manti? The kitchen at the Aldermine Cavern had managed something.

There was also pita bread and feta cheese and three kinds of olives. These were fine, if not exactly what you would get at the Ararat. Gregor restricted himself to those. There was also a big tub of something that was vaguely pink and might have been made of red lentils. Gregor preferred not to ask.

Cary Alder ate as if he were in a dream. He was not focused on the food. He was not focused on Gregor Demarkian. Gregor began to wonder if he had forgotten what they were doing here.

"All right," he said finally. "Marta Warkowski."

"Marta Warkowski," Gregor agreed. "And maybe also Miguel Hernandez."

"Well, I can probably clear one thing up for you," Alder said. "Marta probably didn't shoot Hernandez. I don't think the times would work out."

"You know something about the times?"

Alder nodded. "She was down at our place the night of the, you know, the garbage bag."

"What?"

"She came down to the office," Alder said. "It was after five thirty. I was shocked to shit, to tell you the truth. There were a lot of things you could count on with Marta, and one of them was that she hated going out after dark. She didn't trust the city. She didn't trust her own block, which I don't completely blame her for, because the guys on the street get aggressive. But she came down to the office that night, completely unannounced, and gave me what for."

"And it was after five thirty? And the office was open?"

Cary Alder shook his head. "The girls in the rent office had already gone home. Even Meera had gone home. You've met Meera. She's got that flu or whatever it is lately. She usually stays late, but she went home when the rest of them did, and she saw Marta on the street. Marta didn't see her, from what I understand. It was right outside our building. Meera got home and called me. I came out into the reception area and I could see Marta past the frosted glass in the hall, pacing up and down. I nearly dropped dead."

"She was just pacing up and down? She didn't knock?"

"She knocked. She pounded. She yelled. Then she went back to pacing."

"So you let her in."

"Not at first," Alder said. "First, I went back to my own office and called Hernandez and had a screaming fit, which I had every right to have. This is a long-standing situation. I'd gone out on a limb just to keep Hernandez in that job. I should have bounced his ass back to El Salvador."

"Why didn't you?"

"Because," Alder said, "you may not believe it, but even a low-level building like that one takes a lot of work, and if the people you hire aren't competent, they cost you. And Hernandez was very competent. He got the repairs done. He got the garbage picked up. He got the rents collected. He kept the furnace in order. And he was good at hiring people. The people he brought in could always do their jobs, and they were never drunks or drug addicts or other undesirables."

"Were they always here legally?"

"They were always here legally enough," Alder said. "You get that, don't you? There are people who come here illegally who are total little shits. They're perfectly safe unless they get arrested, which a lot of them do, because they're not that bright. Then there are the kind of people Hernandez hired. They have forged papers out the wazoo. They work hard. They keep their noses clean. They raise families. They might as well be wearing neon signs that say 'Deport Me.' They just stick right out there where ICE can pick them up as soon as they get a traffic ticket."

"How did you know to call Hernandez about Marta Warkowski?"

"It was a long-standing situation; I've told you before." Cary Alder tried an olive. He didn't seem to like it. "Her family's been in that apartment since before Alder Properties owned the building. When we first bought the building, we wanted to break that apartment up into at least two smaller ones. That's what we did with the other large apartments. The kind of people who rent in that neighborhood these days can't really afford places that large, and they're more than willing to crowd into something smaller. So we make more money if we have more apartments, even if it's the same square footage."

"But?"

"But Marta didn't want to go," Cary Alder said, "and our usual . . . ah . . . procedures didn't work. We raised the rent as far as we could. She paid anything we asked and then she went down to housing court and filed a complaint. It's the two things together that killed us. If she'd filed the complaint but hadn't paid the new rent, or only paid part of it, we'd have had grounds for an eviction suit. She never gave us any. So we had her investigated."

"You can't tell me you thought she was a drug addict," Gregor said. "I've seen her. Granted, it was while she was in a hospital bed—"

"Listen, for a while there I was wondering if she wasn't selling the stuff. She always had enough money. Always. And she didn't have a credit rating. She didn't have credit cards or anything to get a credit rating from. So I finally talked to some people with less than stellar reputations for obeying the law, and they looked into it."

"Her case manager at the hospital told me and then told the police that she thought there was something funny about Marta Warkowski's finances," Gregor said. "That she was able to pay her bills too easily. That kind of thing."

"There's nothing funny," Cary Alder said. "It's just not very usual these days. My people found she had four or five million dollars stashed in savings accounts and certificates of deposit in maybe a dozen different banks. She'd been putting money away, every single paycheck, for decades."

"Why all the banks?"

"My guess would be FDIC insurance," Cary Alder said. "This isn't a sophisticated woman. Her savings strategy was idiotic. When she started, she probably got three percent for her trouble. These days, she probably doesn't get one. But she wasn't looking to make a ton of money. She was looking to be safe. FDIC covers the first quarter of a million of the money you've got in the bank if the bank goes bust. She's got her money parceled out so that if there's a crash, she'll still be solvent. The FDIC insurance will cover big chunks of it."

"And she's got enough money so that you're never going to be able to force her out of that apartment," Gregor said.

"Right. So we stopped trying. Once we knew what the score was, we just decided to live with it. Except Hernandez couldn't live with it. He kept coming across these people who needed bigger apartments. He wouldn't stop nagging at her about it. So she didn't just take us to housing court, she took us to regular court. She took him to court. She got a restraining order against him. She got fifty thousand dollars out of us at one point because we didn't keep him away from her. Anyway, as soon as I saw her out there in the hall, I knew he'd been at it again. So I called him and had a fit. I got him on his cell phone, so I suppose he could have been anywhere at the time, but she was here."

"And you did talk to her," Gregor said.

"Absolutely," Cary Alder said. "I let her into the office and did my best to calm her down. We'd managed to go a couple of years without ending up with her in any kind of court. I've got two enormous building projects, both luxury projects. I've got loans. I've got lines of credit. Ending up in court means you end up publicly exposed. Ending up publicly exposed means all kinds of people start looking into all kinds of things. A luxury building project is a balancing act. I didn't want to fall off the high wire."

"Are you on a high wire?" Gregor asked.

Cary Alder ignored this. "If nothing else happens to you, you get the inspectors," he said. "There are hundreds of building and construction regulations in this town, issued by half a dozen different departments, and some of those regulations contradict each other. There is no such thing as being entirely in compliance. Which means the city can bring down your project any time it wants. So you stay under the radar."

Gregor tried the hummus with the cilantro in it, just to know. It was awful.

"Anyway," Cary Alder said again. "I let her in finally, and I talked to her. I must have talked to her for over an hour. She was livid and she was fed up and I don't really blame her. She was also handing out ultimatums. Which she could have made good on, by the way. You know what else happens when you don't fly under the radar?

If some jerk decides to take you down, he's likely to take a lot of your people with you, even people who haven't done anything really wrong. Then the mess gets bigger. And bigger."

"I take it there's quite a lot of mess going on there to get bigger," Gregor said dryly.

"I had the Aldergold in my desk," Cary Alder said. "I gave it to her as a kind of appeasement. I had to explain it to her. She didn't know what it was. I tried to stress that she could use it to come into one of these places and have dinner or whatever. On Alder Properties."

"Would they have let her in?"

"Sure. If you've got Aldergold, they let you in. And they treat you like anybody else with Aldergold. If they don't, they get fired. They might have stuck her in a back booth out of sight, but they would have let her in and they would have served her."

"So she took the Aldergold and then what? She went away?"

"I put her in a cab and paid for it," Cary Alder said. "It was dark by then, really dark. And that's the last I saw of her. I don't know what happened after that. I don't know how she ended up in a garbage bag. I don't know how Hernandez ended up dead in her apartment. Hell, I don't know how Hernandez ended up in her apartment at all. And if she had a gun, it's news to me."

Gregor took an olive. It was a Kalamata olive. There was nothing you could do to ruin an olive. It was just fine.

"Well," he said. "Here's one thing. If Hernandez is the one who put Marta Warkowski in the garbage bag, she couldn't have shot him. And if she shot him, he couldn't be the one who put her in the garbage bag."

3

For some reason, it felt as claustrophobic and suffocating outside the Aldermine Cavern as in it. It didn't help that Gregor's phone was full of messages delayed by the Cavern's thick walls. This seemed distinctly dysfunctional to him. Surely the kind of people who would want to spend time in the Cavern would also want to get their messages in real time. Maybe he had underestimated Cary Alder. Gregor always had some respect for people who bucked the smart phone hegemony.

He looked around with no particular purpose for a while, wondering if he should go home or back to the detectives' squad room or off to a place where he could plausibly pretend to be out of communication. He was slightly disoriented, or he would have realized where he was. He'd been here only two weeks ago, when they were finalizing the paperwork that brought Javier to the sisters and then to Cavanaugh Street.

"Chickie," Gregor said to himself.

Then he checked the building numbers on both sides of the street and headed up the block.

At the door to the building that housed Marshall, Burbank, Callahan, and Freed, Gregor identified himself to the doorman and asked for Edmund George. The doorman got busy and official looking at his switchboard and then waved Gregor to the bank of elevators. It was at the last minute that Gregor realized the man was armed, the distinct bulge not quite concealed under his left armpit. More and more lately, Russ's ravings seemed less like ravings than like prophecies.

And that was very bad news.

Ed George was waiting outside the elevators when Gregor got to the fifth floor. Marshall, Burbank, Callahan, and Freed had that entire floor and the one above it. As usual these days, Ed looked professional, prosperous, and straitlaced. Nobody would think to call him Chickie.

"Are you all right?" Ed asked as Gregor got out of the elevator. "You look a little stunned."

"I was in the Aldermine Cavern," Gregor said. "I am a little stunned.

And then for some reason, I was thinking of you as Chickie. I don't know where that came from."

"It's a blast from the past," Ed said. "I wouldn't worry about it if I were you. I think of myself as Chickie sometimes, too. And I bring Chickie out at least once a year for Pride. Come on back. I can actually carve out half an hour. I just had an appointment cancel on me."

Gregor followed Ed through the maze of cubicles to the back of the floor, where the associates had their tiny little offices, then beyond that to the slightly larger offices reserved for junior partners. Ed was a junior partner. He even had a window.

"You didn't have to come all the way down here," he said. "I told Bennis I'd come up to Cavanaugh Street whenever you needed me. And you should be in good shape, at least for the moment. How's Javier?"

"He seems to be doing pretty well," Gregor said.

Ed had a visitor's chair. He kicked it out where Gregor could get to it and then went behind his desk to sit down.

"What were you doing in the Aldermine Cavern?" he asked. "There's something that doesn't sound like your thing. I'd think Bennis would spit on it."

"I don't think she's that dramatic," Gregor said. "I was talking to Cary Alder."

"That must have been interesting."

"Oddly enough, it was." Gregor hadn't bothered to button his coat when he left the Cavern. Now he shrugged it off and draped it over the chair. "You ever do any business with Cary Alder?"

"No," Ed said. "This is an old-line firm. He's a little too—"

"New?"

"Crooked," Ed said. "I'm not saying I know anything specifically, but there are people around here with connections. The word is the Feds are about to land on him with both feet."

"That's what I hear, too. I think that's what he hears, too. Do you know the case that just came up? The woman in the garbage bag, and then the man they found dead in her apartment?"

"I know about the woman in the garbage bag," Ed said. "It's been all over the news."

"Did you know she had Aldergold on her when she was found? Do you know what Aldergold is?"

"Aldergold is the kind of thing that makes this firm not want to deal with Cary Alder," Ed said. "I had heard about that. But I thought the woman was supposed to be some kind of bag lady. How did she get Aldergold?"

"Cary Alder gave it to her. It's a long story. She's not a bag lady and she's not a highflier, but the police found the stuff and so we're talking to Cary Alder. But forget that for a minute. I'll tell you about it later if you want me to, but it's not what has me up here. Alder said something to me that's sticking in my head. Do you do any criminal law?"

"Pro bono, but some," Ed said. "Not on Cary Alder's level. The firm gets involved in some of that kind of thing. You can't help it when you're dealing with people who make lots of money. Making lots of money makes people truly stupid."

"I can bet. Alder said to me, sort of as an aside, that when there's a big money case like that, when everything starts going south, it isn't just the top guys who get hit. A lot of their employees get hit, too. Get arrested, I think he meant. And prosecuted and put in jail. Even if they weren't necessarily doing anything illegal."

"Ah," Ed said. "Well, you got that wrong just a bit. They'll have been doing something illegal, they just won't necessarily have known it was illegal. Money cases are not like murders."

"I wouldn't expect them to be."

"Financial law is a rat's nest, in a lot of ways. Remember some time back, when Martha Stewart went to prison? You read the newspapers, you'd think she went to jail because she engaged in insider trading. But she didn't. They couldn't convict her on insider trading.

What she went to jail for was telling her stockholders that she expected to be acquitted of insider trading."

"And that was against the law? Even though she was right?"

"Exactly."

"Okay," Gregor said. "Things have changed a bit since my day."

"It's stuff like that that makes all the complications," Ed said. "Let's go back to Cary Alder. What I've been hearing is bank fraud, connected to some building projects he's got going. That almost certainly means he's got a connection at one or more banks. Each of those connections has to be high enough up in the hierarchy to approve a loan, and with enough clout to hide the transactions that need to be hidden. That could be one of the top guys, and sometimes it is, but it also could be somebody a couple of rungs down the ladder. In that latter case, the people above that connection are going to be on the hook at least partway, because the Feds expect them to know. But you've also got the people right below the connection. Almost certainly one of them is going to have done the actual physical moving of the money, and that's going to be a crime even if the guy who did it had no idea he shouldn't have been doing it. His boss said to do it. He did it."

"Right," Gregor said.

"The same is going to be true at Alder's own company," Ed said. "I suppose Alder could be altering documents and sending falsified financial statements with his own two hands, but I'd bet not. He's got somebody, maybe even several somebodies, doing something like inflating his rent receipts, maybe, or overestimating the market value of his holdings. Remember the savings and loan debacle? I think we're talking about Reagan. A guy would come in and take out a mortgage to buy property for a hundred dollars. A few weeks later, another guy would come in and take out a mortgage to buy that property from him for a thousand dollars. Back and forth, back and forth, back and forth until there was some two-acre little sand plot mortgaged for millions of bucks, and then the scammers would disappear. Well, every time they did that flip, there was some second assistant bookkeeper actually doing the paperwork. And that guy got charged along with the rest of them."

Gregor thought this over. "So Cary Alder has a second assistant bookkeeper on the hook somewhere."

"He does, and whoever he has in with him at the banks probably does, too."

"And what happens to the second assistant bookkeepers when the case blows up?"

"Depends on what the second assistant bookkeepers did," Ed said. "And what they did and didn't know. And just how furious the prosecutors are."

Gregor sighed. Second assistant bookkeepers. Bank fraud that the banks participated in. He didn't believe that Cary Alder had himself stuffed Marta Warkowski into a garbage bag, and he didn't believe he had gotten Hernandez to do it and then shot Hernandez in Marta Warkowski's apartment. In fact, Gregor had the impression that not only did Cary Alder know the Feds were about to land on him, but that he wasn't trying very hard to get out from under it. It didn't make any sense.

"You ever see a man who's about to be hit by a freight train and just doesn't care?"

"I know enough about Cary Alder to know you don't want to get too involved with him," Ed said. "What I know may be secondhand, but everybody says the same things, and my guess is that means the things are true. He's a liar. He's a cheat. He's a con man. And he is going to go down, sooner rather than later."

"And all of that may be true," Gregor said, "but I don't think he's a murderer. I don't even think he paid a murderer. And that puts me in a very uncomfortable position."

TWO

1

Tommy Moradanyan was coming down the stairs and through the living room when the landline started ringing. He was carrying five Dr. Seuss books and a copy of *Winnie-the-Pooh*. He threw the books on the couch as he headed for the phone. He looked at the caller ID and came to a full stop. If his mother had been home, there would have been no question. He would have let the call go to voice mail. But his mother was not home.

Past the living room and through the door, Javier and his sister, Charlie, were sitting on another couch, flanking Pickles on each side. They had another book, which they were holding open between them. Every once in a while, Javier would point to the book and say something in Spanish. Sometimes it was Charlie who would point to the book and say something in English. Pickles was sitting up and staring at the pages, looking alert and intelligent.

Tommy dropped down and picked up. He had grown too tall to stretch out his legs comfortably under the coffee table. He thought the knobs of his knees looked like bowling balls. He thought the big house was too quiet around him.

"Russ," he said, when he got the phone to his ear.

Tommy hated landlines. In spite of caller ID, they gave you too little information.

Russ was quiet on his end. Tommy could understand that.

"Russ," Tommy said finally. "Mom's not home. She's not going to be home any time soon."

More silence. Then, "You're there by yourself?"

"I'm babysitting. I've got Javier and Charlie. Oh, and Pickles. We're reading Dr. Seuss books."

"By yourselves. With no adults."

"I'm fourteen."

"I know you're fourteen. Have you at least got the doors locked? Have you got the windows locked? Have you got any means of defending yourself if there's a break-in?"

In the family room, Charlie turned a page and Javier nodded sagely. Tommy liked looking at them. He didn't know why, but they made him feel both safe and hopeful.

"It's like a different world," he said. "Them in there. Next to you in here."

"You're not answering my question."

Tommy twisted around and tried to get comfortable. It was impossible. "I don't know if the windows are locked. Do we lock the windows? I've never thought about it. The door's locked if Mom locked it when she left. As to defending myself, the last time there was a weapon in this house it belonged to you, it was under your bed with three others, and the police came and took it away. I remember that day. They were friends of Mr. Demarkian's and they were as nice as possible under the circumstances and they still gave me PTSD."

"You should have let this go to voice mail," Russ said. "I had a message I wanted to give your mother. I suppose you can give it to her instead, but if you do, it's going to cause problems."

Tommy got up and started to pace. Charlie was sleepy. She had leaned into Pickles and closed her eyes, letting the book fall out of her hands. Javier looked a little sleepy, too, but he was holding on to the book even tighter, and pointing to things, and talking a little to himself.

If Tommy gave his mother a message from Russ, there was a good chance that she'd finally make that phone call that would mean Russ couldn't call here again. Tommy was beyond amazed she hadn't done it already. He also knew he didn't want it to happen.

"Mom's gone out with Mrs. Demarkian," he said. "I don't exactly know why. Something about blue-colored aluminum foil—"

"Is she decorating the house? Has your mother got the house all tarted up for Christmas? It's like putting a neon sign on your heads, here we are, come and get us—"

"Stop it," Tommy said. "Mom doesn't decorate the house anymore. She hasn't decorated the house since, you know, you—"

"Thank God something worked out right with that."

"She just went out," Tommy said. "It wasn't planned. Mrs. Demarkian was here bringing stuff from Ohanian's and they just decided. Call back in about three hours and leave the message yourself."

"I can't just call back in three hours. My schedule isn't in my control. In case you didn't know."

"I know, but I can't help it. I'm not going to give her a message for you. For some absolutely insane reason I'm going to have to live to be ninety-eight to figure out, I don't want her cutting you off. Call back later. Or call Father Tibor and have him deliver your message. She knows you talk to him."

More silence. Tommy watched as Javier put his head down on the arm of the couch next to him and closed his eyes. Now it was only Pickles who was awake.

"What's he like," Russ asked, "this kid Gregor and Bennis have taken in?"

"They haven't 'taken him in,' like the laundry," Tommy said.

"They're being foster parents, however you put that. And what do you want to know for? You're never going to meet him. He isn't bothering you."

"I wish I could see what he looks like."

"He looks like a kid. He's seven. He's kind of short. He likes Dr. Seuss. He likes Pickles. He likes Charlie. He likes me. He likes Big Macs. Don't get started. He's not the apocalypse, come to murder us all in our beds."

"I didn't say he was, Tommy. I really didn't."

"You were going to. But you know what? He's not like that. I'm not like that. Nobody is like that. I've got this teacher who says we shouldn't call people like you crazy, but I think you're crazy. Bald frigging nuts."

"Does your mother know you use words like that?"

"I told you. I'm fourteen. She can probably guess. And I wish she would decorate the house. I wish she'd put one of your neon signs right up there and let everybody know where we are. You know why? Because they wouldn't be the apocalypse either. They wouldn't storm the house and take us all hostage. They'd probably bring casseroles."

"You're too young for this," Russ said. "I understand you're too young to understand."

"I understand a hell of a lot more than you do," Tommy said. "And yes, I said 'hell,' and no, I don't care. I'm going to hang up now. They've fallen asleep in there. They need a blanket."

"I need to talk to Gregor," Russ said. "I need to talk to him face-to-face. It's important. It's not information I can get to him through a third party. I have told Father Tibor about this. I thought I'd leave your mother a message and she could tell Gregor the same thing—"

"You know what thinking the way you do got you? You killed two people. You killed two people, Russ, and you nearly killed Mr. Demarkian, which is like eviscerating a teddy bear. And then what? You blew up Mom's life. You blew up my life. I don't see a civil war in the streets, Russ, but I sure as shit see what you did to us. And don't tell me not to say—"

"Tommy, for God's sake."

"I'm going to hang up, Russ. And to hell with you."

Hanging up was the one really good thing about a landline. There was a solid, definitive bang when the handset went back into the receiver.

Tommy got the books from where he'd dropped them on the couch. The two of them really did need blankets. Pickles would probably like one. He went on into the family room and put the books on the table there.

He felt better than he had in nearly two years. Lighter. Less tense. Maybe not tense at all. He thought he could work on his physics problems without being too distracted.

He got a couple of throw blankets from the chair across the room and put them over Javier and Charlie.

Next year, he was going to go out to Hardscrabble Road and buy a six-foot pine tree for Christmas—and if his mother wouldn't decorate it, he would decorate it himself.

2

Clare McAfee was not a sentimentalist. She did not believe in the American dream, or the melting pot, or the happy fantasy of all people living together in peace and harmony. There was a Lithuanian neighborhood in Philadelphia. She had visited it once and hated it. There was another Lithuanian neighborhood in the suburbs, where a distant cousin lived with a Polish husband and a thoroughly execrable child. She had gone out there one day for a barbecue and hated the place even more. She did not want people to have warm, fuzzy feelings about her. She didn't want cards on Christmas or baskets of eggs on Easter. She wanted people to make sense.

Cary Alder wasn't the first person Clare had engaged with in extracurricular activities. He wasn't even the only person she was engaged with now. The extracurricular activities made perfect and uncomplicated sense. Some people had money and some people didn't. Most of the people who had money were idiots. Your problem was to get their money away from them without turning into an idiot yourself.

Clare didn't think Cary Alder was an idiot, but she was beginning to think he was something worse. Crazy, maybe. Or involved in something secret and irrevocable, like gambling. She had checked him out as carefully as it was possible to check anybody out. She had found nothing. She had asked people at the bank. She had asked other people, people she had only gained access to by stealth and persistence. The closest she had come to finding a secret life was the persistent rumor that he ran "a coyote operation," which apparently meant that he did things to make sure he had people here illegally to work on his properties. Clare had come to the United States legally and on her own, so she wasn't sure how this worked. The best she could figure it out, people who wanted to come here paid you a lot of money. You made arrangements for travel and transportation and all the rest of it until they landed on US soil and took a job. You charged them much more than it cost to get them here. Then you paid them much less than you would have to pay anybody else. There was nothing in any of this that would cause anybody to hemorrhage money like water.

There were things Clare knew she couldn't do, so she didn't even think about doing them. She couldn't ask Cary Alder himself. She had tried. He wasn't going to tell her anything. She couldn't go down to the neighborhoods where Alder had his bread-and-butter properties. Like many Lithuanians, she was pale-skinned and fair. She'd stick out like a sore thumb in four solid blocks of people from Central America. And what could they tell her, anyway? What did they know besides whether they were being evicted this week or whether they could get someone in to fix the furnace?

Cary Alder kept a couple of accounts at the bank, as did most people who had their loans there. The bank encouraged it. Clare had checked into this and found that there was about half a million dollars sitting there. It had been sitting there, untouched, for over a year. Obviously, that was not a main account. She had checked through Alder's loan documents and come up with accounts at four other banks, including JPMorgan Chase and Barclays. Those had been checked into at the time the loan was made. That was years ago. To check into them again would be to send up red flags she wasn't interested in launching just yet.

She had only one chance. She had to go to the main offices of Alder Properties and hope that Cary Alder was not there himself. This was an insane idea, but it might work out. She had seen Cary Alder at lunch. He had looked positively immobile.

She even knew who it was she wanted to see. Assuming the woman would talk to her. Assuming the woman knew anything.

Here was another red flag she didn't want to send up: being out of the office too often or too long on a workday. She would have to invent a tooth abscess.

She got to the offices of Alder Properties and looked around. There was nothing to see. She went into the building and then up in the elevator. There were ordinary people doing ordinary things. Clare couldn't see a police presence, or a security team. Most places these days were armed and ready for mass shooters. Alder Properties didn't seem to be.

Clare had been to this building once, and to this office once. She went through the frosted-glass doors to the reception area and stopped at the desk of a middle-aged woman working at a computer. Past this desk there were several others, and past those there were more frosted-glass doors. The one at the very back belonged to Cary Alder. It was open and the lights inside it were off.

"I would like to speak to Ms. Agerwal," Clare said. "Do you think you could tell her it's Ms. McAfee calling?"

"Of course."

The woman got up and scurried away. Clare wasn't sure Meera Agerwal would remember who she was. They had met exactly once and talked on the phone twice. In all those cases, the subject matter had been casual and peripheral.

Meera Agerwal came out of the office closest to Cary Alder's own. Her heavy black hair had been braided down her back and twisted into a bun at the nape of her neck. The skirt of her crisp blue suit went significantly down below her knees. The middle-aged white woman was scurrying back to her desk at the front of the room.

"Yes?" Meera Agerwal said.

Clare didn't waste any time. She could see it in the woman's face. Clare thanked the woman now back at her desk and marched to the rear, moving as swiftly as if she were late to catch a bus. She went through the door of Meera Agerwal's office without stopping and closed it as soon as Meera herself stepped over the threshold.

"You know who I am," she said. "I'm sure you know who I am."

"You're from one of the banks," Meera said. "Is there something wrong at the banks? Are you looking for a property for yourself? I am almost certainly not the person you should be talking to in any case."

Clare dropped into a chair. "You're the only person I can talk to. I came up here on a hunch, but I was absolutely right. I can see it in your face. You're just as scared to death as I am."

Meera Agerwal's body stiffened. Clare did all she could to not make a face. She didn't like Indian women. She never had. They were sly, and they were almost always dishonest. They were worse when they were tarted up in Western clothes like this.

"He has to have somebody moving the money around for him," Clare said. "He isn't going to give that to somebody in accounting unless he's got an accomplice, and I don't believe he has. That means he has to give it to somebody who is used to dealing with the accounts but won't know what it is she's doing when he starts pulling fast ones—"

"I can assure you I am fully competent at my job," Meera said stiffly. Clare could practically feel the starch rising up out of her bones.

Meera sat down behind her desk. Clare thought a certain kind of man would find her beautiful, but that she wouldn't care.

"This week," Clare said carefully, "Cary Alder failed to make one of his loan payments. Not on one of his regular loans, you understand. On one of the loans we made— Well, I'm not going to go into all that. Let's just say he's got half a dozen loans with us that are more than the bank would have stood for, but they're disguised as loans to other people, and all of that works fine as long as nobody gets off schedule. But he got off schedule. And that set off alarm bells all over the bank. It took the devil's own time for me to fix it."

"I'm sure I don't know what you're talking about."

"I'm sure you do," Clare said. "What's more, now that I'm looking at you, I think you've always known. If you haven't known what was specifically going on with the loans, you've known something was and you've known you were moving around money to facilitate it. Because you're the one. You've got to have access to his payout accounts if you're going to do your job. You have to know what money goes in there and what money comes out. Accounting will get hold of it all eventually, but on a day-to-day basis, it's got to be you. And that means you have the information I have to have."

The stiffness in Meera Agerwal's bones was now so complete, she actually seemed to be taller. "I am not the person you want to talk to about accounts," she said, staring straight over Clare's head to the opposite wall. "We have an accounting office that deals with all aspects of our financial arrangements, including loans and cash flow. You should make an appointment—"

"Don't be an idiot," Clare said. "Don't you realize we could both end up in the penitentiary if this blows up in our faces? It may be too late to do anything about it as it is. I need information and I need it fast. And you need to cover your ass. Because if I could figure out who was involved, it's going to take the FBI about ten seconds to do the same."

3

In the second-floor principal's office at St. Catherine's School, there was a floor-to-ceiling bookcase, a yard and a half wide, filled with St. Catherine's School yearbooks. The ceilings on that floor were fourteen feet high. At some point, somebody must have come in with a ladder to fill the highest shelves. The bookcase itself had been bolted into the wall in three places. That was to prevent a repetition of the time in 1973 when it fell over onto the principal's desk during a police raid that was tearing up the street. On the very top shelf, the "yearbooks" were not exactly books. They were thick pamphlets recording the life of St. Catherine's when the school was first founded in 1891. There hadn't been many students then. The nuns had been dressed in their original, traditional habit, complete with a white linen pie frill framing the face.

"Bet that thing wilted like dead dandelions every time it got wet," Sister Margaret Mary said to herself every time she saw a picture of a nun in that old habit. By the time she'd joined the order, they were wearing this modified thing, where the veil was held back away from the face by a stiff headdress that needed no attention at all.

Sister Margaret Mary had spent over an hour looking for the yearbooks that contained pictures of Marta Warkowski, and she had found them. Here was Marta in 1952, one of eight children in the brand-new St. Catherine's kindergarten. Here was Marta in 1954, in her white first communion dress and veil. Here was Marta in 1959, getting ready to graduate from eighth grade. The nuns were still wearing their pie frills.

Sister Margaret Mary had no idea what she had expected to find in these old yearbooks. She could see the changes in the neighborhood through the changes in the children in the school. In Marta's day, the children had been not only white, but white and fair. Now, of course, the only blondes you ever saw around St. Catherine's were people's mothers with dye jobs. From what Sister Margaret Mary could tell from YouTube, there were plenty of real blond women in Central and South America. They just didn't seem to move north to Philadelphia. The child Marta Warkowski was plain and glum and very solemn. Her clothes looked as if they had been handed down or bought used. They probably had been.

None of this told Sister Margaret Mary why Marta Warkowski had ended up in a garbage bag, or what they should do about her if she ever got out of the hospital and came back to the parish.

There was the sound of footsteps clattering on the stairs. Sister Margaret Mary put the yearbook she was holding down on her desk and looked up to see Sister Peter rushing in, flushed.

"Sister," Sister Peter said. "Father Alvarez is downstairs. We've been looking everywhere for you."

"I've been wasting my time," Sister Margaret Mary said. "What's the problem?"

"ICE just hit St. Rose's. They've got a daycare over there. ICE was waiting when the parents showed up."

"For the children?"

"Father Alvarez can explain," Sister Peter said.

Then she turned around and disappeared out the door. Sister Margaret Mary put her head in her hands and counted to ten. Then she moved herself out into the hall and down the stairs.

Father Alvarez was standing in the school's front foyer, his coat open, his collar looking as if it were too tight for his throat. Sister Margaret Mary called out to him. He looked up to watch her descend.

"Are they coming here?" Sister Margaret Mary asked. "We don't have anyone here. We don't have a daycare. We're on break."

"They may be coming to the church," Father Alvarez said. "That's where I put him."

"Him?"

"A man named Tomas Domingues. You may have met him. He works as a janitor over at the Glendower Arms. He helps out with the Cub Scouts."

"I know Tomas," Sister Margaret Mary said. Then it struck her. "Tomas is undocumented? He's been here forever. He's been here longer than I have."

"Thirty-two years," Father Alvarez said.

"For God's sake," Sister Margaret Mary said.

Sister Peter cleared her throat.

"It's not just him," Father Alvarez said. "He's got a wife, Maria Cristina. She's American born. So are all four of his children."

"But shouldn't that help?" Sister Margaret Mary asked. "Isn't there something about sponsorship? Couldn't they sponsor him?"

"Second or third year he was here, he had a DUI," Father Alvarez said. "He totaled a car he didn't own and put a teenager in the hospital with a broken leg."

"And they're just arresting him for that now?"

"They're not arresting him for that at all," Father Alvarez said. "He was arrested at the time. He went to court. He pled guilty. He got probation. But he got probation on a felony."

"Oh, Lord," Sister Margaret Mary said.

"We got him out a back door at St. Rose's," Father Alvarez said. "I thought we'd try something I've seen on the news. I don't think we can do it without your help. All of your help. The whole convent and maybe some of the other parents."

"What?"

"They did it at this church in Connecticut," Father Alvarez said. "They declared the church to be a sanctuary, and then the man lived there. I think for months. It worked for at least that long. I don't know why. I'm sure there isn't any law in the United States that allows churches to serve as sanctuary spaces for people trying to avoid law enforcement, but I do know the man managed to stay in the church for a long time, and ICE didn't raid the place. At one point, I think they gave him amnesty for a week so he could spend Christmas at home with his family. I don't know if they would do that here."

"Do they know he's here?" Sister Margaret Mary asked. "I mean, do they know you've brought him to this parish?"

"They didn't when we left," Father Alvarez said. "Now I've got him over in the church basement, in one of the Sunday school classrooms. And I tried calling around. I think this would work better with a suburban church, where most of the families weren't Spanish. I even asked the Carmelites. I don't know if a cloistered convent would count as a sanctuary, but all I could think of was that this is all about public perception. ICE wouldn't want video of the news of them storming into a consecrated monastery no man has set foot in for fifty years."

"Have you talked to the cardinal archbishop?" Sister Margaret Mary asked.

"I've been avoiding it," Father Alvarez said. "He's going to blow his top, and we both know it. I just don't know who he's going to blow his top at."

"All right." Sister Margaret Mary's head hurt. First things first. Everything had a practical dimension. Concentrate on that. "Sister Peter," she said, "round up everybody except Sister Margery. Go over to the church and stand in front of the front door, or just inside the front door in the vestibule. You want to form a barrier they won't want to move. Put Sister Marie Bernadette out front and center. She's strong as an ox, but she looks ninety-two. They're not going to want video of some ICE idiot manhandling her. And we want video. We want the news stations. Father, really, you need to call them and maybe set up a press conference. We need—"

The sounds outside were unmistakable. There were two heavy

vehicles moving too fast. Then there were doors opening and closing. There were no sirens. Sister Margaret Mary didn't know if that made things better or worse.

"Go," she told Sister Peter. "They don't need a warrant to enter the church. It's open to everyone twenty-four/seven."

Sister Peter took off, down the front steps and up the street to the convent. Sister Margaret Mary and Father Alvarez went out to see what was going on. The ICE people were wearing bright yellow vests, the kind of yellow that would glow in the glare of headlights if it were dark. There had to be fifteen of them.

Fifteen people to arrest one middle-aged man. Sister Margaret Mary did remember Tomas Domingues. He didn't have the strength to beat up a puppy.

"I'm going down to hold the fort at the church," Father Alvarez said, taking off.

Sister Margaret Mary watched him go, her head full of all those practicalities: sheets, blankets, pillows, cot, food, water.

The ICE people had come in vans, but they were white vans, and they had logos on them.

The plain black van parked up near the church, the one that looked exactly like the one from the night Marta Warkowski was dumped in that garbage bag, seemed to have appeared out of nowhere.

THREE

1

The big black van belonged in St. Rose's Parish, not to the parish itself, but to the Glendower Arms, where Tomas Domingues worked. Gregor saw it as soon as he and Morabito and Horowitz rounded the corner on their way to "check things out." It was Horowitz who wanted to "check things out," and Horowitz who was unhappy with the entire situation.

"The way this thing stacks up is crazy," he kept saying as the three of them walked along. "We've got real bad guys in these neighborhoods. We've even got real bad guys who are here illegally. They're never the ones being hunted down by ICE and hiding in church basements."

"I don't see why a church ought to be a sanctuary," Morabito said. "Aren't we supposed to have separation of church and state? Or maybe we just have separation of church and state when churches are doing stuff you don't like."

Horowitz ignored him. "The guys who come here and do everything right are the targets. They get jobs. They settle down. They raise families. And there they are, right out in the open where ICE can find them on a second's notice."

This time the street in front of St. Catherine's Church was not empty, in spite of all the law enforcement everywhere. Men and women were out on the doorsteps and the sidewalks, watching. Nuns were lined up in front of the church's front doors. Gregor broke away from the two detectives and went directly to the van. He wasn't great at identifying vehicles, but it looked to be the very same make and model as the one in the police garage. It even had Jersey plates.

"It looks like the same one, doesn't it?" Sister Margaret Mary said, appearing at his elbow. "I asked around, though, and it's not. It's the one Tomas uses for the Glendower Arms. The priest from St. Rose's drove it over here with Tomas in the back, because it doesn't have any windows. That way, no one could see him if they passed an ICE vehicle."

"Is the Glendower Arms owned by Alder Properties?"

Sister Margaret Mary nodded. "I was thinking the same thing. Maybe all the Alder Properties buildings have one of these vans. Except, if they do, I don't know why I haven't seen one before."

The man who came up to them now was huge; tall and fat. Gregor had the impression he'd seen the man before, and then nailed it—it was Juan Morales, who had been in the hall on the morning they found Miguel Hernandez's body. Juan Morales, who had been Hernandez's handyman or second-in-command or something similar.

"The vans are kept in the garages," Morales said politely. "Unless we need them for work. To bring things in or take them out."

"Things like what?" Gregor asked.

Juan Morales got that look on his face that Gregor had learned to interpret as: *I don't speak a word of English.* This was not a look restricted to speakers of Spanish. Gregor had known a wide range of Armenian immigrants who had that look down flat.

Besides, Gregor thought, he'd been asking a stupid question. The reason you didn't want windows was to make sure nobody could see inside, and the reason you didn't want anybody to see inside was because what you were transporting was people.

"So," Gregor said. "How many of these vans are there around here? One for each of the buildings?"

"No," Juan Morales said. "We have one for all the buildings. We have a garage to put it in. We don't need more than that in one barrio."

"And your one, is it in your garage right now?"

Juan Morales shrugged. "I don't know. I haven't been to look at it. I haven't needed it."

"Are you going to need it? Are you taking over as super from Miguel Hernandez?"

Juan Morales shrugged again. "You never know what they're going to do, those people. Maybe I'll be the super. Maybe they'll bring in one of their own."

"And you're not one of their own?"

Juan Morales looked around. "I was his right-hand man. That's the term, *sí*? I was always the first one he went to. I was always the one he could count on."

"You should show the police that garage," Gregor said. "Either the van they've got is the one that belongs there, or it isn't. If it is, they're going to want to make a search."

"This isn't going to work," Juan Morales said, looking back up the steps to the church doors. "I saw this on the television. White people, in that church. They don't use tear gas on a bunch of white people."

"They're not going to use tear gas here," Sister Margaret Mary put in. "The cardinal archbishop is on his way. Nobody uses tear gas on the cardinal archbishop."

Juan Morales gave her a long look. Then he let out a stream of Spanish he obviously expected her to understand. Yet another van drove up in the street. This one disgorged a dozen uniformed men in riot gear. Juan Morales disappeared.

"Well," Sister Margaret Mary said.

Morabito and Horowitz were standing on the far corner of the block. Gregor excused himself and went back to them, crossing through the lines of ICE officers and police and nuns. The mood of the people of the neighborhood was ugly. Gregor could feel the waves of anger coming at him from every side. Television camera crews were setting up all along the sidewalks, always looking for a good angle to catch the front doors to the church and the line of ICE officers. If Gregor had caught this scene out of context, he would have thought he was in a war zone.

"It doesn't make any sense," Horowitz was telling Morabito as Gregor came up to them. "All this crap for one guy. It's one guy."

"He could be armed to the teeth," Morabito said. "Nobody knows what he's going to do."

"He's a janitor," Horowitz said. "He's got to be fifty years old."

"Whitey Bulger was eighty years old," Morabito said.

Over at the church doors, an ICE officer climbed the steps and stopped in front of a very old nun. He tried to pass her. She didn't move, and three other nuns moved closer to her. He put out his hands, grasped her on both shoulders, and moved her aside. By now, everybody in range had a phone out and was recording.

Would they break down the doors of a church? Were those doors even locked? Weren't Catholic churches supposed to stay open twenty-four/seven, for anybody who wanted to come in to pray? Javier liked this church. He especially liked the Lady Chapel, where there was a statue of Our Lady of Guadalupe.

After the first ICE agent passed the old nun, two more followed him. They reached the great double doors and opened them without resistance. They had not been locked. One of the agents propped open one of the doors and went inside. The other two agents followed him. Then six more followed them.

Out in the street, a limousine pulled up, plowing through all the rest of the traffic as if it wasn't there. It didn't park so much as just come to a stop across the entire width of the street. If there had been any vehicles moving, it would have blocked them. Nothing else was moving. The limousine's back door opened. The cardinal archbishop climbed out, dressed in the full red regalia of his office, including the cape.

"It's not going to make any difference," Morabito said, sounding immensely satisfied. "They're going to get him and they're going to send him back where he came from."

Marta Warkowski in a hospital bed. Cavanaugh Street on Easter Sunday. Bodegas with their ceilings hung with piñatas in the shape of donkeys.

"Listen," Gregor said. "I'm not sure who tried to kill Marta War- kowski, but I can tell you how she got into that garbage bag, and I can tell you who killed Hernandez."

2

Javier saw the story about the "hostage situation" at St. Cather- ine's Church on the news before dinner. Gregor came home to find him pacing back and forth between the living room and the kitchen, talking out loud in Spanish but not directing the words at anyone. His night was bad, tossing and turning, getting up to pace, sitting next to Pickles and talking in Spanish some more. Gregor didn't think Pickles could understand Spanish any more than he could understand English, but, like Tommy Mora- danyan, he seemed to understand Javier.

By the next morning, when Bennis took her turn walking Pick- les, Gregor had come to the conclusion that Javier understood more English than he was letting on. Maybe it was just passive vocabu- lary. Maybe he just understood more of what he heard than he was able to express in English words. What Gregor was sure of was that he was able to get the basics of what had happened with Tomas Domingues, and that he knew what ICE was.

John Jackman called while Bennis was out, and got to the house before Bennis got back. Javier gave him a good looking over when he came to the kitchen table and grabbed a coffee cup.

"Hi," Jackman told him. Then he looked at Gregor. "I don't think this kid likes me."

"I don't think this kid knows you," Gregor said, "and there was a lot on the news about the mess over at St. Catherine's. In case you've heard about it."

"Everybody's heard about it," Jackman said. "Washington talked to Father Alvarez. He'd seen something about a church in Connecticut that kept an illegal immigrant for months and declared itself a sanctuary, and ICE put up with it. I think he was hoping that would happen here."

"And it didn't."

Jackman snorted. "That church was in Connecticut. Congregation was rich as Midas and had a lot of Yale faculty. They had leverage. St. Catherine's doesn't have any. Neither does St. Rose's. Even the cardinal archbishop couldn't get through this bunch."

Gregor poured coffee. "I take it it isn't the mess at St. Catherine's that brought you here."

"Of course not," John said. "I got word you talked to Cary Alder. One-on-one. Face-to-face."

"I did."

"And?"

"It's like I told you before, John. I don't know what you want out of me. To get the evidence you're looking for to nail him for bringing in illegal aliens, you need the accountants the bureau has already got on this, and if they can't find anything, I won't be able to. As for Marta Warkowski and Miguel Hernandez . . ."

"Yes?"

Gregor pointed across the kitchen table to a large stack of papers.

"More information from the Philadelphia police department," he said. "Arrived right after dinner last night. For what it's worth, Washington or no Washington, I don't think Morabito and Horowitz want my help. They know the commissioner wants them to want my help. And they're looking for a way to cover their asses in case of a screwup. But they think they can handle this themselves, and they probably can. I gave them my view of it yesterday. If they hadn't figured it out for themselves before that, they would have in the next few days."

"And what was your view of it?"

"Hernandez put Marta Warkowski in that garbage bag," Gregor said. "He probably had the help of a man named Juan Morales, who serves as his second-in-command for the Alder Properties in that neighborhood. Hernandez had a few other assistants, so it could be one of them instead, but my guess would be Morales. I think they put her in the garbage bag thinking she was dead. Then they put the garbage bag in the van. Then they drove the van back to the neighborhood and put it in the garage."

"Back to the neighborhood?"

"She can't have been killed in St. Catherine's Parish," Gregor said. "Too many people would have noticed. Besides, Father Alvarez saw her leave the neighborhood after Mass, and Meera Agerwal saw her down near Alder Properties headquarters not an hour later. Cary Alder actually talked to her down there. So she wasn't in the neighborhood."

"She was at Alder Properties headquarters?"

"Right. I told Morabito and Horowitz to get a warrant to search those premises. Cary Alder's office. The reception area. Pay special attention to the carpets. Anyway, they put her in a garbage bag thinking she was dead, then they put her in the van."

"And they got the van?"

"I'm not a hundred percent sure," Gregor said, "but there was another van just like it from St. Rose's yesterday, and the Glendower

Arms over there is another Alder property. I think every little clutch of Alder Properties probably has one."

"Then wouldn't the van have been known in the neighborhood?"

"Depends on what it was used for," Gregor said. "If it did general errands, yes. But if it was just for special occasions, bringing in those undocumented workers, say, or maybe heavy equipment when it was necessary, then maybe not. And we know it wasn't parked on the street until somebody wanted us to find it. There has to be a garage."

"I take it you sent out Horowitz and Morabito to find that, too."

"I did," Gregor said. "I think they brought her, still thinking she was dead, back to the garage so they could work out what to do with the body. I don't know what they decided. But I think they went up to Marta's apartment and went looking through it. We didn't find any identification on her. Maybe it was that. They went up there, they had some kind of fight, and Morales killed Hernandez."

"Then?"

"Right then, while Marta was still parked in the van," Gregor said. "That's the only thing that makes sense. Otherwise, getting rid of the body could have waited until the weather got better. But Morales killed him. Then he went to get the van and the body and get rid of them both as fast as he could. But the accident happened, so he couldn't do either. Marta was on the street and he had to put the van away before he got picked up. So he did, and left it there, until he started to worry that the police would do a house-to-house and find it where it could be tied to him. I don't think he's very bright."

"It seems like a lot of trouble to go through to kill one middle-aged lady," Jackman said. "Are you sure she wasn't running drugs or something?"

"She's just untouchable, that's all," Gregor said. "The case manager at the hospital mentioned it to both me and the detectives. She always had enough money. The department got a search warrant and her records. Cary Alder didn't bother to get a search warrant, but he had her checked into when he first started having trouble with her, too. She seems to have spent her entire working life putting one-tenth of her salary away every single paycheck without fail, in savings accounts and certificates of deposit in different banks. By the time she retired, she was up to putting away closer to thirty percent. No credit cards. No loans. No extravagances. It doesn't sound like much, but if you do that for forty years, it adds up. So there was no way they could get rid of her. She could always afford increased rent. She could always afford lawyers to go to housing court. She could always cause trouble. And she caused a lot of trouble. And Cary Alder was sure that was going to call attention to Alder Properties and whatever the hell else they were doing."

"Funny," Jackman said. "I don't think it did. I mean, I don't think it was anything Marta Warkowski did that put the Feds onto him. It wasn't anything she did that put the Philadelphia Police Department on to him."

"Are you on to him?" Gregor asked.

"They're going to arrest him," John Jackman said. "At least the Feds are."

"I think he knows," Gregor said. He poured himself another cup of coffee. Javier was staring at the two of them, eating his way methodically through a slice of bacon. It was his fourth. Gregor poured him another glass of orange juice.

"It was an interesting talk I had with him," he said. "Interesting and very odd. I think he fully expects to be arrested. I think he's doing absolutely nothing to stave it off. I think there's something very, very odd going on here."

"Odd, how?"

"If I knew that, I'd feel a lot better," Gregor said.

There was the sound of the front door opening down the hall. Bennis called out, "I'm home," and Pickles came running into the kitchen at Javier. Pickles was wearing a bright red woolly coat, a matching hat, and four matching booties. He looked like the reincarnation of Doris Day.

3

Bennis came in taking her coat off, saw John Jackman at the table, and smiled.

"This is unexpected," she said. Then she turned to Gregor. "I ran into Tibor. He wants you over at his place at ten o'clock sharp. It's an emergency. I think he really means emergency. He sounded like it, anyway. I told him you'd be there, so if having John here means you can't be, you'd better call him. We don't see you much, John. Aren't you supposed to be in Washington?"

"Everybody asks me that," John said. "We're on recess."

Javier was snaking a strip of bacon down toward Pickles on the floor. Bennis cleared her throat.

"Javier," she said, holding up two fingers. "Two."

"*Dos*," Javier said solemnly. "*Sí*."

"That dog will eat an entire pound of bacon on its own and then throw it all up on the carpet," Bennis said. Then she dropped her coat over the back of a chair and sat down herself. "Am I cleared to hear this conversation, or should I leave the room and let the two of you talk stuff you need warrants for?"

"You only need warrants for the particulars," John said. "The general stuff, you probably already know. We were talking about Cary Alder."

"Ah," Bennis said.

Gregor got himself more coffee. He was beginning to feel more than a little wired, and the message from Tibor was making him uneasy. He watched Javier feed Pickles the second slice of bacon. He wished he knew what the boy understood and what he didn't. He wished he wasn't so sure that Javier understood ten times what any of them suspected him of.

"Didn't you talk to Sister Margaret Mary about the circumstances of our getting this one here?" he asked.

Javier didn't look up at him, but Gregor knew immediately that the kid had hooked into the conversation. Bennis didn't seem to notice.

"I did talk to her," she said. "It was weird, the circumstances were, I mean, but it wasn't bad. He checked out medically. And he looks healthy, doesn't he? He's not too thin. He eats like a horse. I'm pretty sure Sister Margaret Mary said he came to the Maryknoll sisters that way."

"We're trying to figure out how something works," John said.

"John thinks Cary Alder is running a coyote operation," Gregor said. "I've looked at the paperwork, and I think so, too. Sort of."

"Coyotes bring illegal aliens into the country for a fee," John said. "If you're sitting in Guatemala or El Salvador or wherever—Venezuela a lot, lately—if you're sitting there and you want to get here, you pay them and they guide you up here and get you across the border. Most coyotes are freelance. They operate on their own. But there's a downside to that. They get you across the border, and then what?"

"There are other coyote operations," Gregor said, "that are centralized. They're run by business guys who have specific jobs to fill. They hire coyotes to find and recruit people. They pay them a salary, and then the coyotes get more money from the guys they take for the jobs. If you're an immigrant, it's supposed to be a better deal. You know you have work when you get here. You know where you're going. When you get across the border there will be contacts you can use to make your way. You're much less likely to get caught and deported."

"And Cary Alder is running one of those?" Bennis asked.

"We think so," John said.

"There ought to be a paper trail of money," Gregor said. "Not just money going out, but money coming in. Remember, you collect from the immigrant and not just Alder himself, and some of what you collect from the immigrant has to go to Alder. If it doesn't, the whole operation collapses financially. But we've both looked over all the paperwork, and so have dozens of forensic accountants at Homeland Security and the FBI, and we can't find any money coming in."

"So maybe he isn't running a coyote operation," Bennis said.

"Practically everybody in the high-end resort and restaurant businesses are involved one way or the other," John said. "And it's going to get worse. With all the pushes for a fifteen-dollar minimum wage, we think the population of undocumented immigrants working in the US is going to explode."

"Because you don't have to pay them the minimum wage," Gregor explained. "They can't complain about their situation or their working conditions without being in danger of being deported. So they put up with it. It takes some fancy accounting to make it look right on paper, but some of these guys are only paying their people two or three dollars an hour."

"And Alder Properties is definitely doing that at some of their places," John said. "Lawn and landscape workers on their gated communities on the Main Line. Pool boys at the resorts. Dishwashers and other out-of-sight personnel at the Aldergold venues."

"But if you know all that for sure," Bennis said, "why don't you arrest him? Or arrest somebody? Or move into the operations and do something?"

"Nobody wants to," John said grimly. "The Republicans know if they lower the boom, a lot of their donors lose a lot of money. The Democrats know that if they lower the boom, the result will almost certainly be a wave of mass deportations. The situation is politically intractable on both sides. And no. Opening up to mass immigration wouldn't work. It would just push wages ever further south. And ending illegal immigration will result in businesses finding ways to hire as few people as possible. Automation is a wonderful thing.

Self-checkout lines in supermarkets. Self-checkout lines in fast-food restaurants. Mass unemployment from one end of the country to the other."

"Well," Bennis said. "This sounds cheerful."

John shook his head. "To tell you the truth, I don't know what I'm doing myself half the time. I don't know what we'd accomplish if we sent Cary Alder to jail for the coyote operation as well as for the bank fraud. Another operation would open up next week. I can't fix the world. I can't fix the country. I can't even fix the Commonwealth of Pennsylvania. I just—hate these people."

John finished his coffee and got up. "The SEC is going to file indictments next week," he said. "And the FBI is coming in right after them. Are you expecting to talk to Cary Alder again?"

"I was," Gregor said. "But not over this."

"Over the Marta Warkowski business? Well, do what you can. And thanks for coming in on this. I know you're been staying out of it ever since, ah—"

"Russ shot me?"

"Yeah, that," John said. "Good to see you, Bennis. Good to see you, too, Javier, even if you don't like me much. I'll let myself out."

He got up, got his coat, and went out into the hall. Gregor watched him go. It had been years since they had first met, all the way back to the days when John was the first African American head of homicide in Bryn Mawr. His hair hadn't been that gray, then. His shoulders hadn't been so firmly set.

The front door opened and shut. Javier reached for another piece of toast from the stack.

"You ever get the feeling that the whole world has gotten a lot more depressing than it used to be?" Bennis asked. "I was actually feeling pretty good when I came home today. The sisters have this plan for St. Catherine's. They want to provide free hot lunches for everybody, not just the kids whose parents can't pay. Sister Margaret Mary says that that way, there'd be no stigma to getting a free lunch, everybody would be the same, and if they could fund it themselves and not take government money, they wouldn't have to follow government guidelines and a bunch of kids brought up on tortillas wouldn't have to eat quinoa. And I was thinking—I have money."

"Lots of it," Gregor said. "Most of which you made before you ever met me. Do what you want with it."

"It's a good idea," Bennis said. "It's a good approach to that problem. You know what else is? Okay, different problem. Providing money so everybody can go on field trips and no parents have to pay. Even for kids whose parents could pay."

"Those are good ideas," Gregor said.

"I know," Bennis said. "And I can help do something about them. But things are still more depressing than they used to be. And I'm getting really tired of it."

FOUR

1

Meera Agerwal was not good at planning ahead. It was not what she had been brought up to do, and it was not something she had ever imagined she would need to learn. By both caste and environment, she was used to having things done for her, anticipated for her, arranged for her. At home, someone else cooked and cleaned and took care of the clothes. Someone kept tabs on the weather and got the house and grounds ready for storms. Someone monitored the movies and shows and vetted the young men who were hoping to marry her and her father's money.

If everything had worked out the way it was supposed to, Meera would never have come to America. Her biggest problem would be checking out the women who would be her mother-in-law. Then her father's money had gotten low and her brother had brought it lower. Then everybody's money had gotten low, which had something to do with politics. Meera knew nothing about politics, and she didn't care. She cared only that she now had almost as much as she needed set up in bank accounts back in India and secret places here. The only reason she couldn't go home on the next available aircraft was that she'd never get away with it.

It was maddening. The other thing Meera knew nothing about was law enforcement. In Mumbai, the prominence of her family and their position on the right side of the political divide meant she needed to know nothing about law enforcement. They would concern themselves with other people and leave her alone.

Here, law enforcement concerned itself with everyone. Too much of who she was and what she was didn't matter. This was one of the things she had figured out from her talk with Clare McAfee. Law enforcement already knew what had been going on at Alder Properties. They knew about the false reports to the banks. They knew about the money being shifted from one account to the other so that it seemed like there was always more money than there actually was. The question was not what they knew but how they interpreted it. It was one thing to know that the money had been shifted around and that some of it had been siphoned off. It was another thing to know who had done the siphoning.

The method Meera and her mother used to get money back to India was simple. First, someone in India who needed money here, but didn't want anyone to know he had it, deposited that money in Meera's mother's accounts. Then he came here and threw a house-warming, or a welcoming party, or another event that looked like typical Indian over display of wealth and influence. People brought gifts. In the gift Meera brought there would be cash, lots and lots of it, enough to cover what had gone into her mother's account. Nobody knew anything. Nobody could prove anything. Meera's own money was magically safe in Mumbai.

Meera was not worried about the money. That was why she had the gun. When you carried money around with you all the time, in a city like Philadelphia, you had to have a gun. She'd been an idiot to lose the other one in the apartment that night after all that trouble with Marta Warkowski. She should never have gone out there when Hernandez demanded she come. Still, that wasn't too bad. Nobody could trace the gun to her. She never handled it with her bare hands. She hadn't bought it legally. That one was like this one, a blank you picked up on the street from some man standing in the shadow of a doorway or at the edge of an alley. Guns were everywhere.

When push came to shove, Meera was sure Cary Alder would say she had tried to kill Marta Warkowski—if he got to talk first. He hadn't seen her do any such thing, but he was in the same position she was. He had to have someone to deflect it all on.

The whole thing got more and more convoluted, the more she thought about it. Hernandez standing in Marta Warkowski's apartment. That Juan Morales man lurking in the hallway. Marta just gone, disappeared, as if she'd never existed. Then Hernandez dead on the floor, and that Morales man—

Who would say what about what? Would Marta Warkowski wake up and tell the world what had happened to her? What *had* happened to her? Had Cary Alder hit her? Had Hernandez? Had Morales? Would she remember? By the time she got back on the scene, Marta was gone and nobody was explaining anything. Cary Alder was gone, too.

One thing at a time.

First, Meera told the girls in the office that she had another meeting. She called from just outside the place where she had met Clare McAfee. Then she went back to her apartment and went carefully through the drawers and cupboards. The money was gone. She had been clearing it out for weeks. She didn't think a stray bill here or there would make much difference. Nobody had been jotting down the serial numbers.

The next thing was the gun. There were too many checkpoints in too many buildings these days. There were metal detectors. Meera got the gun out of the Bundt pan where she kept it. When she had one of her internal fits about how stupid Americans were, the Bundt pan was high on her list of evidence. What would an Indian woman do with a Bundt pan?

She put the gun in her purse and left the apartment. On the street, she walked slowly and deliberately. She was not in a hurry. She didn't need to run. She turned in the direction opposite to the one that would take her back to her office. She walked four blocks, then took a right, then took another right. The weather was still very cold. The day was beginning to wind down, even though it was not that late. Eventually she found a stretch that was deserted, and a series of narrow alleys. Those were deserted, too. You always had to worry that the alleys would have junkies in them.

She went down one and walked about half the length of it. There were garbage cans, tall metal ones, stuffed so full their lids couldn't settle on the rims. One of them smelled so bad, it made her reel a little. She took the lid off a different one. There were orange rinds and carrot peelings. Meera looked up and down the alley. There was no one there. There was no one passing on either street at either end.

She was wearing thick winter gloves. She took the gun out of her purse and put it in the bin, in among the rotting vegetable matter. Then she stripped off the gloves and put them in there, too. The last thing she wanted was the smell of the rot on her hands.

A moment later, she was out of the alley and back on the street. She was walking purposefully now. She made a left turn at the next corner. Now she was on a street with people on it, pedestrian traffic, office buildings. Men were wearing suits. Women were wearing high heels that skidded on the pavement. It was just a matter of keeping her cool, of sounding plausible, or being the heroine of this thing and not the villain. She'd never been a villain in her life. You couldn't be a villain if it was just about money.

It was four more blocks before she found the building she wanted. There was indeed a checkpoint at the door. She had expected it.

The man at the desk was old and tired looking. Meera put her purse down so that he could search it.

"I would like to talk to the Federal Bureau of Investigation," she said, as crisply as she could. Her voice had just a hint of British accent. That was because she had gone to a good school. "I have information about a crime."

"What kind of crime?"

Meera almost blanked. "A crime about money," she said, dredging it up from somewhere. "A crime about a bank."

"A bank," the man said.

Meera thought the whole thing was about to blow up in her face. Then the man picked up the phone next to him on the table, talked into it rapidly, and hung up.

"Take those elevators," he told her, pointing across the lobby. "Go to room three sixteen. Ask for Madelyn Pertwee."

2

Father Tibor Kasparian did not believe the things Russ Donahue believed. He did not think the United States was about to explode in a bloody civil war. He did not believe that there was going to be blood in the streets, and that everybody would be the victim of everybody else. He did not believe these things because he had once been in a place at a time when they were true. He could smell them coming. He did not smell them now.

At the same time, he could smell something, and he did not like the way it made him feel. Something was . . . off, these days, and it wasn't just that Russ had gone crazy and begun to behave in ways that would have been unthinkable when they first met. He knew the tones in that man's voice. He knew when ideology was running thought and when reality was. And he had known, since Russ began insisting on this, that here was something connected to reality.

When Gregor knocked, Tibor let him in, then went into the living room and let him follow. He had the landline out on the coffee table, speaker button blinking red to show it was on, sitting on top of Aristotle's *Poetics* and a novel by Jackie Collins. It made him wonder what had happened to Jackie Collins. There had been novel after novel. Then it had all stopped. Tibor appreciated silly novels. They relieved the tension in his back.

Here was one thing about Gregor—he showed up when he said he would. Tibor watched him sit down in the big overstuffed chair. The clock on the wall said one minute before ten.

"That's a phone all ready to go on speaker," Gregor said. He was pleasant, but Tibor knew he was not happy. "And if you're doing what I think you're doing, I'm going to walk out of here."

"I need you to stay," Tibor said.

"The man shot me in the face," Gregor said. "He nearly killed me. He meant to kill me. God only knows what he thought he was going to get out of it, but he did it. I have nothing I want to say. And if he has something he wants to say, I don't want to hear it."

"You want to hear this," Tibor said.

"I take it you've already heard it. Why don't you tell me yourself and we can skip this part."

"You may have questions I haven't thought of. Questions I can't answer."

"I have a million questions, and nobody can answer them."

The phone shrilled on the coffee table. Tibor leaned forward and hit the switch that activated the speakerphone. Then he said "Hello," and there was static.

"Father Tibor?" Russ said.

Father Tibor watched a crease of pain cross Gregor Demarkian's face.

This was the real problem with crime, and with evil of all sorts. It changed people. It changed the people who committed it, and it changed the people who experienced it. In all his years as a priest, Tibor had not been able to figure out how to handle that part of it.

"I am here, Russell," he said. "Krekor is also here."

"Damn," Russ said.

"I'm not interested in being here," Gregor said. "So this had better be good, because if it isn't, I'm going to leave."

"I have said nothing about it so far," Tibor said. "I have left it up to you."

"Damn," Russ said again.

There was a sound on the other end of the line of scraping and coughing. Tibor wasn't sure where Russ was when he made these phone calls. Some of these phones were out in the open where anybody could overhear the speaker. Others were more private. There had to be rules for who got which phone when, but Tibor didn't know what they were.

"Listen," Russ said. "I told Tibor. I'm not promising anything. This is just something I heard."

"We know," Tibor said.

"And this is a state penitentiary," Russ said. "The people here, they're here because they've committed ordinary crimes. Robbery. Murder. Lots of drug violations. But just because they're here because they got convicted of some state thing doesn't mean they haven't done other things. You get that? Lots of other things. And some of those things could be federal crimes."

"I think we all understand that," Gregor said.

"Okay." Russ was taking big gulping breaths. Tibor tried to hear noise in the background, but couldn't. "Okay. There's a guy here, in for selling narcotics. Bad guy. Scary as hell just to look at. I'm not going to give you the name. There are gangs here. He's a big noise in one of them. I'm not in any of them. I don't feel like getting whacked right at the moment. You understand that?"

"Yes," Gregor said.

"Okay," Russ said. "I've been thinking about all this, Gregor. If he'd shot at you, you'd be dead. Although I don't know what good it would have done him, either."

"Russ—"

"Never mind," Russ said. "Listen. This guy keeps telling this story.

Back in Central America, this guy says he hired himself out as a coyote. He took money from people to bring them into the United States illegally. He charged whatever the traffic would bear and then on the trip he said there were . . . perks. Do you want to know about the perks?"

"I can guess," Gregor said.

"Yeah," Russ said. "He can be explicit about the perks. Anyway, the deal was the more money people could put together, the more likely it was that somebody would bring them up here. But there was this situation. The coyotes run with gangs, just like the drugs do. And the gangs took care of their own. There was this guy named Roberto Rodriguez. He was an up-and-comer with the drug guys. He had a girlfriend, let's not talk about the girlfriend and how he got her, but he got her. And he kept her. And she had a child. His child. They weren't married, but he damned well knew it was his child. Got all that?"

"I said it was not an unusual story," Tibor said.

"She was fifteen when she had the kid," Russ said. "And Rodriguez took care of them. Set them up in a place. Got her mother to stay and help out. The mother was very religious and hated him, but Rodriguez must have figured that would help. The mother wouldn't put up with any shenanigans. So they're all living together in this house, and the mother gets sick. Really sick. It gets to the point where she's lying in a room in the dark, praying the rosary nonstop, that's all that's happening anymore. It's getting inconvenient, right? And Rodriguez is getting to be a big noise. He has responsibilities."

"Just like a CEO," Gregor said dryly.

"Don't laugh," Russ said. "You don't think that's how these guys see themselves? Anyway, comes a day, the mother's feeling a little better, she can look after the kid while Rodriguez and the girlfriend go out. So Rodriguez and the girlfriend do go out. They go to a restaurant or something. I don't know what it was all about, but they go. They're gone a couple of hours. Maybe longer. The girlfriend's supposed to be a real piece of work. Maybe that's just my guy talking. He thinks all women are real pieces of work. It doesn't matter. They went out. They came back. And when they came back, the mother was stone-cold dead in a back bedroom and the kid was gone."

"What do you mean, gone?" Gregor asked.

"Gone," Russ said positively. "Just plain gone. Disappeared off the face of the earth. And it's Rodriguez's son, right? He went looking. He had his people looking. Nothing. Nobody saw anybody going in and out of the house that day. Nobody saw the kid. Nothing. They start fanning out across the landscape. They talk to everybody. They invade people's houses. They torture people. They intercept coyotes and caravans and everything else you can think of. Still not a thing. But they do get hold of a rumor."

"This is the part," Tibor said. "This is what I wanted you to hear for yourself."

"Rumors aren't facts," Gregor said.

"Just listen to me," Russ said. "The rumor says there's an operation out there that will get you into the United States, clean. Women and children only. Mostly children. The coyotes are paid to make sure these people make it to the US without having had to put up with any of those perks. They're paid a lot more than they can get for any regular trip, but everything is checked out as soon as the passenger arrives across the border. And the people who run this thing are not kidding. Deliver damaged goods and you could end up dead."

"And the kid went with this group of people?" Gregor asked.

"I don't think they know," Russ said. "According to my guy, they checked, everywhere. They looked for people with lots of sudden cash. Nothing. They chewed up the landscape. Still nothing. Rodriguez is completely ballistic. The old lady couldn't have paid for something like that. Even an ordinary coyote costs twenty thousand dollars or more. Something like this would have cost three times this, if not more. Rodriguez is like all these guys. He set them up at stores all over the place, let them charge groceries and clothes and toys for the kid, paid off street vendors in advance, but he never gave them much in the way of cash. You don't want your people to have cash. Some of them are going to stash it and then try to take off."

"But the kid is gone," Gregor said.

"And the rumors could be untrue," Russ said. "Maybe my guy just wants to sound big. Maybe it's nothing. But here's the thing. Here's what I've got for you in exchange for shooting you in the face."

"Tcha," Tibor said.

Russ gave a hollow little laugh. "The kid they're looking for," he said, "is a seven-year-old boy named Javier."

3

The meeting with Meera Agerwal had been a mistake. It had been so much of a mistake, Clare McAfee couldn't believe she had made it. She had survived this far in her life by making very few mistakes, and none of the kind that put her immediately at risk. The problem was that, in her mind, motivations were simple and straightforward, no matter how complicated they appeared on the surface. People wanted money, and power, and freedom. Sometimes they also wanted fame and prestige, but that was less likely. Prestige was fleeting. Fame was its own kind of problem, complete with people you'd never heard of who suddenly wanted a piece of your hide. Clare McAfee preferred to be anonymous. That way, if something went wrong, it took the people who were after you a little time to figure out who you were.

There was no time to do too many of the things she should have done to prepare for flight. She wasn't going to kid herself. Time was very short. She had a single suitcase packed and ready at her apartment. Her everyday purse had all her identification already in it, plus half a dozen credit cards in its regular pockets and another half dozen (in different names) in the security pockets in the folds. If she hadn't talked to Meera Agerwal, she wouldn't have to move anywhere near this fast. She could do what she originally planned and go down to Nashville before taking a plane out of the country. It would be weeks before the bank figured out what she had done. She could have made it even longer if she had been able to cook up an excuse to take off for a while—a business meeting in Prague, a sick mother in Lithuania, her vacation time. She had been very careful about the system she had set up. She had used that system for other people as well as Cary Alder. Cary Alder was the only one of her special clients who knew for certain she was the one who was facilitating—everything.

It was always better to take a plane from an airport that did not fly directly out of the country. Nonstop international flights always originated at airports with lots of extra security, and lots of extra agency personnel to provide it.

She had her suitcase. She had her purse. She had her ticket, bought on the Internet and printed out right there in the office. First, she'd done it. Then she'd gone back and carefully wiped the memory of everything she'd done. She'd been very careful not to leave even a scrap of paper behind. Then she'd first double- and then triple-checked that her special-boarding-security thingy was up to date. She'd gotten one of those years ago, on the very first day they'd been offered. The last thing she wanted was to hang around in lines while she was being searched by the TSA.

Indian women, she thought, as she allowed herself to be processed through to the plane. The suitcase was not small enough to count as a carry-on. She got it stamped and tagged at the counter. Indian women might as well have come from a different planet. They cared about money—oh, dear God, they cared about money—but they only cared about money after they cared about all these other things, caste, public humiliation, the mere idea of having to touch anything they considered "unclean." Dear God, what would these women have done in Lithuania or Kosovo or any of the other countries of the collapsing Soviet Union, when everybody was at war with everybody else and if you ate, you ate out of garbage cans? Welcome to the world, Clare thought. The real world. The world where an American prison would be the Plaza Hotel of bad situations.

Sometimes they held the plane on the tarmac while they were sorting out their information. Then law enforcement would come on and get you right out of your seat. They tracked you down through your ticket or your cell phone—but Clare had been smart about that, too. She had left her regular cell phone in her office, as if she'd just forgotten it on her desk. All she had with her was the Tracfone she'd picked up at Walmart and registered to her Marilyn Borden credit card.

She had bought the ticket as Clare McAfee, though. It had never occurred to her that she would have to leave in such a hurry that her name would matter.

"I don't care where you're from," Meera Agerwal had said. "You're like all the Americans. You think everybody in the world is a thief."

Nobody got on the plane. The flight attendants fanned out to demonstrate safety procedures. Clare buckled up and ignored them. Then the pilot said something. Then the plane began to move.

Thief, Meera Agerwal had said.

Clare McAfee wanted to scream. Of course, the woman was a thief. She was a bad thief. She was so obvious, Clare had picked up on the activity the first time she'd run into it, and that was at the very beginning of the scheme. She would move the money from one of Cary Alder's accounts to another, carefully, day by day, and the banks would report the real-time value of each of the accounts as they were asked. What was really $100,000 would look like $600,000 in no time flat. Then what was really $3,000,000 would look like $18,000,000. Anybody could do it. It took a rank idiot to skim off the edges of it so that the numbers never added up exactly.

Meera Agerwal was a rank idiot.

She was a rank idiot with a persecution complex and a sense of entitlement that rivaled—well, anything. Entitled to the money. Entitled to get away with it.

JFK airport was not very far. The plane went up and almost immediately began to come down. It was just a puddle jumper. She would have been better off if she had been able to get a plane she could stay on. Now she would have to change planes, check in at another counter, do something about the suitcase. Maybe she could leave the suitcase. The airlines were supposed to move it for you, but usually she checked. Just in case. She didn't trust the airlines. She didn't trust anybody. She should be in Nashville on the way to Atlanta.

The airplane was rolling to a stop. She had been so far into her own head, she had barely noticed it landing. She waited until the stop was complete and the flight attendants came out to wish them all a happy day. Her flight out of JFK went to Brussels—a nice bland European country, no red flags for politics or religion. On that flight she had a business-class seat. That was bland, too.

I think I'm going to be sick.

Clare got out of her seat. The plane was not crowded. She clutched her purse against her body. She walked up the narrow aisle to the disembarkation door. The flight attendants were standing in a row near the door. The sweat was coming out of her scalp in pulsing waves. It made the roots of her hair feel as if they were falling out. All the muscles in her body were shaking.

Nobody can tell I feel like this, she promised herself, making herself walk faster. There was a deep, hollow echo in the disembarkation tunnel.

In the airport itself, there was a different echo, but Clare McAfee didn't notice it.

What she did notice was the four men waiting at the door. All of them were dressed in black. None of them had on one of those flashy vests that identified them to the world at large.

She knew who they were anyway.

FIVE

1

Horowitz and Morabito had information. They had stacks of print-outs, computer screens full of the same information, form after form of impenetrable jargon accompanied by footnotes on subjects Gregor couldn't identify. What it came down to was this: the blood and hair on the tire iron was mixed. Most of it belonged to Miguel Hernandez. Some of it, near the curved end, belonged to Marta Warkowski. That suggested that Hernandez had died from being hit, not being shot. The coroner concurred. What had looked at first sight like a bullet hole was a gash from the small hook near the tire iron's curve. The gun on the floor of Marta Warkowski's room had not killed Hernandez. The rest of the forensics team had come up with a set of fingerprints from the gun, but little else. It had not been recently fired. It had not left a bullet or a shell in the room.

Gregor's feeling that he was only being consulted on this case because Horowitz and Morabito thought the brass wanted them to consult was stronger than ever. These were two experienced detectives. They knew how to do their job.

He tried anyway.

"You have to assume she was attacked somewhere outside her apartment," he told them. "There doesn't seem to be anything in these reports about finding her blood or skin or hair in the apartment, other than what would be usual because she lived there. If what caused the coma was that she was hit on the back of the head with the tire iron, there would be something."

"She was hit on the back of the head with the tire iron," Morabito said. "The reports say so."

"They do," Gregor admitted. "But that blow could have been secondary. If she was hit with something else, or if she fell against something else, and everybody assumed she was dead—"

"Right," Horowitz said. "They moved her. They were going to dump the body. They realized she was still alive. They decided to finish the job and make sure, so they hit her again."

"I don't know that they hit her the first time," Gregor said. "Cary Alder said she came up to the office that evening. He says Meera Agerwal will corroborate that. I don't see Hernandez coming up to the office here on his own. I really don't see Juan Morales going there, or anyone like Morales. There wouldn't be any point. But if Marta Warkowski was hit, or fell, in the office, the person who hit her or caused her to fall—"

"Cary Alder? Meera Agerwal? You don't think they would have called the cops?"

"If they thought she was dead?" Gregor asked. He had to remind himself that these two men didn't know all the circumstances, although they'd heard rumors. "It would depend on what happened and who did it. But you've got to keep a sense of place. These men don't belong here. It was late. Most of the building would have gone home. If they parked in the back and came up the service elevator, they wouldn't look too out of place. I'm sure that happens all the time. But now consider St. Catherine's Parish. Cary Alder *would* look out of place there. So would Meera Agerwal—in fact, she did, when she let us into that apartment. Remember? And the people in the parish wouldn't tell us anything about Hernandez or Morales. They're their own people. There would have been somebody in the vicinity who would have been more than happy to give up Cary Alder."

"Somebody legal," Morabito said sarcastically.

Gregor ignored him. "The van was mostly clean except for the tire iron," he said. "That means they must have parked the van in the local garage and then cleaned it, then brought the tire iron with them to Marta Warkowski's apartment. With the tire iron as sticky as it was, there was no way they could have made that van look as clean as it appeared to us if it had been sitting in the back there after it had been used on Hernandez. Still, I can't believe they're *Good Housekeeping*. Forensics went over the van?"

"With tweezers and black light," Horowitz said.

"Some of the crap they find there should belong to Marta War-kowski," Gregor said. "I wonder where they were taking her. A public park, maybe? Somewhere without people and without too many surveillance cameras. Maybe they thought they'd bring her to Jersey and the sea."

"That's a long drive," Horowitz said. "They could have been stopped at any time."

"They could have secured the body so it didn't roll around and secured the doors so they didn't pop open," Gregor said. "They didn't."

"You're saying they also didn't hit Marta Warkowski," Morabito said. "Which means we're not going to be able to get them on that."

"True," Gregor said. "But I've been receiving updates from the hospital, which means you must be, too. She's actually in good condition. She could wake up. If she does, she might be able to tell us what really happened and who did it."

"I wonder what's going to happen to her now," Morabito said. "Would you go back to that apartment if all this had happened to you? People who try to force you out. People who treat you like garbage. People who act like you're invisible. That's the thing, isn't it? She doesn't even have anybody there she can talk to. And it's supposed to be her home."

"Things change," Horowitz said.

"Things only change as much as we let them," Morabito said.

Gregor had the feeling he had just walked in on the middle of an old and continuing argument.

"I think there are things I'd better make myself do," he said, getting up from the desk where he had been looking at the forensics reports. The stack looked like hyperbole. There was something that had changed in the forty years since he had first joined the Bureau. He could remember crime scenes with agents pacing back and forth through the area, flicking the ashes from the cigarettes they were smoking right into the grass or the carpet. He could remember car phones that hooked up to receivers that couldn't be removed from the dashboard.

Some things changed, and that was a good thing. He didn't want to go back to polio epidemics, or women who died in childbirth because antibiotics hadn't been invented yet, or men screaming in battlefield hospitals because anesthetics hadn't been invented yet. He didn't want to go back.

He gathered up his things. Horowitz actually had a plate of doughnuts on his desk, as if he were trying to reinforce all those stereotypical jokes about the police. Gregor cocked an eyebrow at Horowitz, got permission, and took one. There were, of course, things he did not want to change. Doughnuts were one of them.

Out on the sidewalk, he realized the weather was actually better. The sun was out. It was warmer. Days had been going by, and he had not noticed them. He did not like this part of Philadelphia. In spite of being on the edge of half a dozen vibrant neighborhoods, it was overindustrialized and dead.

Even Cavanaugh Street had changed in the years he had been away from it. It was just a change for the better.

He got out his phone and called Bennis. Then he wondered what would have happened to her if his wife had still been alive, and he had still been married, when he had met her. But that didn't make sense. If his wife had not died, he would not have retired from the Bureau. If he had not retired from the Bureau, he might never have come back to Philadelphia at all.

Thinking about that kind of thing could make you a neurotic.

Bennis picked up.

"Hey," Gregor said. "Are you home?"

"I am."

"Is Javier there with you?"

"He is," Bennis said. "And Tommy Moradanyan is here, too. And Pickles. They're going through the first communion catechism."

"Even Pickles?"

"Absolutely. Pickles is very fond of being read to."

"I'll let that one pass," Gregor said. "I was wondering if you could do something for me. I'm going to be another couple of hours, I think. It might be longer, but I don't think it will be. Could you by any chance stay in the house and not go out until I get back, and not let anyone in unless they're somebody you know?"

"I could do it. You could tell me what's going on."

"Don't let them in unless you know them well," Gregor said. "Don't just open the door because you've seen the milkman a couple of times before."

"We don't have a milkman," Bennis said. "Are you sure you don't want to tell me what's going on?"

"I will when I get home."

"Am I supposed to be expecting someone to storm the place with AK-47s?"

"Keep Tommy there with you if you can."

"I really don't like the sound of this," Bennis said.

"It'll probably be fine," Gregor told her. "I just need a piece of information I don't have."

Gregor Demarkian did not know the exact timetable the Feds intended to use to arrest Cary Alder for bank fraud. He didn't know if that timetable included today, or next week, a direct raid on Cary Alder or a subpoena delivered to his lawyer. It didn't matter, because the issue for him was now Javier. He had to get that out of the way before anybody did anything else.

It took him nearly an hour to find Alder, and when he did, he felt like an idiot. He'd gone to the office first, then to one Aldergold venue after another. In one or two places, he was sure the young men at the reception desks were lying to him. They were that kind of young men—affable enough, but with an air of obstruction. They stood between the outside world and their employer like a lead wall between Superman and Lois Lane.

Javier had been watching *Superman* this morning. That was why he was thinking about Superman. Superman and drug kingpins in Central America.

Gregor finally found Cary Alder at home, in his own apartment. There was no wall of any kind between them. Gregor gave his name to the doorman. They doorman sent him right up. It was as if Alder had been waiting for him, maybe for a long time.

Alder let Gregor in by himself. Gregor could tell, from the feel of the apartment around them, that they were alone. He followed his host through a magnificent foyer with a patterned parquet floor, then into an even more magnificent living room with a cathedral skylight. Standing in the middle of the living room, it was possible to see across most of the city.

Cary Alder dropped into a chair next to a side table with a bottle of scotch on it. There was a glass on the side table, too. It was full.

"I'm surprised," he told Gregor. "I expected to see you with a couple of cops. Those two detectives who came to see me. Uniforms. Somebody."

"I wanted to talk to you before they put you out of circulation. Assuming they're going to put you out of circulation. The last I checked, they didn't have anything on you one way or the other."

"But you do?"

"About the Marta Warkowski business? I have common sense. You hit her. You had to have. She came to your office. You blew up. Then what? She hit the back of her head on the sharp edge of one of those desks?"

"Something like that. I don't think I meant to do it. She was just . . . she was just being Marta. Angry. Threatening. Impossible. And a complete wall of noise. When that woman got talking, God Himself couldn't get a word in edgeways. And I just—went."

"Which is where the common sense comes in," Gregor said. "We know enough about what happened after that for me to know you were the only one who could have set it up. Hernandez wouldn't have taken that body out of there for anybody else. It would have been too much of a risk. Did you see who he brought to help him?"

"No," Cary Alder said. "I barely even saw him. I thought she was dead. She looked dead. I tried to figure out if she was breathing, but I didn't want to get too close to her. It was one of the girls' desks she fell against. I wiped the edge down. I didn't do much. Nobody knew she was there. Nobody was going to know she was there. I didn't think there'd be any reason for anybody to check. In some ways, I'm quite an idiot, Mr. Demarkian."

"In some ways, you seem to be a saint."

The glass of scotch was two-thirds empty. Cary Alder drained the entire thing in one swift gulp.

"Never think that, Mr. Demarkian. You know the jerk and the asshole you read about in the press? Well, that really is me. Little Cary Corporatist. Donald Trump's mini-me. Do you know why I really didn't get close enough to figure out she was still alive? Because I couldn't stand being near her. I can't stand being near any of them. They smell, poor people do. The poorest ones smell like they've shat on themselves. Marta smelled like camphor. And they're all ugly. My God, their women are unbelievably ugly."

"You rent apartments to them."

"I rent apartments to anybody who can pay their rent on time and without a fuss. I employ people to collect those rents. I don't—deal with those people unless I have to."

"Then you should have stayed out of the coyote business," Gregor said. "I don't know if you realize it, but if it hadn't been for that, the chances are good that you'd end up with a form of probation or house arrest."

"For bank fraud? Really? Because I did some really spectacular defrauding of banks. I think I'm into one bank for close to eight million dollars. Hardly a Trump-level operation, but not bad for a local boy."

"The agencies kept picking up on information that said you had to be running a coyote operation, but they could never nail you for it, because they couldn't figure out where the money was coming in. But that's the whole point, isn't it? There was no money coming in. You were bringing people into the country and you were not charging them. Not a dime. They were, what? Children?"

Cary Alder poured himself more scotch. The stuff was disappearing like smoke.

"Do you know what goes on, on those trips north? Oh, you hear a lot of garbage in the press, long lists of all the crimes committed against 'unaccompanied minors.' But they're not unaccompanied. They have those coyotes with them. They have those guides. Guides. Do you know what it's all about? It's all about sex."

"Sex?"

Alder nodded. "Six-year-old boys. Twelve-year-old girls. Anybody, really. All traveling north and all of them getting nailed night after night after night. Sometimes by one guy. Sometimes by gangs of guys. Sometimes getting rented out to the guys in the towns they pass through. It's the price of getting across the border."

"And the parents send the children unaccompanied anyway?"

"I don't know if they know," Cary admitted. "I expect some of them do."

"So you did something else," Gregor said. "You paid to get the children up here, and you paid enough to get them here without—all that."

"It was very expensive," Cary Alder said. "They like all that, the guides do. It's what they're in business for. The money is just . . . dessert."

"But you did it."

"I made a lot of mistakes in the beginning. I'm not good at knowing who to trust."

"But you know now?"

"I know who'll do what he's paid to do."

"What happens to the children when they get here?"

"There are people waiting for them," Cary Alder said. "People who have been through the drill. People who know what goes on. And no, Mr. Demarkian. I'm not going to tell you how those people found me or how I found them. There are considerations in too many of those cases. Other people in other places who might want to get the children back."

"That was mostly what I was interested in."

"Then you should get uninterested in it fast," Cary Alder said. "In fact, if we do get raided by half the law enforcement in the United States, it might turn out that I don't know anything about this at all. Why should I? Half the midlevel businessmen in this city are running some kind of coyote operation. Why shouldn't they? They need the labor and they sure as hell don't want the hassle that comes with hiring legal. Or hiring black people."

"Black people," Gregor said.

"They smell, too."

Cary Alder got up. Gregor realized that the bottle of scotch on the side table was now empty. There was a bar along one wall of the room. Alder went there and got another bottle of scotch.

"I'm getting thoroughly plastered here," he said. "I think it's the right thing to do."

3

Tommy Moradanyan was pacing in the family room when Gregor got home, watched intently by Javier from the couch. Bennis was sitting at the kitchen table, going through yet more stacks of papers. Gregor never ceased to be amazed at how many stacks of papers there were, for everything. Was that something else that had changed over the last however many years?

Tommy and Bennis both stopped what they were doing when Gregor came in. Javier put down his book and threw his arms around Pickles.

"There you are," Bennis said. "Are you all right? Are we in some kind of an emergency?"

"You almost sounded like Russ to me for a minute there," Tommy said. "Don't leave the house. Don't let anyone in. Lock all the doors—"

"I didn't tell anyone to lock all the doors," Gregor said mildly. "And I didn't talk to you at all. Are you in a hurry to get somewhere?"

"I'm in a hurry to get back to my house," Tommy said. "Assuming my mother is going to let me back in."

"Your mother has locked you out?"

Bennis coughed. Tommy shrugged.

"She's on the phone. She told me to come over here and make myself useful for at least an hour." His backpack was on the kitchen table. He went over to it and started to zip up compartments. "She's on the phone to Russ," he said.

"Ah," Gregor said. "I take it she did that on purpose."

"The phone rang, she got the caller ID, she picked up."

"We've been talking about it," Bennis said. "Tommy doesn't know what it means. I don't know what it means. It must be two years since the last time they talked to each other."

"I even want them to talk to each other," Tommy said. "I keep thinking we could get some of this straightened out, people could get more back to normal, if they'd just talk to each other. Once, even. Except I don't want him to talk her into anything."

"Do you think she's going to talk him into something?" Gregor asked.

"If you mean do I think she's going to talk him out of thinking the world is about to set itself on fire, no," Tommy said. "I've been thinking about my trip up during visiting hours. It was one of the things I wanted to know. I don't think he's making it up. I don't think it's an act. I think he really thinks the whole world is about to explode in civil war and people like my mom and Charlie are going to be targets and we all have to do something to protect ourselves. I think he believes it. I think he may believe it even more being where he is. I think there might be a lot of other people who agree with him in there."

"Then I don't understand what you think your mother is going to talk him into," Gregor said.

"Maybe I just don't want him to talk her into what he's got going," Tommy said. "I don't know. I just want to get home and make sure she isn't buying assault rifles on the Internet. I'm talking crazy. I'm feeling crazy."

"If it helps any," Gregor said, "I've met quite a few people over the last few days who have . . . let's just say similar ideas. There seems to be a lot of this kind of thing going around."

"To tell you the truth, Mr. Demarkian, that *doesn't* help." He went over to Javier and patted him on the head. "Keep studying the catechism. You're going to need it for the first day at school. I'll see you tomorrow." Then he gave Pickles a scratch between the ears. "Father Tibor says Pickles is going to stay here with Javier and he's going to get another rescue dog. That would be good. Thanks for the cookies. I'll see everybody later."

He took off, faster than Gregor had expected him to be able to go. Gregor and Bennis listened while the front door opened and shut. Then Gregor shrugged out of his coat and sat down next to Bennis.

"It's New Year's Day the day after tomorrow," Gregor said. "Which makes New Year's Eve tomorrow. Did you know that?"

"I hadn't really thought about it," Bennis said. "We don't usually do much of anything for New Year's Eve. And I never really liked New Year's Eve parties. Too many people getting drunk and too many people getting stupid. Why? Is there something you want to do tomorrow night?"

"No. Maybe Javier would like to see the ball come down at midnight."

"Javier will be fast asleep at midnight, even if we don't put him to bed. You want to tell me what this was all about? You really did sound like Russ for a minute there, like we were the Bastille and somebody was about to storm us."

"Well, it's an interesting situation," Gregor said. "I don't think we have to worry about anybody storming us, at least for the moment. I don't think anybody knows what's happening here, with one exception. Unfortunately, that exception is Russ."

"Russ knows something."

"Russ knows who Javier is, and how we got him."

"And that's a problem?"

"It could be. It depends."

"It depends on what?"

"On whether Russ is still mostly Russ, or if he's become mostly this new conspiracy theorist who seemed to pop out of nowhere two years ago. Except that can't be right, either. People don't change that drastically if something doesn't happen to them. I don't think they change that drastically short of a traumatic brain injury. If this is a part of Russ, it must always have been a part of Russ, down there somewhere where the rest of us couldn't see it. So I don't know."

Bennis got up and started clearing things away reflexively, because it was something for her to do now that he'd made her restless. Gregor watched her move. The cloud of black hair hovered over her perfectly symmetrical face. The long fingers ended in blunt, unvarnished fingernails meant for typing and doing and not display. Gregor could remember the first time he'd ever seen her. She was older now. He didn't care.

He got up himself and started to help her clean up. "Let's go down to the Ararat for dinner tonight," he said. "We'll take Javier with us and let him eat his way through the appetizers menu. He can order three desserts. We'll get Tibor to come with us."

"You can have yaprak sarma," Bennis said. "Do you think he misses it? His home? His people? I can't believe he was some orphan living in the streets. He was too well cared for."

"He wasn't some orphan living in the streets," Gregor said. "But you'd better give some thought to this. He can't go home again. If we're going to take him on, we should assume we're going to take him on permanently. I don't know how you envisioned this when we first started it, but that's where we are now. Either we decide right away that we're going to keep him, or we find somewhere else for him to go immediately. And I know you never particularly wanted children. We never talked about it, but I know."

"I never particularly wanted children in the abstract," Bennis said. "I think I could want this one."

They both turned to look at Javier. Javier was looking at them.

He was very happy.

EPILOGUE

1

Marta Warkowski woke up at 4:17 on the morning of New Year's Eve day, less than fifty minutes before Cary Alder's houseboy found his employer dead and twisted on his living room couch. Gregor heard about these things as he was taking Pickles for her morning walk up and down Cavanaugh Street. It was six o'clock in the morning by then. Cavanaugh Street looked the way it had always looked since Gregor had first moved back home from D.C. Old Mrs. Ohanian had opened Ohanian's Middle Eastern Market and hung a string of garlic bulbs near the door. Linda Melajian had taken down the dinner menu on the Ararat's plate-glass front window and put up the menu for breakfast. Lida Arkmanian had rushed into the street through the fancy front door of her town house and found Hannah Krekorian waiting for her on the sidewalk. The only thing that didn't look quite right was the Moradanyan house, down on the far end of the neighborhood, still blank and gray and devoid of even the slightest signs of decoration.

The call about Marta Warkowski came in from Horowitz, who sounded both elated and dismissive. He was elated about Marta waking up. He was dismissive of Gregor, and Gregor found his belief confirmed that the two detectives had never wanted him on the case to begin with. It didn't matter that much. Gregor and Bennis had been talking for a year now about whether Gregor would go on working. They had come to no definite conclusions—except, maybe, they had. Given this gray morning not quite at the beginning of January, Gregor couldn't see himself chasing around like a Peter Lovesey hero in the wake of some idiot who wanted to murder his wife.

"Of course, she isn't exactly giving evidence yet," Horowitz said over the phone, as Gregor steered Pickles into the wide alley that led behind the Armenian church to Tibor's apartment. "And maybe I'm getting away from myself. Maybe she'll have amnesia. The doctors don't want us in there until we absolutely have to go in. But still. She could tell us everything. She could tell us what happened. We could even get a guilty plea."

Everybody wanted a guilty plea. Gregor made noncommittal noises. It was as he was signing off that the phone brought up the news alerts and he saw the headline about Cary Alder. He almost stopped halfway down the alley. He made himself keep going. Cary Alder was dead. Gregor had a feeling he knew more about that than anybody else ever would.

Tibor came down to meet him and took the little brown bag full of Pickle's . . . uh . . . business to put in the trash can. It was Tibor at his most Tibor-ish: the three-quarter-length woolen overcoat, the heavy hat with its ear flaps, the scarf wound tightly enough to strangle him around his neck. He was even wearing thickly padded leather gloves, the kind men wore when they trekked through the tundra. Sometimes it felt as if Tibor had never left Yerevan.

"Burberry," Gregor told him when he came up, bag gone, to meet Gregor and Pickles in the wide courtyard.

"What?"

"You're wearing Burberry," Gregor said. "The coat. The scarf. I don't know about the hat. If you weren't wearing Burberry, you'd look like you were right off the boat."

"It was a Christmas gift from Bennis the year after the two of you got married," Tibor said. "It's a very good coat."

"It ought to be. It probably cost as much as a small co-op apartment."

"You are talking about inconsequentialities," Tibor said.

This was true. They came out of the alley onto Cavanaugh Street again. There were more people now. Most of them were headed for the Ararat. Some of them were headed farther down the street to where the buses stopped.

Pickles was wearing her little red outfit, complete with the booties and hat. Tibor leaned over and gave her a scratch behind one ear.

"So today Tommy and I will go to the shelter and pick up the other dog," Tibor said. "That is also an inconsequentiality, except not for the dog. I will enjoy having a dog in the house again. Is there something I should be worried about when it comes to you?"

"Not really," Gregor said. "We've got a fairly calm day planned. Bennis wants to take Javier to the Liberty Bell. I think there's going to be shopping, and also probably lunch. I think she wants to go to a bookstore."

"And that is all?"

"I've got a theoretical question."

"I do not trust theoretical questions, Krekor. They are never really theoretical."

The Ararat was coming up fast now. Gregor could see the door to the restaurant opening and closing, opening and closing. Maybe they should make it part of their routine to bring Javier here every morning for breakfast before school.

"So," Tibor said. "A theoretical question."

"About good and evil," Gregor said. "About people and good and evil."

"Are we discussing Russell Donahue again?"

"Maybe. Partially."

"I do not think Russell Donahue is evil, Krekor. I think he is tortured and I think he is lost. I think he believes the things he says. I think he is terrified for himself and for his children and for Donna. I think he lives in a nightmare that will never disappear. But I do not think he is evil."

"I don't think he was evil before all the craziness started," Gregor said. "He was a kind person. He was a person of integrity. He's those things now in a lot of ways. Even if it's all pointed in the wrong direction."

"I do not think you have to worry about it, Krekor. I do not think they will allow him out of jail ever again. I think that is sensible."

"I knew somebody else for a while," Gregor said. "And in a lot of ways he was evil. He was not a kind person. He was almost comically selfish. He hated—I almost don't know how to describe it. He was like one of those idiots on the Internet. It was as if he wanted to see harm come to people. As if seeing harm come to some people made him feel better."

"You make him sound like a cartoon," Tibor said.

"Maybe he was."

"Was?"

"I think so."

"People are not cartoons, Krekor. They are not all good or all bad. They are not agents of heaven or agents of hell. They are not all of a piece. That's why your Internet idiots cannot stand the thought of history. The great civil rights leader turns out to be a serial rapist. The Nazi saves abandoned dogs in the wilderness and ships Jewish children to the camps. God knows these things, Krekor, the rest of us do not."

"I'm pretty sure that this particular evil person did a very good thing," Gregor said. "Did it more than once. Did it often enough so

that he ruined himself doing it. He told me I should be careful not
to give him too much credit for doing it."

"Krekor."

"We're at the Ararat," Gregor said. "I'd better get Pickles back
to Javier."

Tibor paused just at the Ararat's door. Then he turned away and
went inside. Gregor could hear Lida Kasmanian calling him over to
her table.

It was only when the door closed all the way that Gregor realized
that the front of the Ararat was awash in Christmas decorations.
There were shiny golden bells and silver tinsel and big red bows
made out of shiny synthetic satin. They had to have been here all
the time. They had to have been here for weeks.

Gregor hadn't noticed them before.

2

Bennis was making waffles when Gregor got home, pouring batter into the big no-stick waffle iron Hannah Krekorian had given
them for their wedding. As far as Gregor knew, it had never been
used before. Looking at it now, he wondered if it would ever be used
again. Bennis was very enthusiastic with the waffle batter. It went
everywhere, and when the waffles were done it had to be cut off the
edges.

Javier didn't seem to mind. He had four fully cooked waffles
with butter and syrup, a glass of orange juice, a cup of hot chocolate, and a banana. He also had two strips of bacon he had kept for
Pickles. He held them out as soon as the dog came in.

Bennis frowned at him. "Two," she said.

Javier nodded. "*Sí. Dos.*"

Gregor thought it was a good thing there were only the two
strips left.

Bennis waved him to a chair and went for the coffee. "Maybe we ought to take him down to the Ararat for breakfast after all," she said. "I know we discussed it, and it sounded more like a real home to do it all here, but the Melajians are all better cooks than I am and we can't live on pancakes, waffles, and bacon. Not that Javier seems to mind. Yet."

"Javier seems to be having the time of his life," Gregor said, sitting down. "I got a phone call while I was out."

"I listened to the news. Is it all the same thing?"

"I doubt it. The news was probably Cary Alder. My phone call was about Marta Warkowski. She's out of the coma, or whatever it was."

Bennis poured orange juice for herself and sat down, too. "If she's awake, she'll be able to tell you what happened to her. Do you think she'll say what you think she'll say? That Cary Alder hit her?"

"I don't know," Gregor said. "She's awake, but I don't think she's talking yet. She may never talk. She may never remember. If she remembers anything, I hope it's who was with Hernandez when they stuffed her in the van. Whoever was with Hernandez must have killed Hernandez. But she might never have seen him. She might have been out cold by the time Hernandez and his helper showed up."

"But you're sure Cary Alder hit her."

"He admitted that much, not that my word for it is going to constitute admissible testimony. He got angry, lashed out, and she fell back against the corner of a desk. Horowitz and Morabito have search warrants and forensics people all lined up. The only question becomes who killed Hernandez, and Morales had the motive. He also had fingerprints on the gun. There's something the two of them should have checked out first thing."

"You really aren't happy with the crime consulting thing anymore, are you?"

Gregor shrugged. "It's hard to tell what I'm happy with anymore, aside from you and the peanut here," he said. "Something's gone out of this for me since Russ—well, since Russ. I was thinking it might be a good idea, once school is out for the summer, to take Javier here to see something of the country. Maui, maybe. You like Maui."

"I do," Bennis said. "But I think Javier would probably have a better time at Disney World. Especially if Donna would let us take Tommy with us. Or maybe all three of them would come. We could stay at that side resort they have in Florida with all the wild animals."

"What would we do with Pickles?"

Bennis sighed. "I suppose he'd end up getting eaten by one of the cats. We'll figure something out. The news said they thought Cary Alder might have committed suicide because he was about to be arrested for bank fraud. They've already arrested these two women they think were part of it. One of them is cooperating."

"I'll bet both of them will be by the end of the mess," Gregor said. "And bank fraud is as good an excuse as any."

"Not a potential murder charge?"

"That, too."

Javier had finished all his food. He bowed his head over his plate, made the sign of the cross, and said a short little prayer in Spanish. Then he made the sign of the cross again and hopped down to collect Pickles.

Bennis got up and started to clear the table. "It's been a weird morning already," she said, "and now you're back and it's just as weird. Donna talked to Russ last night. I don't know what about, but she's been revved and crazy ever since. And you've never been secretive about your work before. I really don't need any help these days, feeling like I don't know what's going on in the world."

"You know what I noticed this morning?" Gregor asked her. "There are Christmas decorations everywhere. The entire facade of the Ararat is covered with them. Lida has silver bows on her living room window."

"Is there really something odd about that? It was just Christmas, just before we got Javier."

"I know it was. But I didn't notice it. Things were going on right in front of my face, and I didn't notice them. Maybe it's time for me to retire for other reasons besides being sick of it."

Bennis started stacking dirty dishes in the sink. Gregor watched Javier and Pickles go into the living room and get up together on a large, wide, stuffed armchair. Javier had books. Pickles was wearing that alert expression that said she was a very smart dog and willing to indulge the humans in anything they did, no matter how senseless.

"You know," Gregor said, "I remember Cavanaugh Street when I was in high school. Before the tenements got renovated into town houses and floor-through apartments. When everybody spoke at least some Armenian, and we had an old priest at the church who would go on and on and on about the Armenian Genocide. Displaced persons. People who belonged here and didn't belong here at the same time. But I wouldn't have belonged in Armenia, either."

"You belong here now."

"Oh, yes. Yes, I do. I'm perfectly at home in this place, even though it's a lot different than it was when I was growing up. And I have a theory. I think it's what we're all looking for. A place where we're perfectly at home. We build neighborhoods. We build whole nations. Just so that we can feel we fit. And when we lose that, when we don't fit anymore, anywhere, I think we go crazy."

"I think you're beginning to sound pretty crazy yourself," Bennis said.

Gregor shook his head. "I belong in this place, even if I'm not so sure I belong in this time anymore. But all around us there are people who gather together in small little knots and try to re-create the familiar and the comfortable and the safe, and if they get the formula right, it sometimes mostly works. But some people can't do that. The world falls apart around them and there's nothing they can do to get it back."

"You're talking about Cary Alder again," Bennis said.

"Hell," Gregor said. "I'm talking about Russ."

3

Father Tibor's new rescue dog was a "sort of" Samoyed. At least, that was what the woman at the shelter said while Tommy Mora-danyan was putting on the dog's new collar and fixing the leash to it. The collar had a name on it, as well as all of Tibor's informa-tion. The name was "Spot," which Tibor explained to anybody who would listen was meant to indicate the white spot that covered the dog's entire body. This, in turn, was a literary reference. There was a Samoyed named Spot in one of Tibor's favorite mystery series.

Tommy only cared about getting out of the shelter as fast as he could. It wasn't what he himself would have called a shelter, which would be a place where dogs were kept safe and comfortable until someone wanted to take them home. That could take a few days or a few years or forever. It wouldn't matter. In this shelter, it mattered. Animals had three months. After that, they were dead.

Tommy understood why Father Tibor wanted to adopt his dog from a place like this. It still amazed him that the little priest could chatter on and on to the woman at the counter as if he didn't know she had murder in her heart.

The one positive note in all of this was Spot himself. He came out from the back looking bedraggled and depressed. He got steadily happier and more lively as the proceedings went on. He liked his collar. He liked his leash. He put his front paws on Tommy's shoul-ders and licked Tommy's face clean of anything that had ever been on it, ever.

"I do hope this will work out," the lady behind the counter said. "When those other people brought him back, I thought it was all over. Then you came in and wanted a dog right away. I'd say it was a miracle. If I were you, I'd call him Lucky instead of Spot."

"I think he goes with God," Tibor said seriously.

The woman behind the counter gave a tight little smile and let them go.

Out on the street, Tibor stopped to give Spot a pat on the head. Spot gave Tibor's face the same treatment he'd given Tommy's.

"I'll have to get him some things," Tibor said as they started walking again. "I understand that he is not a tiny dog and he has more fur than Pickles, but he shouldn't have his bare feet on these pavements. They're cold and there are chemicals on them, to keep people from slipping."

"I wonder who decides what dogs go to what shelters," Tommy said.

They had to pass through a corner of the Somali neighborhood to get to Cavanaugh Street. There were no Christmas decorations up there, and no signs of an impending New Year's Eve. Cavanaugh Street was different. The little newsstand at the edge of the neighborhood was decked out in shiny plastic Christmas balls and New Year's noisemakers, the kind that unfurled when you blew them. Tommy remembered smacking more than one of his classmates in the face with them at holiday parties. He would have to teach Charlie how to blow one. She would love it.

There was a bench right in front of the steps to the Armenian Christian Church. When they got to it, Father Tibor sat down and began petting Spot again. Tommy sat down, too. It was crazy in this cold, but Spot didn't seem to mind, and from the bench Tommy could see his own house several blocks away. There was something odd about it. Tommy couldn't put his finger on what.

"Tcha," Father Tibor said finally. "You are going back up there? To the prison? To see Russ?"

"Eventually. And don't ask me what I'm doing. My mom asks me what I'm doing. I can't explain it. I mean, I know I can't change what he did. And I know he's never going to get out of prison. Part of me thinks maybe I can show him how wrong he is about everything that's happening. And if I can do that—" Tommy threw his hands into the air. "I don't know. I don't know what that's supposed to fix."

"Do you know why I became a priest?"

"If you think you're going to talk me into that—"

"Tcha," Father Tibor said. "In one way, it was the same reason as the other men in my seminary class. We did it because the Soviet authorities didn't want us to. We did it because we were Armenians and we wanted to remember that. But I couldn't have chosen this life for only that reason."

"So?"

Spot had been sitting quietly on the ground. Now he jumped up and put the front half of himself into Tommy's lap. Tommy laughed.

"Listen," Father Tibor said. "We wanted to remember we were Armenian and there was nothing wrong with that. But there was nothing right with it, either. Armenians are no different than anybody else. There are good things about us and bad things about us, and the worst thing about us is the same as the worst thing about everyone else. Do you know the joke, about the Catholics in heaven?"

"No."

"There is a new arrival in heaven," Father Tibor said, "and Saint Peter shows him around. Over there are the Methodists. Over here are the Muslims. Over in that other place are the Lutherans, and next to the Lutherans are the Jews. The new arrival sees a group of people behind a high wall and asks, 'Who are they? What are they doing behind a wall?' 'Oh,' Saint Peter says. 'Those are the Catholics. They think they're the only ones here.'"

Tommy laughed again.

"But it's true of all of us," Tibor went on. "We all think we're the only ones here. But there is a place in one of the epistles of Saint Paul, where Paul is talking to a group gathered to hear him preach, and what he says is, 'You are neither Jew nor Greek, neither slave nor free, neither male nor female. You are all one in Christ Jesus. You are all sons of God.'"

"My mother would give you a four-hour lecture about sexism."

"No," Father Tibor said. "It is not sexism to put it that way. In the culture of the time, sons could inherit but daughters could not. Paul is saying that in Christ, there will be no such divisions. We will not be the only ones here. We will all inherit the kingdom of God. And when I heard that, I thought it was what I wanted to be a part of, what I wanted to see happen in the world. That we will all inherit. That we will all be part of each other."

"I may not be as crazy as Russ is, Father, but I don't think that's the direction the world is heading in."

"It is never the direction the world is headed in. It is only the direction the world should be heading in."

"In the opposite direction of Russ."

"Think of yourself as part of a tide," Father Tibor said. "If enough people are going in the right direction, more and more people will be dragged along with them."

Spot got down from Tommy's lap and tried a similar maneuver on Father Tibor's. Father Tibor scratched him behind the ears and stood up.

"You should go home. Your mother will be worried about where you've gone."

"Yeah."

Tommy stood up. He was looking down Cavanaugh Street at his own house again, the tall brownstone walls, the peaks and whorls of the roof facade. Spot pranced around his legs, happy to be out in the air, straining against the leash to get a better sniff at the feet of the few people who came by.

And then he saw it.

He really saw it.

The roof facade was glinting, and as he watched he saw a cascade of gold foil paper come down the house's dull stone front.

"Tommy?" Father Tibor asked.

"I've got to go," Tommy said. "I've got to go. That's my mom."

"Tommy."

"She's decorating the whole damned house."

And that was true.

After two years of nothing, of barely tinseled twigs at Christmas and blank walls at Easter and all the lights out and the doors locked for Halloween, Tommy Moradanyan's mother was doing her thing again. She was wrapping their entire house in gold foil paper. She was *celebrating*, and that meant she could now see something to celebrate.

Tommy figured he'd better get over there and help.

AFTERWORD

Matthew DeAndrea

This was a lot harder to write than I thought it was going to be.

In July of last year my mother, Orania Papazoglou, who you probably know better under the pen name Jane Haddam, died. I started writing this afterword a little bit before she passed away, sitting in the hospital after the doctors told us she wasn't going to wake up and it was only a matter of time. Because one of the things she made me promise, in that time when she was sick but we all thought the time she had left was still measured in years, was that this book would eventually get published. I promised her a lot of things in that time. I've been able to follow up on almost all of them. Most of them I wasn't taking too seriously, you know? Because Mom had been known to fret, and she had at least another year.

Except of course, she didn't.

Mom was diagnosed with stage four metastatic breast cancer about one year before she died. She spent that year undergoing various forms of treatment, from hormone pills to injections to chemotherapy. For a while even, a lot of it was working. She complained about the constant pink, which she described as "the worst part of having breast cancer." She taught another semester. And, of course, she wrote one last Gregor. The one she'd been talking about writing for years. It was suggested to me that I should describe this book as a gift to the fans. And it is certainly that. Mom had no intention of leaving everyone hanging, especially after *Fighting Chance* ended with questions left unanswered.

But more than anything Mom was somebody who bulled through. Well before the cancer Mom had faced (and she'd yell at me for the cliché here) her fair share of tragedy, starting when she was young, going through the death of my father (William L. DeAndrea, also a mystery writer) and raising us alone and right into the disease itself. She'd yell, she'd complain, she'd argue, and she could get inventive with the colorful language as only someone who writes for a living can, but she'd get to the other side. Often she wouldn't believe she could do it herself, and be almost confused at the far end.

She got us through an awful lot that way, more than she should have had to. So this book really is a gift. A gift to all of you, for reading and loving her work over the years—or for picking it up to give it a try, if this is the first time you've touched a Gregor Demarkian novel. A gift to me and my brother, because she always wanted to pass these stories down to us in time. And finally, corny as it may sound, a gift to herself. Just like the last semester she taught. Bulling through one last time, to prove she could. Even though Mom being Mom, she started bulling not really sure she would bull to the end.

And Mom being Mom, of course, she did.

I've used the first person a lot in this, because I'm the one sitting here typing, but I've got my brother hanging over my shoulder. We're both writing this, really. And as to what we're getting at, well, I guess it's that we hope you enjoy the book. And that Mom was one hell of a lady. And that when you're done with it maybe hand a copy to your mother, or someone else you care about, or at least give them a call. Because the world is a funny place, and you don't always have another year.

Matthew and Gregory DeAndrea